I asked, "Why? Does it matter? No one seems to care. People apparently want to be lied to. That's what politics is. That's why they go to the movies, isn't it?"

Otto was firm in his answer. "Truth matters. You have to look for it. What our children know is our only legacy. That's why I make my movies."

Biedermeier

his identity, both mistaken and true

Other works by Vincent McCaffrey

Hound
A Slepyng Hound to Wake
The Dark Heart of Night
The knight's tale
John Finn
A Republic of Books
I Am William McGuire and other unexpected stories
I Imagine My Salvation
A Young Man from Mars

Biedermeier
his identity, both mistaken and true

by Vincent McCaffrey

Avenue Victor Hugo Books
Lee, New Hampshire

This one is for Bill, and the movies he loves

Biedermeier is a work of fiction, based on the facts as I know them. Any resemblance between the characters herein and actual people, living or dead, is unintended and most likely accidental.

ISBN-13: ISBN-13: 978-0-9897903-5-2
ISBN-10: 0-9897903-5-5
Avenue Victor Hugo Books

As always, the typos are my own speciality and are in no way the fault of those friends who helped to get the manuscript into shape. For the fact that there are not more, I thank them all again, especially the mindful and diligent Dan Karlan and Pamela Siska.

Chapters

Otto Biedermeier, 1939? – 2016

October 19th, 2016. A Hollywood Tab exclusive by Thomas
Lenz

"I don't make parody. Life itself is a parody and I
attempt to capture that," the quote that he is most famous for,
is itself a parody of the original statement made to a Chicago
film critic in 1984. The transcript of that interview reads, "I
don't make parody. That's cheapjack and just another form of
plagiarism. Life itself is a parody, and too often counterfeit. I
attempt to capture that and offer an alternative."

Otto Biedermeier has died, and it is perhaps parody
that killed him.

The headlines that screamed with minor variation from
most major newspapers during the past forty-eight hours,
'Hollywood Icon Murdered,' have now been replaced by news
of the latest suicide bombings in the Middle East. The further
possibility that this was no murder at all has already dampened
early enthusiasm for lurid details and diminished the point size
of follow-up ledes. Though nothing more has been learned, the
unsalaried spec writers now move to the carcass of the story
like a wake of vultures seeking morsels the hyenas have left
behind. Thankfully, due to past associations, the *Tab* has
generously assigned me to follow the story to its conclusion. As
of Tuesday evening, this is what we know.

As his own brand of humor would have it, the budget-
comedy-horror director and producer, Otto Biedermeier, aka

Lincoln Kelly, has been found dead under Mysterious Circumstances. Miss Circum-stances, the female lead of Biedermeier's most famous film, *The Drool*, called both police and ambulance to their shared residence in Malibu at 2 am, Sunday morning, immediately after returning from a party. She has had no further comment. Given the circumstances, police are uncertain, but still suspect foul play.

Mr. Biedermeier's own movie oeuvre makes any reverent discussion of the events surrounding his death difficult for film fans. *Fowl Play* was Mr. Biedermeier's second film, released in 1966, and though a mystery more than a horror film, it featured a British rock band, unable to actually play their instruments, who murdered any female groupies that learned their dark secret. In the age of The Monkees, the film did well despite a budget of barely $100,000, most of which was borrowed from the actors themselves so that the director could pay union scale.

Importantly, it is with *Fowl Play* that Biedermeier firmly established what was to be his characteristic directorial 'style.' The opening pan shot refocused in passing to some intimate detail; the closing pan to a telling freeze-frame; and his tendency to direct the camera elsewhere while an actor speaks are just a few examples. Though he liked the idea of such directorial devices, he called all of his tricks 'merely habits,' and repeated most of them in each film he made. His use of chiaroscuro harkened back to the work of Carol Reed and early Hitchcock. His forthright characters might have appeared in an Archers film from Emeric Pressburger and Michael Powell. His straightforward sense of humor reminded many of the films of Alexander MacKendrick. But that one trick of not directing the camera to the speaker had been learned while filming his very first effort, the holocaust documentary *Lost Circus*.

Otto Biedermeier became famous for producing low-budget movies 'ripped from the headlines,' and frequently in production, after furious bouts of writing, only weeks following an event. Responding to an inquiry about one often used device that some viewed as an idiosyncrasy, he told me, "A journalist cannot be faulted for respecting a subject's own habits. I learned long ago that people often look away when they are speaking, usually out of embarrassment or shame. I turn the camera to what they might see. But when they look me in the eye, I never turn away."

Early police reports are that Mr. Biedermeier's body was found on his bed, with a knife wound to the chest that likely penetrated his heart. Murder was immediately suspected, but not confirmed, because the weapon used was part of a collection that Mr. Biedermeier kept as movie props. The house was well-locked and always barred in that way against the many fans frequently trying to get close to the moviemaker in the hope of hooking a part in an upcoming film. "I go out to my balcony in the morning to drink my coffee and they are sitting on the beach like sea lions, staring back," he once said.

The knife in question, found at the scene, was especially constructed with a slide-blade that retracted directly into the handle, and lacked the locking mechanism that would keep it fixed in place. There is speculation that this mechanism may have rusted, offering the possible explanation that Mr. Biedermeier, known to practice action scenes on his own in order to avoid wasted time and added expense, may have accidentally killed himself by mistake when he fell on the bed. The script for a new movie, *The Perch* currently in pre-production, and calling for a knife murder, was also present on the floor at the scene.

The Malibu house, designed by his daughter Audrey to compliment the sea-torn cliffs of nearby Point Dume, is cantilevered above the beach, and as this reporter can testify, the entire home, including the bedroom and its sweeping balcony are essentially inaccessible except by the front door. As a N.Y.U. graduate student in 1996, I spent some days there interviewing Mr. Biedermeier for a Ph.D. thesis that was subsequently published by the University of California Press as a monograph on the moviemaker's work. It should be addressed here that this generosity in giving a young film student his time is still warmly felt to this day.

It was the success of *Fowl Play* that allowed for the larger budget that is readily seen in Biedermeier's third effort, *Tryst Trap,* released in 1967. Using an all-European cast, Biedermeier tried to save money by shooting *Tryst Trap* on location in Trieste, Italy, and dubbing sound in the Italian manner. This was Mr. Biedermeier's first and only financial failure. However, many ascribed the poor response of American audiences not to the dubbing but his attempt to make a horror-comedy based on the holocaust, still too sensitive a subject.

"I came back from Europe and people were watching a weekly comedy on television about a prisoner-of-war camp. It gave me the wrong idea, I suppose."

A well-received 2008 'Ottobiography,' *Double Take,* chronicled Mr. Biedermeier's fortunes and a life-long search for his own origins. Given the subject of his 1989 film, *A Deadly Projection,* it is clear he had little use for psychological therapy, and the realizations in *Double Take* appear to have been the culmination of a slow process resulting from his personal efforts to understand his past. Admittedly, this was a background subject hardly mentioned in my own monograph and much needed in reconsideration.

However, the personal details offered to this reporter 1996 were only bits and pieces. Otto Biedermeier usually addressed his nightmares on film, in a droll but never sardonic manner. At the time of our interview, he had been famously silent about his childhood, and the details that he suddenly presented to me then seemed out of character. Given certain fantastical aspects, related in that quiet and often uninflected voice he used on the set, and allowing for the fact that I was, after all, in Hollywood, the land of make believe and self-promotion, I had wrongly supposed Otto might be 'putting me on' and I failed to include more of the material—in retrospect, a matter of my own inexperience as much as an impending deadline, or the lack of ready secondary sources. It appears to me now that his admissions to me were just the beginning of a larger self-examination.

But one quote I did use was this: "I have always started each film in the mind of a six-year-old child awakened from a deep sleep; a child with nothing—empty of hope, illusion, delusion, or any understanding. I must discover everything from the beginning."

In fact, the filmmaker was born to a Gypsy father and Jewish mother during World War Two and later found abandoned among thousands of homeless refugees by United States Army soldiers in Trieste. As an orphan, he was eventually given passage via War Relief Services to Chicago. I believe it was this plane ride into what must have appeared to that young mind to be a fantasy world that he later recreated in a failing DC-3 for the 1979 film *Flight Response*.

Otto was subsequently adopted into the heart of Illinois farm country, raised by an Irish Catholic family named Kelly, and given the name Lincoln. It was as Lincoln Kelly that he was to later graduate from New York University in 1961. And it was this name change that was the reason why records for the better-known Otto Biedermeier were not to be found at that school when I attended there.

It was the lack of academic training in film production

that led this reporter, when still a grad student, to simply suggest that his stylistic innovations were the result of a natural genius for the moving image. In fact, it was his work as an intern at local television stations, particularly the innovative WNTA, and his firsthand experience working with a U. S. Army film unit that I now believe directly influenced his style in filmmaking. Genius he was, nevertheless.

The number '16' plays an added part in all of this. Perhaps for lack of a better name, and long before the invention of the rifle of that designation, 'M-16' was the identification given to a redheaded child, apparently mute, but estimated to be only six years old by his U.S. Army and Red-Cross caretakers. Biedermeier was the 16th nameless male child to be processed at the facility on a single day, October 16, 1945. It was later learned that children had often been forbidden by their parents to give family names to authorities for fear of being swept up in the arrest and genocide of Jews, Gypsies, and others. Each of Mr. Biedermeier's films ends with the white hand drawn 'M16' on the exposed film, a designation he also applied to his production company.

Immediately following graduation, and with little money, the young Mr. Kelly kissed his adoptive mother goodbye, shook his father's 'calloused hand,' and sallied forth, accompanied by his college sweetheart, Jesse Fleming, packing two borrowed 16-millimeter cameras and one change of clothes, to discover his origins in Europe. Though the evidence for his actual birthparents was slight, and much of that constructed around his own vague memories coupled with a surviving two-page circus program from Vienna in 1939 (which had been found along with other paper, sewn into his clothing, perhaps only for added warmth). A Red Cross report on the child known as 'M16' states that the program was the only whole and undamaged piece, and thus kept and filed as such by a thankfully bureaucratic clerk. Biedermeier's determination was that this program was a clue and the key to his identity. His search extended from Trieste to Vienna and then to Prague as the determined filmmaker peddled a bicycle the entire distance to achieve the slow progress of the original caravan, while following backwards the faint trail of a one-ring circus, by that time almost forgotten.

Among other performers, that brief circus program featured a Josef Biedermeier, magician, and one Alma Klage, his assistant. I believe this small document is, even now, framed and visible in Otto's second home near Red Rock Canyon. That filmed journey of 1961 ends at the Clementinum in Prague with Biedermeier's discovery of a three-line newspaper wedding notice in the *Lidove Noviny* which offered the added information, in bold letters, that his mother was a Jew and his father a gypsy. This, with his own hands holding the bound newspaper up to the dim light of a storage room, was to be his first final freeze-frame, yet another signature in all his movies.

The Selective Service draft caught up with him in 1962 and Lincoln served in the Army for most of the next three years. His previous experience with 16-mm film had resulted in a posting with an Army Special Bulletin crew and an existential experience of war when often flown by helicopter onto the scene of engagements. I asked him about this period of his life, and he specifically refused to offer detail, saying, "I was not doing what I wanted to do and I had no control of what I shot or how it was used, so there is nothing much to say."

However, Jesse Fleming spent this intervening time very well, editing and re-editing the film they had made together and speaking with anyone who might be interested in what they had done, finally getting the attention of an associate of David Susskind in New York.

Lincoln Kelly assumed the name Otto Biedermeier in

1965, when their cinema verite collection of interviews with the last aging witnesses to the passage of the *Lost Circus* was first broadcast as a documentary on New York's WNDT Channel 13 television and later released to local television stations nationally.

Many years later, I wrote Otto a letter after the publication of *Double Take* and told him how thrilled I was with the larger accounting of his personal discoveries. Perhaps presumptively, I asked if it was possible that, given the times, both his parents' names were also assumed. He answered, "I have no complaint with that proposition," clearly, I realized later, a double entendre on his mother's name, 'Klage.'

It has long been reported that Biedermeier still had a large collection of 16-millimeter film covering his first twenty years as a director and taken by him on the various sets he used. These were originally thought to be a kind of pre-video age 'continuity,' or test shots, used during filming, but in June of this year one of these clips, with revealing footage of actor George Rooney and actress Sylvia Place, was somehow stolen and later came into the possession of the *National Enquirer,* causing a still unresolved legal contest.

As a young actor, Rooney had starred in the Biedermeier production, *Apples for Oranges,* a 'beach party' film made on location in Fort Lauderdale, Florida in 1978 and now famous for its mix of cheesecake and horror as well as the comic circumstance of New England private school students set loose in the Sunshine State. The clip, mere minutes in length, contained what appears to be a secretly filmed tryst between Mr. Rooney and actress Sylvia Place. A copy of this was only recently released on the internet by the *National Enquirer* when Mr. Rooney sued that paper for defamation of character after being called a 'profligate and promiscuous womanizer,' among other colorful slander. Miss Place was only fifteen at the time the movie was made.

As unlikely as that is, speculation is now rife that many more of the clips contain similar compromising circumstances. These films have been carefully kept in a 19th century Wells Fargo safe in the bungalow and former stagecoach stop owned by Mr. Biedermeier near Red Rock Canyon, Nevada. Several aging Hollywood 'A-list' actors, who had their own beginnings in Biedermeier productions, and are now possibly in need of attention and or publicity, have expressed concern. A motive for murder is certainly suggested there, but the circumstances previously mentioned make this unlikely.

Interestingly, that bungalow, as well as the cast-iron and steel safe, have been filmed many times by other directors over the years for various television and movie productions and were a steady source of additional income for Mr. Biedermeier's own low budget efforts. The property, originally purchased for the film, *The Cattle and the Cowed*,' a political comedy made in 1974 and featuring vampire zombies among the saguaro cactus and Joshua trees, was as close to a 'western' as Mr. Biedermeier ever made. The 'hanging tree' scene, a direct homage to *The Oxbow Incident*, with the mob arguing among themselves about the best way to tie the rope until the prisoner himself ties the knot correctly, has been viewed millions of times on YouTube. Both house and safe can also be seen in the later classic, *The Drool.*

The 'bungalow,' as he himself referred to it, had been a long-abandoned wreck when Biedermeier purchased the property in 1975. He rebuilt the structure, assisted by his wife Jessie, his ten-year old son Jason, and long-time friend Josh Green, "post by post and plank by plank" with the added purpose of making films on the property. The family lived there until 1987. The Malibu house was built in 1996.

It is known that Miss Circumstances, Otto

Biedermeier's third wife, changed her name following the surprise success of *The Drool* and just prior to their marriage. She had previously been a circus performer—an unusual combination of magician and funambulist, with the Barnum & Bailey western touring company, performing then under the stage name Dolly Dare. Her birth name is not known to us at present. Mr. Biedermeier discovered the actress working on location, prior to making *Three Rings, but one Wife* in 1994, her mysterious past being just one more coincidence in a life apparently filled with them.

Mr. Biedermeier's brief second marriage to French actress Michelle Babineaux, star of the 1991 political farce, *White House, Black Dog*, resulted in one daughter, Alma. Miss Babineaux has since remarried. Both mother and daughter are now living in Paris and have refused any comment, but my interview with the filmmaker in 1996 included the information that they had been long estranged and were uninterested in being contacted.

Mr. Biedermeier met his first wife, Jessie Fleming, at New York University. "We both loved photography and things sort of developed in the dark room," she once said to an interviewer concerning her work behind the camera. She later accompanied the director on his bicycle adventure to Europe in search of his birth parents and they married in1965, soon after his return from the Army.

Jesse Fleming was the sound technician and primary film editor on all the Biedermeier movies until her accidental death in 1987. They had three children together, two sons and a daughter. Jason, a Lieutenant in the United States Marines, died in Iraq in 2005. Kenneth, the youngest, died in the same automobile crash that killed his mother. We have been unable to contact his daughter, Audrey, an architect in Santa Monica, for this report.

Long ago, when I had already been made cynical by a shallow education but was still young enough to be looking for answers, I asked the great director what he meant by that quote, 'I don't make parody. Life itself is a parody and I attempt to capture that.' Of course, I had taken it simply as a statement of futility and cynicism in keeping with the age.

He told me then, "Journalism fails when it only reports what it wants to hear. That fellow who wrote up that interview did not listen. What I was saying then was that I don't make parody because life itself is a parody. A satire. A burlesque. We humans mock better than we appreciate. It's why we love cartoons. What makes slapstick funny. The distortion of reality is easier to see than the reality. We imitate our parents, you see, without knowing what they know. We copy our teachers, without learning what they have learned. We repeat what we hear but not what was said. It is how we learn to fail. Few will stop and think. Those few who care, try to add something. They try to build. But then, too often, what we are told is false, or what we see is only one side of a larger picture. Worse, much too often, it's counterfeit. Pretense. Hollywood is all about the pretense. I have tried to turn the pretense on its head. I have attempted to show what is true by contrast and make that clear. I try to show what is false and offer an alternative."

I asked, "Why? Does it matter? No one seems to care. People apparently want to be lied to. That's what politics is. That's why they go to the movies, isn't it?"

He was firm in his answer. "Truth matters. You have to look for it. What our children know is our only legacy. That's why I make my movies."

Further developments in this case will be carried right here in the *Hollywood Tab*.

Notes: Mysterious Circumstances
Identity as destiny

She is a larger woman now, standing about 5'10" and, at the age of 46, nearing 200 pounds. But when I first met her at the house in Malibu many years ago, she still had the lean look of a tightrope walker. The magic act she performed for Barnum & Bailey was mostly the tried and true. As Otto once happily related, "what made it unusual was, because she's black, and she wore only a black, skin-tight leotard while suspended twenty feet in the air, she appeared to audiences as a prancing silhouette in the lights. She used powder to take the shine off her skin, and the leotard left nothing to the imagination, so it truly made you imagine everything. Objects seemed to appear from nowhere."

The skin of her face is just light enough to show freckles—the result she says of too much time spent on the balcony or the beach. She also admits to the necessity of dyeing an onslaught of grey in her hair to keep it black.

Mysty is no longer staying in their home, but I asked a friend at the *LA Times* to find out where she might be. I called her Monday morning. Amazingly, she remembered me, and I was greeted at the door with a hug, and her saying, "You've gained weight!" The smile was sly and said everything else.

"My wife is a very good cook. But I blame the kids. Men always seem to gain weight after they have children."

This got the throaty laugh I remember.

She was temporarily renting the small second floor apartment of a friend near the center of Malibu and, instead of waves, at that hour there was the constant drone of traffic on U.S. 1, so she closed the window against the sea breeze and the noise, turned on a fan, and we sat in a breakfast alcove overlooking the potted key lime tree on her landing.

"I'm afraid I don't have the children for an excuse. And I was always the cook. Otto could never boil water. He was too easily distracted. Everything burned. When I went away, he ate cold cuts. Not sandwiches, mind you. Just the meat and the cheese and the bread. Like a European. He loved liverwurst. I can't stand it myself. And baloney! Sometimes we used to eat out at a nice restaurant, and he would order a sandwich. Pastrami. That sort of thing. He likes the efficiency of a sandwich—He liked that . . . But never—I'm sorry. That's not what you came here for. I was just . . . How many children do you have?"

"Four. Three boys and a girl. And a dog."

She seemed genuinely delighted with the facts. "Good! I'm glad. I'm so tired of childless couples. They're boring. Everything is just about them. They live in the present. Only the moment. The past bores them. The future bores them. And they always assume I'm one of them by choice . . . ah! . . . Tell me about yourself. What do you do now?"

"I still write. Mostly for internet magazines."

"There's a living in that?"

"No. Sadly. But my wife has a clothing shop in Santa Barbara. She pays the big bills. And I stay home and mind the dog. The kids are all teenagers now and usually off doing whatever they do."

"Very good!" She said it as if she were enthusiastic about such small facts. She asked about Laura's shop. I told her about that, and she sat up at my answer. She had been there.

Because Laura specializes in recreations of fashion design from classic movies, I thought she might have.

"You know, I always wished I could dress like Ingrid Bergman in *Casablanca*." She giggled at the idea, "Can you imagine? But I don't have the body for that anymore."

She asked where I lived now, which is only a half-mile from Laura's shop so that we only needed the minivan because one of the kids is usually driving the Toyota. She liked that. She said she hated to drive.

"Otto's first wife and his son were killed that way, you know, driving the 15 down from Red Rock in that desert at night. Lord, how he hated that road."

The best I could do was complain about the traffic in Oxnard and the hour and a half it took me to make it down the coast on Route 1. She suggested taking the Ventura Freeway through Camarillo, the most boring road in the world. I told her I preferred the traffic to tract housing.

"Very good! Yes. And the ocean. You get to see the ocean your way."

I reflexively looked at my watch. The small talk suddenly felt like a waste of time.

I said, "You worked for Otto's production company, I believe. What will you be doing now?"

The smile on her face fell as if she were hit.

"I don't know."

"I'm sorry. It's too soon for questions like that."

"No. No. It was the very first question I had. Odd— Waiting by the door for the ambulance, it was the only actual thought I had."

Now I was suddenly in the midst of what I wanted to hear about.

"You must have wondered what happened?"

"I didn't know, you see. I didn't understand. It was just

a lot of blood. Everywhere. I froze. I go over it now in my head, again and again. A stupid thing to do. If the person who murdered Otto was still there, he could have murdered me without a peep. I just froze."

"You think he was murdered?"

"Oh, yes! He was murdered. I told the police that."

"What about the knife?"

Her dark eyes are large and search your face thoroughly.

"You mean, was the knife rusted? Yes. It was. The police showed that to me because I wouldn't believe it when they said so. And I told them, it couldn't be. Impossible. Otto was meticulous about his props. He'd used that knife three or four times before. He bought it in Italy, you know, years ago. It was especially made for him at one of the oldest factories in Maniago, where they specialized in that sort of thing—what they call stilettos, but we call, 'switchblades.' That knife was a favorite. And taking care of it was my job too. After a production, I always cleaned the props we were keeping. It's been a long time. I think we had it out for *The Man Who Laughs*. But that knife was not rusted when I put it away. Period! The blade was opened, and that knife was oiled just like Otto wanted it. That was my job. I know! I was assistant producer but what I actually did was find locations and props and clothing and whatever else he thought we should have. It was a wonderful work. I loved it! I even went to your wife's shop a few times looking for the right clothes. He put me down as 'assistant producer' just so I could take care of things if something . . . Well, I was never good at numbers. I was hopeless. But I loved playing with the sets. I loved to find the little thing—the prop that made a scene work. He would tell me. He would say, 'We need a distraction. If they're all looking at the face of the monster, they'll see the makeup. Get a hat for the girl! Something that'll grab the eye of the audience, like

15

those skin-tight leotards you wore. Something I can focus on.' And I would find it!"

She gripped her hands together atop the table, with her head dropped low between her shoulders. She suddenly looked exhausted.

"Where are the props kept?"

"At the M-16 warehouse downtown. 'Otto's Garage' on San Julian over by 6th."   "That's Skid Row. I remember that. It was an old taxicab garage. He took me there."

"He did. You were very excited, I remember. Well, there's more there now. He only had the place a couple of years back then. But I'm always spending my time there when we were getting ready for a shoot—was . . . One of the street people spray painted a great big brown spider on the door. You can't miss it. A spider with red eyes and long eye lashes." She reacted to my face. "Yes!"

"Could somebody have broken in there and taken the knife?"

"Could have. But Otto has the place pretty well locked up. We were just about to get ready for a new picture and the knife is in that script. There is a knife in that story. I'll bet Otto had already gone down there and gotten a hold of it and it was just around someplace when everything happened."

"Otto hadn't spoken to you about it?"

"Not yet. We were still on vacation, you know. The rule was not to talk much about production when we were on vacation. That was the rule. But Otto did what he wanted. You couldn't tell him."

"You spoke to the police about it."

"I gave them the keys and the alarm code and the prop number too. I keep the list. Not too sophisticated. Small stuff like that's kept in plastic bins and they're all alphabetical. That one was just 'k' for knife. We had half a dozen different types

16

of knives in that one. And they are not just thrown in there either. Each one is wrapped in a towel. Carefully. I saw to that myself."

I'd called her as soon as I got a response from my friend at the *Times*, and with echoes of the past—"I remember you! You were that skinny boy that ate us out of house and home," she'd asked me to come over immediately. With my own kids in school, I had the neighbor's kid keep an eye on the dog—he graduated last spring and I knew from his father's complaint's that he still hadn't found a job. But Laura expected me to do the shopping for dinner and I was feeling a bit rushed. All of that was just my own stupidity, of course. I took a breath.

"Could he have killed himself?"

"No! Sure, he was unhappy about some things. He was in a legal match with *Lightwave*, the distributor he's been using. They've been cheating him. They wanted to go direct to TV with the next picture. To cable. Youtube. Netflix. Whatever. Otto was very upset and adamantly against that. There is always time for that after the screen release, you know. But they'd only booked the last picture, *The Big Cheese*, into 1200 theaters. Not even enough to cover the bills and they wouldn't pay their share of the advertising before dumping it onto HBO. Otto doesn't have the pull of someone like a Woody Allen or a Clint Eastwood. Independents are at the mercy of the distributors. Those guys all want open contracts so that they can dump a film that doesn't get an immediate reaction or keep it exclusively for themselves if it finds an audience. They make money one way or they other."

"How were they cheating him?"

"Same old, same old, I think. Reporting lower numbers. Especially on the streaming. The internet is pure theft, I can tell you that."

"Do you think someone from the distributor might have had a reason to kill Otto?"

"You're kidding. You don't kill the cow. You milk it. That's like the loan shark in a bad TV show that kills the guy who doesn't pay on time. It's not a winning proposition."

I pressed that thought.

"Do you think Otto owed anyone money?"

"Ha! No. You mean like a loan shark? No. He usually spent everything he had but that was it. No, that was me. When he first met me, I was in debt up to my ears. Try to tell a bank you're a magician—a magician who works the high wire at a traveling circus, and you want to borrow money. My very first car was repossessed. So, I borrowed money to get a new one because I thought I had a deal in Vegas about to happen. We were going to be there in another two weeks. Then I had an accident, and I was laid off while we were in Denver. The circus paid my medical bills and a little slack pay but that was it. Otto came to see me there. I remembered him, of course. He'd come to see me before. Like a kid. He was very sweet. He said he'd gone to our next tent in Vegas to see the show and I wasn't in it so he found out where I was. Otto paid every dime I owed, before he married me, and didn't tell me about it until after. That was the kind of guy Otto was."

I wanted to know more about that, but I felt as if I was already way out on a limb with this. I didn't understand. I'd intended to come by and pay my respects and maybe set something else up so I could add some detail to my old thesis and get it republished. Otto had accomplished a lot in the twenty years since—and then the darker thought. His death would make it more saleable. Very Hollywood. Very mercenary. And suddenly I was way out in very deep water. Out on a limb in very deep water.

"Okay," I knew I was running out of time. "Mysty, why

did you want to see me? I didn't really expect you to respond so quickly."

She was shaking her head before I finished the question.

"Why did I want to see you? Because he liked you. Otto thought very highly of you. Didn't you know that?"

"No. We only really spoke that one time when I was here, and that was nearly twenty years ago. I wrote him a couple of times after that. Once about his book."

"He liked your book about Warren William too. But one reason Otto liked you was because you didn't say anything about his private matters in your book. You were respectful. Most reporters can't get past my name. My skin color is next. Everything to them is a joke."

"That's more flattering than I think I can take."

"But he liked you most because you came to see him. You made the effort to come, instead of sitting home and speaking with him on the phone."

"Or maybe choosing to write about him first instead of Warren William."

That surprised her. I did not realize the implication of my words.

"No! It was nothing to do with that. It was because you came. You made the effort. You tried."

I had to turn the direction of the conversation again before more of my own motives were under inspection.

"Mysty, can you tell me about your name. I remember even Otto called you 'Mysty,' when I was here that time. I was surprised. I thought it was just a stage thing."

"The name I was born with was 'Georgia Whitehouse.' Can you imagine a black woman living with that? Well, my mother did. But she was a saint and I'm no saint. I never even finished high school. And I had no idea what love was. So, I married the first boy who asked me. Wallace Martin. I was Georgia Martin, then. But he was not a very nice fellow. A crummy magician. He drank too much. He liked to hit. His one gift to me was that he worked with the Shrine Circus. And I got a taste of that. The circus. It was all magic to me. But then I had a bad miscarriage when we were still in Detroit and it spoiled my chances for that part of life, and after that, Wallace left me. He left me with the medical bills. I loved the circus, though. Still do. So, I took a bus down to Florida and tried to get a job with B&B. Nothing doing. But I was already practicing my act and I worked in a coffee shop in Orlando for six months before I got another audition by using the name Dolly Dare. They liked that. Names matter. So, then I changed my name again. Easy enough. I didn't have as much as a driver's license at the time. I couldn't drive. Well, that went well for awhile. I even bought a car. And all the time I had guys telling me I should be in Vegas. I was perfect for Vegas. Guys will tell you anything, but I started to believe it. Until I fell. Until Denver."

"What happened after that?"

"Otto had already asked me to do the film, *Three Rings, but One Wife*. Then, when I recovered, we did *The Drool*. It was a hit. I got the bad idea that I was famous, and I really could do Vegas, and I told him I wanted to try. But Otto knew better. He explained it to me. He took me to Vegas and explained it all to me. So, I guess I fell twice that year. And then he made me a better offer. It was all Otto after that."

I wondered, "Did you ever regret not doing Vegas?"

"You're kidding? Vegas? That's like Broadway. You need money to make money. No. Not a bit. Never."

"So, tell me why you wanted to talk to me?"

She looked me in the eye.

"I should remind you that it was you who called me,

shouldn't I? But you're right. It's because I think I need help. And I'll tell you something else. Except for Otto's family, I don't really have a lot of friends. Not close ones. Hollywood isn't a place for that. . . . Otto was my friend." She twisted the knot of her fingers tighter on the tabletop. "And I can't find his will. I looked. It's not in the safe in Malibu. I drove up to the bungalow at Red Rock to look there too. And all the 16-millimeter film reels were gone. All of them! At least forty reels. I don't know what's going on. And Josh wasn't there—Josh Green is living there now, but he's been staying somewhere down here since he heard about Otto. I told the police about it. But that's all I could do."

An odd thought occurred to me. I had one of those 'family matters' conversations with Laura once. She told me to remember, if anything ever happened to her, that all the papers were at the accountant's office. She knew I would forget something like that.

"Maybe the will is somewhere else. Do you have a lawyer, or an accountant?"

"Truman. He's Otto's lawyer. I called him. He's the one that told me that Otto kept his papers in Malibu. I'd never even thought about it."

"But it wasn't there?"

"Nothing. Absolutely nothing. Not even my engagement ring. Otto spent a small fortune on that. And he told me once that if I ever had to, that the ring would pay for almost anything I needed. It was an antique he bought at an auction in New York. We kept in the safe, but I have no idea how much it was worth."

"You told the police about that as well?"

"Yes."

I knew right then that this limb was out in very deep water, indeed.

I asked her what else she knew about the missing films, but in fact, those were all from well before her time. Sometime in the early 1980's, Otto had started using videotape instead of film and she had never even seen the old 16-millimeter stock outside of the metal cans. I asked her if Audrey might know anything, as the only other member of Otto's immediate family. But Mysty had called the daughter first. Audrey said that her father had never mention the will to her.

I asked Mysty a little more about Truman Donitz, in that it appeared Truman had been Otto's lawyer forever.

"Truman wasn't very helpful. He didn't seem to know very much. I know he'd been talking to Otto a lot lately because the new film in pre-production. There's always a lot of legal strings to tie. But Tru said he hadn't seen the will since Otto signed it, and that was years ago. . . . And I called Philip as well. Philip Reeves was Otto's accountant. He said he had no idea about any of it."

"Mysty, when you're going over it all in your mind, what do you think? Someone did this, and you don't know who, but maybe you know something that'll give us a clue."

She was staring at me, expressionless, the tears thick in her eyes.

"You don't understand. I don't know anyone that would kill Otto. No one! Even his enemies liked him."

We could both hear the sounds on the stairs that went down the outside of the house when the police came, but the knock was still abrupt, as was the voice.

"Miss Circumstances? It's the police. Can we speak with you?"

She looked at me. "I had a feeling. I'm sorry. I guess that's the real reason why I asked you to come over. I needed somebody to be here."

Naturally, they were very interested in just who I was,

and kept me there on the landing for at least fifteen minutes after they'd taken Mysty away. Traffic on Route 1 was snarled even worse by the double-parked patrol cars. A small crowd stared up at us from the street and made me wonder how anyone could perform in front of an audience.

Notes: True man or false
Grease in the wheels of justice

Monday was cool, which I frankly prefer. Most of Santa Monica was looking very green but the picket line of palm trees on Wilshire Boulevard was as incongruous as ever above the low storefronts and steady stream of cars. The GPS on my cell phone had Arty and me standing in front of a party-goods store. After the fact, I realized I could have found Truman Donitz's office just by triangulating between the Krispy Kreme, the In-N-Out Burger, and the nearest pizza shop. His office is down an alley, in a house close behind the storefronts, and I see my mistake only when I'm actually standing in the alley, out of the flow of pedestrians with the leash tight to keep Arty's nose out of places it shouldn't be and wondering what I did wrong. The numbers and arrow are on the wall just above my head. Many of the original houses of the old residential neighborhood are still there, behind the newer stucco storefronts occupying what were once front yards. It makes for a secret world of sorts.

'Truman Donitz, Attorney-at-law' is on the brass plate above the mail slot. I rang the doorbell just like any door-to-door salesman.

Arty was anxious over several of the palm trees he missed on the way from the parking meter, and I kept him reined in close. I only had him with me because the neighbors' kid saw me coming. His dad is all for teaching his son to take on responsibilities and earn some pocket money, but the boy is more interested in learning how to hide from anything that smacks of work. He's eighteen. In a year or two, when his needs enlarge a bit, he'll be game, perhaps. Girls like it if you buy them things. That is, if he's still living in his parents' basement. Arty doesn't particularly like the kid anyway, but I can't afford a regular dog sitter.

I rang the doorbell again.

My own father, a man of undenied imperfections and readily admitted self-delusion who has had dozens of jobs through the years, is usually correct in his assessment of others. He has a phrase that is appropriate here. 'Of course, lawyers are slippery. They're the grease in the wheels of justice.'

The woman who finally answers the door does not look like a lawyer, nor a receptionist—too oddly dressed for that. She's slight of build and dressed in a multi piece outfit with no apparent theme of style or color, and has a small gold ring in her nose—something I'd more readily expect from someone ten or fifteen years younger. She has dark hair with purple streaks. Her shoulders are exposed, and both are tattooed in what at first appeared to be a floral design that makes me think of Georgia O'Keeffe, with what I took to be thorns.

She says, "What is it?"

"I'm looking for Truman Donitz."

"Do you have an appointment?"

I did not.

"Then you'll have to wait."

Arty gave her a good sniff, but she ignored him. She did not exactly invite me in but left the door open and so I entered.

What was once a living room was now an office, complete with several vinyl covered 1950's style chairs, a coffee table with magazines several months old, and a plant with dusty leaves. The woman sat down behind an L-shaped desk and proceeded to scroll through several venues on her computer screen. I couldn't see what she was shopping for.

Before I could settle myself, or Arty, the hallway to the back of the house darkened as it was filled by the large shape of a balding man in a gray suit.

The first impression the man I still understood to be Mysty's lawyer makes is not good. Nor do I believe he intends it to be. I have actually heard of Truman Donitz before. His love-hate relationship with reporters is well established. He is overweight to a degree that makes his health immediately questionable. His belly proceeds him, and the stain on his shirt by the buttons betrays this, as well as does the fall of his tie to one side of the burl of flesh beneath. He wears expensive clothes that do not fit him well. I'm thinking thrift store finds. The growl in his voice is that of a cigar smoker who inhales. As always, my first thought is of the movie star he most resembles. This is a bad habit; I am well aware. Laura reminds me of that, constantly. But then I am thinking that Sidney Greenstreet was a bit thinner, before I stop myself. No matter how good the actor, you can't learn anything about anyone by seeing them through that sort of veneer.

I told him my name and that I had just come from speaking with Mysty.

As the assumed lawyer for the accused, he is not interested in giving me the time of day. But I insisted. We remained standing in the outer office, supposedly because he doesn't want any dogs on the premises.

His first words were, "I don't want any animals in here."

Arty is perplexed at the tone of voice so I shortened his leash even more. While we talk, Donitz's secretary is playing with the computer keyboard with one finger at a time, as if it might explode.

He wanted to know how I knew Mysty.

Finally provoked, I asked him why she'd hired such a disagreeable fellow to be her lawyer.

He told me to "fuck myself."

I left with Arty trying to get one last sniff of the young woman.

Arty really doesn't care for me any more than the neighbors' kid. But at least he usually minds me. His primary interest in life is finding a harem of his own and protecting them. To my knowledge, he has never met a girl he doesn't like.

I then went up to the Lost Hills jail on Agoura Road without an appointment. With no chance to see her, I simply left Mysty a note describing my encounter with Mr. Donitz, along with the advice that she should get another lawyer.

On Tuesday, attorney George Peal, of Gregory and Peal, called me and asked if I could come to his office in Malibu. I have to take Arty with me again because the neighbors' son is still in hiding.

I am immediately put in a better mood because the secretary there tells me the dog is welcome. Arty is pleased with her. She is dressed nondescriptly, in gray and white, with no tattoos visible and no nose ring.

Peal is the sort of fellow you hear about in Hollywood all the time and, sight unseen, I assumed him to be a slick operator. He is not fat but has the neat beard of a successful middle-aged man, impeccably fitted black suit, pressed white shirt with crisp collar. The piece de resistance is neat suspenders, much like the ones Fredric March wore in *Inherit the Wind,* and he displays these to me in taking off his jacket and loosening his tie (by way, I think, of trying to make me feel more comfortable. I was wearing jeans.) And he had a ready smile. He speaks with the gravel of a long-time smoker who has quit and he keeps a root beer candy in his mouth. He offered me one. I like root beer but I am avoiding candy these days.

I tell him, "My wife has told me to drop twenty pounds, or I can sleep alone."

He says, "Listen to your wife. Mine told me to quit smoking almost every day until she divorced me. Now I have some kind of growth in my throat. Can you imagine? If I had listened to her I would be healthy and still married to the most beautiful woman in Southern California. Well, maybe not. Her new boyfriend smokes too, and he's a good deal younger than me. But at least I'd be healthy." As he says this, he gets a hand down on Arty's sweet spot, just behind his left front leg. "What kind of dog is he? Chocolate Lab? A mix?"

"Labrador and Pit Bull Terrier."

"Excellent combination. And I'll bet he's as friendly as a puppy."

"More."

He tells me again that Mysty has engaged him to represent her against the murder charges. He readily informs me that she has no funds to pay him at present, but that it should be a high-profile case, a rainmaker, and business has been slow. Except for drug arrests and the underage sexual escapades of various children of the rich and famous, his docket is not full. He is working pro bono and is happy for the work. This sort of apparent honesty of motive makes me think Mr. Peal has something up his sleeves beyond the cuffs and the links.

I told him, "I have to remind you that I'm a reporter, and my first allegiance is to my paper and getting the facts, maybe even the truth, but I do like Mysty, and I'd like very much to discover that she is innocent—of these charges, at least. But I won't pull punches."

He smiled. Cats, Cheshire or otherwise, don't smile in

my experience, but if they did, his would be that smile. My dog does smile, however. A dumb grin that is not easily resistible. Especially around the dinner table. That's why Arty is a little overweight, just like me.

Mr. Peal nods, "And I can relate to you that Mysty is a very trusting sort of person, a little naive I think, but she has settled on you as the one reporter she will speak with. In fact, she told me to tell you that. Her story is now in your hands."

"Christ!"

"You may need to call upon the Lord before this is over. I have a few more things to tell you. I'm putting you down as a legal assistant in this case. On an interim basis, you understand. No payroll. But Mysty wants to be able to talk to you. She trusts you. The only way you'll have that kind of access is if you're working with me as part of her counsel." I sat back against the cool green leather of my chair and tried to absorb this. Arty sprawled himself on the carpet between us, unimpressed. Peal squinted at me. "I have never done anything like this before, but I see some advantages. There is no money here for the kind of private investigation that might dig up any dirt. Most of that will be a matter of phone calls. But you can actually help. Mysty is still in shock. She starts crying and then she can't talk. You can keep Mysty calm. You might even come up with some leads. Two heads are always better than one. And then again, you'll have access to the sort of information that your editor may be looking for."

"I'm not sure I bargained for this. I'm just trying to write a couple of newspaper pieces and re-write a book. I'm a writer. Where would I start?"

"I can't tell you. But you can help her just by telling her story, I think. Get a little sympathy going for her. I can't do that." He uses his hands very effectively when he talks, emphasizing a word here and there. But I suppose Peal is successful because he can read faces. He is studying mine when he says, "Did you know that Wallace Martin has hired Truman Donitz to represent him?" I suppose my face fell. An easy read there. "No? Well, Truman was Otto's lawyer first, not Mysty's. That's the rub, here—Now, I've known Truman for many years. He does not like to lose. Worse, he seldom takes a client if he thinks the case is not in his favor. Whatever Wallace Martin's involvement in the murder of Otto Biedermeier, I suspect it is peripheral. And I already think I know what that is. I will tell you more if you'll promise to keep it under your hat."

I especially like old expressions you usually only encounter in black and white movies, but I wasn't even wearing my baseball cap.

"This is going to get complicated. Are you going to warn me that I can't report on it every time you tell me something?"

"No. I'm just not going tell you what I don't want you to know. I'm actually telling you this as a favor to Mr. Donitz. One hand washes the other, you understand. Are you agreed?"

"Okay. For now."

"Truman wanted you to understand--evidently you've met recently. Yes?"

"Encountered."

"Right. I know what you mean. But he thinks you might have misunderstood something and would like that cleared up so the story you do report doesn't get things wrong." George Peal stretched himself liberally in his own chair. You could see his mind working over the words. "It seems Wallace Martin moved out to California specifically to extort Mr. Biedermeier. He's had a 'bad run of luck' you might say, and, like the more colorful George Washington Plunkitt, 'he's seen his opportunities and he took 'em.' Mr. Martin was aware that his divorce from Mysty had never been properly approved. Likely as not he purposely made that not happen. But, according to the laws of the State of Michigan in 1990, when they officially separated, the divorce was never finalized. Therefore, as a legal matter, Mysty was not, in fact, married to Otto Biedermeier."

Having thought this through in about thirty seconds, mouth open, I had only one question.

"Did she know that?"

"I don't know. She hasn't told me."

"But most of that will soon be public knowledge, if it isn't already. What part am I supposed to keep under my hat?"

"The part about the extortion. Mr. Wallace is bargaining for a lesser charge. He evidently approached Otto Biedermeier with the information about the marriage some time ago. Otto paid him what he could—about twenty thousand dollars—with the agreement that Martin would not tell Mysty or contact her in any way. It was made clear to Otto after the initial payment that more money was wanted. Truman found out about all this, and—perhaps skirting the law—interceded on Otto's behalf. Blackmail being illegal, if Martin wanted more money, he had to do it according to Hoyle. Money doesn't grow on trees. As of that time, Martin was employed by Truman Donitz for temporary services. The money would be paid out on that basis. All apparently legal. Otherwise, they would simply go to the police, report the attempted blackmail, and take the heat for the mistaken marriage. Martin agreed. He's been in regular contact with Mr. Donitz since."

George Peal did the old pencil bounce on his desk to give me time to digest all that. I kept quiet until he picked up the thread of his revelations again.

"But Otto was putting them off. Truman wasn't sure why, but he thought it just might be a money matter. On Saturday evening Martin got impatient with just talking to Truman on the phone, and a little drunk, and he went to speak with Truman in person about the situation. Truman convinced him that he understood. Martin has debts to cover. Some people can't wait. That sort of thing. But Otto would do what they could, sooner than later. And Truman gave him a thousand dollars cash for a few weeks rent out of his own pocket and Martin left. That was just before 1:30." Peal studied Arty for a moment. Arty raised an eyebrow but kept his jowls on the carpet. I had my own thoughts, but I wanted to hear the whole presentation first. Peal finally realized I wasn't going to ask a bunch of silly questions and he continued. "More importantly, Martin had no motive for killing his golden goose. On the contrary, the previous payment has been confirmed by the police. And finally, Martin was seen earlier that evening— actually very early on that Sunday morning--about 12:30--at his apartment, in Oxnard. Otto was murdered in Malibu between 1 and 1:30 according to the coroner. It is possible Martin could have raced over and killed Otto, before going to see Truman, but highly unlikely. He was in fact arrested by the police for speeding over on the Ventura Freeway at 1:45 that same morning. He had no blood on him but did have a load of about six ounces of tequila in his blood stream and a thousand bucks cash in his pocket."

All that wasn't important.

"First off, it's not a race. Especially at that time of night. I drive the coast highway a lot. But the point about killing his golden goose is good. In any case, unless any of that information is released by the police, I won't repeat it. What I'm more interested in is if you are going to do a good job defending Mysty, or is there a old boys' club thing going on here."

That brought a smile to the Peal's face. Not a cat smile. Sort of a doggie grin.

"Yeah. I'll give Mysty my best effort. And by the way, I

32

compliment you for your effort to drag George Rooney into this. In your story in the *Tab*. It's a good ploy. I don't think Rooney has the balls to kill anyone, despite his reputation as a lothario. But it might be useful for casting a little doubt on what otherwise might appear to be a very certain case. And as for the 'boys club,' I can tell you that nothing would please me more than to make Truman lose again. Even now. I hear he's had his own hard times lately. But he's up on me at court right now, three games to one."

Notes at a funeral
with a cast of characters

Truman Donitz reached me with the obvious effort of a fast waddle, arms pumping, legs stiff, barging with obvious purpose across a closely trimmed swath of bright green grass at the Woodlawn Cemetery in Santa Monica. This was in broad sunlight and still well away from the funeral party.

"What are you doing here?"

"I was asked to come."

"By whom?"

"Mysty."

"She has no standing here."

"She is Otto's wife, until proven otherwise, and not his murderer until proven guilty."

"You are not welcome."

"Nevertheless."

"I want you to leave."

"I don't respect your wishes."

"I'll have you removed."

"I checked in at the gate and showed them my invitation."

"You're a reporter!"

"I also knew Otto, and Mysty, and I've agreed not to cover the funeral beyond basics.

He stood in my way for a moment longer before turning to waddle back to the open tent. Before the service began, with arms chopping the air, he conducted a whispered conversation with a tall, rather thin woman, dressed simply in a black skirt and blouse. This was Audrey Biedermeier, Otto's daughter with Jessie Fleming. She continued to glare at me, green eyes flashing, even as she greeted several other members of the party with hugs as they arrived.

The late arrivals include one younger woman that I soon learned was Alma, Otto's younger daughter by his second marriage with Michelle Babineaux. She is cinnamon-haired, blue-eyed, and very good looking. Following her, an elegant looking middle-aged woman arrived just before the service began, as if they might in fact have been waiting. This was the actress and model, Tamara. She is a regular in fashion magazines now because she has her own designer-line of clothes. Everyone present appeared to know her and she hugged each of them with the exception of the representative from the cemetery and myself. She gave me the passing glance I might expect from a stranger in the street. The oldest person present, a heavyset women enveloped in bunting-like folds of black, who might be in her eighties, stood at the other side of Truman Donitz. Her face is pink as if steadily flushed and framed by billows of white hair pinned by black netting. She wears rimless octagonal glasses set low enough on a wide nose that she could stare back at me over the tops.

The ceremony is surprisingly brief. The prayer read by a priest is from common Catholic liturgy, though I don't believe Otto was a practicing Catholic and there is to be no funeral Mass. No one of the party spoke at the graveside, though the unhappiness was palpable. I looked around for other unwelcomed guests and counted about half a dozen malingerers, several with cameras, all within earshot. I recognized one of them as a regular at the *Los Angeles Times*.

A function room in a small stucco and Spanish style

house in the midst of the cemetery served as a gathering place afterward. There was a short table in the largest room, with plastic cups containing warm apple juice and a white and tasteless cake cut in neat squares and arrayed on paper plates so as to fill the table space but only serving to further exaggerate how few people were present.

Those few gathered in knots until one of the other guests, Philip Reeves, produced a bottle of fine bourbon from a paper bag that had conspicuously shown from his jacket pocket at graveside. Clear plastic cups were supplied by the official, and everyone was offered a slug before the first toast was made.

Philips Reeves is maybe 60 to 100 years old, a thin man, with a comb-over on sun scorched scalp and a walnut tan. My guess, given the look on his face, is that this has something to do with alcohol. His black suit is loose on his shoulders. I'm thinking: borrowed. He was Otto Biedermeier's longtime accountant and evidently knew everyone present as well, even addressing me by my first name as he filled my cup.

He spoke loudly to the assembled as he raised a hand, "Goodbye, Otto. You will be dearly missed, and the world is already a much poorer place. God rest."

The bourbon was top-notch.

The young woman Reeves had addressed as 'Alma' as he served, raised her cup immediately after. "I am most unhappy now that I never met this man. He was truly my father. He gave me life in ways I did not understand until recently. Now I must live with the regret. But here's to that man I never knew, may he rest in peace."

There were a few whispers. The white-haired woman stepped forward.

"The truth is, I loved Linc more than a brother. God forgive me for the thoughts I once had. He came to us already a man at eight years old. I was twelve. Lincoln was my first love, though he never knew it. He couldn't have replaced our John, who died in the war, but he was a true brother to my sister and me, and a good son to my parents when they most needed . . ." She slipped a hand beneath the netting to wipe her eyes. "Goodbye, Link."

She could not quite get the cup to her lips and stood there a moment in silence.

Audrey Biedermeier stepped forward. She was ignoring me now as her eyes slid over the other faces.

"I loved him dearly. He was a good father. That was all I ever expected of him, I suppose. I wish I had asked for more. I always thought there would be time. And now that chance is gone. . . . Goodbye, Dad."

She drank the entire contents of her cup in one swallow and put it forward to Philip for a refill.

Phillip Reeves started to cry. My own eyes were pretty teary.

A broad-shouldered man who had been addressed as Charlie stepped up. He was at least in his 60's, with a deeply tanned face behind a short grey-white beard. I didn't know his relationship to the family but he looked familiar to me.

"Here's to you, mi compadre. I'll go without you this year but there'll be no pleasure in it. Anyone wants to come down to drown the sorrows with me is welcome."

I asked afterward and found out that Mr. Parrot ran a fishing boat out of Puerto San Carlos and had been taking Otto out for over thirty years. He had also been an extra in a number of Otto's films.

Tamara, dressed in a neck-to-ankle black silk dress, stepped forward. She was in her fifties by my eye, and still elegant in posture, but I suspect she is older. Following a short movie career in Italy, she had appeared in one of Otto's films before becoming a *Vogue* model in the 1970's. She is often seen on TV now as 'The older woman.'

"Addio, amore mio. I should have married you when I had the chance. My loss is now forever--."

But before she could raise her glass, she started to cry in a way that was unexpected, her face collapsing behind a white linen handkerchief pulled quickly from his jacket by Mr. Donitz. She sobbed. There was a moment then that we all stood still. Finally, she managed to add, "Ti amero per sempre . . . And I know, whatever happened that night, that Mysty loved you too."

That brought on a renewed wave of loud whispers. Another fellow stepped forward. Josh Green was an actor, frequent driver and handyman on many of Otto's movie sets. A jack of all trades. It was rumored, and I later read, that in order to keep the picture on schedule, Josh Green had shot the beginning of *Runway* in 1987. That was shortly after the death of the director's wife and son, when Otto could not get out of his chair at Red Rock. The picture did well, but many sequences were awkward, and the editing was crude by Otto's standards, and the sound uneven. I suspect he might have done more than was rumored, but it kept Otto from financial difficulties.

Green is in his fifties, and balding, but as lean as a twenty-year-old. His eyes most frequently fixed on Audrey. He said, "That's a fact. Mysty loved you. And I loved you. We all loved you. I have no idea what I'm going to do with my life now, you son of a gun. I'll have to get a real job." He was crying profusely as he reached the last of his words. Tamara passed Donitz's crumpled handkerchief to him but had to retrieve it when she started to cry again herself. Audrey did not move from her place a few feet away.

Truman Donitz stepped up.

"You made it tough on the rest of us, old boy. Standards high. Expectations higher.

You made my career, but now I think I'd better retire and smell the roses, while there's still time."

Only a representative and I from the cemetery had not spoken.

Smaller groups formed again around the room. I stood alone in a corner observing at it all until Alma Biedermeier came over.

"They are talking about you. You're a reporter?"

"Yes. But I'm here as a friend."

"You knew Otto?"

"A little. I interviewed him for a book quite a few years ago. But I came today because Mysty asked me to. She wanted me to tell her all about it."

"Oh! I read that! I was reading your book just yesterday! At the library. And that was you, then! I sat there for hours and read almost the whole thing. I knew so little about him. I suppose now that's just another a hole in my life."

There was little I had to say in return. "I often wonder how much any of us know about anyone else."

"That's the truth. I thought I knew my mother, but I was wrong. Very wrong."

"I'm sorry."

"It's like losing two parents with the one death."

"How does that happen?"

She looked around the room before speaking. Mr. Donitz was watching us.

She leaned toward me and whispered, "What are you doing for dinner?"

I instantly calculated the kids could fend for themselves. They usually did.

"Nothing."

"Will you meet me about seven? Someplace?"

"How about Abalone Joe's? It's a cafe in Malibu."

"Fantastic! I'll speak to you there."

It occurred to me again on the drive home that the brief ceremony had been caused by the nature of Otto's death and Mysty's arrest. Certainly, the man deserved more than he got.

Notes: Alma Biedermeier
and the young girl

She is taller than she first appears. Or perhaps she had been slumping under the weight of the sad occasion at the cemetery. She wears flat heels and stands straight and square shouldered. I'd say about 6'1". She looked me directly in the eye as we spoke, just as the father she never knew had once done, except these eyes were a sharp blue instead of walnut-dark, and Otto was not as tall.

Alma was sitting at a table on the patio when I got there but I called her over to the sidewalk. With the food so close, Arty pulled forcefully at his leash.

"They allow dogs on the patio but I'm afraid my being away for most the day has made Arty a little anxious. I'm not sure it's a good idea."

She immediately went down on eye level and let Arty lick her face. I pulled him away when he started to get friendlier, and she stood again.

"But I'm famished! Where can we eat?"

"There's Kelpy's around the corner on Route 1. It's just a hot dog stand, but it's pretty good and they have tables and umbrellas. Arty loves Kelpy Dogs. Both types."

"Hot Dogs! An American hot dog? Incredible! I haven't had one since I was in school!" She has a tendency to speak in exclamation. Very cute.

She tells me her mother is a food Nazi who would

never let her eat anything that wasn't whole grain, pesticide free, and guaranteed to have no genetically modified content.

"Except for the vegetables, everything was stale! Everything! Like cardboard!"

The Kelpy Dog is an unfair comparison to most frankfurters, but they charge accordingly. I philosophized aloud that hot dogs were not all the same. Here it was the addition of kelp relish as much as the beef they used. But still, even with having to buy one more for Arty as well, it was within my budget.

By way of breaking the ice, I told her about my difficulty finding a sitter for Arty. Laura's shop is only open until 9 on Thursdays. But as soon as Alma found out the sorts of things Laura sells, she wanted to go there immediately and check it out.

I told her, at that time of day it would be a good hour and a half drive. We hardly had time enough. But Laura's was open tomorrow.

"I'll be there! I have to fly back to Paris on Saturday. My mother says she's very ill. She gets sick when she's upset but I really don't care if I ever see her again! She's a selfish bitch! And I think she's lying. But I'm all she has. She probably just wants me back to tell her about the funeral. I guess that makes us both reporters now. . . . So tell me about my father."

I told her what was easily said. At first I spoke about the filmmaker I had pursued years before. The man who had welcomed me into his home. I took a break from that to ask about her mother.

"I have a story for you about her," she says. "A good one!"

"Tell me."

"Only if you tell me about Mysty."

"Tell me about your mother first."

42

She finished her first hot dog and ordered another, got a second root beer, adjusted herself on the plastic seat and said, "So, Otto Biedermeier wasn't actually my father!"

Someone at the next table looked over in our direction. I patted at the air for her to lower her voice.

"What about what you said at the funeral?"

"That was true! He was my true father because he is responsible for me even being alive. He married my mother to keep her from having an abortion. She came to him when they were finished with filming *White House, Black Dog* and told him she was pregnant, and she was going home to have an abortion. He told her he would help her if she wouldn't. He told her he'd marry her if she wouldn't. And he did. They never even slept together! Never! Not even after they were married!"

"Who was your father, then?"

"She wouldn't tell me but I think I know. I want to speak with him tomorrow. He said he would talk to me. I think he knows what it's about. He looked very sheepish."

"Josh Green."

"Yes . . . But you won't write that! You won't write about any of this, will you? Promise! You told Mr. Donitz that you were at the funeral as a friend."

"This isn't at the funeral, but how do you know that?"

"He told Audrey that. I heard it."

This information was relevant to the man, Otto Biedermeier, but perhaps not the films. I couldn't make such a promise. I changed the subject.

"What do you think of Audrey?"

"She's wonderful! I'm going to have breakfast with her tomorrow. I'm going to tell her about Josh."

Another turn in the story presented itself.

"That might be a problem."

"Why. Because Josh has his eye on her. Everyone could

see that. He's just an old—what do you call it? Lothario? Goat. Or just a dog! Some men can't help themselves. I'm sure she has him pegged."

She struck me as having unusual common sense.

"Why do you speak English so well? Actually, American English."

"My mother married an American after she divorced Otto. Todd Amory. She has a weakness for Americans, I think. That and stale food. I grew up with both. Todd has family money. He has a public relations firm. He liked to throw parties and invite all his pals. We lived in Meudon in Paris. Right at Bellevue on the Rue Marcel Allegot. Do you know it?"

"No. I've never been."

"But I went to school in Boston. Todd graduated from Harvard so that was an easy pick to get away from my mother."

"Ah. But you never tried to speak to your father—to Otto?"

"She forbade me to. She told me it was part of the agreement when they separated. He evidently gave her money and made her promise. She said he was very crude. Very difficult. But then, Todd was a good enough father for me, I thought. At least he was there when I needed him to be. I was far more upset when my mother divorced Todd than she was, I think. He never said a bad word about her. But that started me thinking. I already knew she was a bitch." Alma shrugged as if the fact was an accepted truth. "I thought that maybe I didn't know the truth about Otto either. But I took my time. I thought there was time! And then the papers had the news about his murder, and I went to her and she didn't want to know anything about it. She just didn't want to know! It wasn't her business, she said! I think someone had already called her. She had the look, just before. Like she had been slapped. So I said I was going to the funeral. It was my father after all. I was going. And that's when she told me. She told me the truth. I wasn't even his child, she said! I couldn't believe it, but then it made so much sense. So I came anyway. And I'm glad I did!"

"At the funeral, you said that his death was 'another hole. ' What did you mean by 'another'?"

"Oh that!" She waved at the air. "That was just me being dramatic, as my mother says. Any display of emotion to her is being dramatic." She paused a moment, took a deep breath, looked around to see that she wasn't going to be heard, and looked at me again. "And selfish! I get that from her too. But when I was a kid, I wanted to have brothers and sisters. That was what I wanted more than anything. I didn't want toys. And Todd wanted that too. I heard them talk about it over and over. And I just wanted it more and more. And then, Todd discovered that she had been taking the pill! All those years! He must have found something. I don't know. Anyway, she admitted it! She said she never wanted to have kids. Ever! And that was when Todd divorced her. She liked his money, and the sex, I suppose, but she didn't love him. I think he was heartbroken. . . . Still, Todd paid for me to go to Harvard. She wouldn't have done that!"

"If she was so mercenary, why didn't she just stay with Otto? He had money."

"Otto was Jewish."

"What?"

Alma offered me an exaggerated sigh and a face to match. "It's the way she is. I don't think she knew it when she married him, but she found out soon enough. Otto was Jewish! You know. From his mother. She thought he was just German. My mother is a terrible anti-Semite! Her father hated the Jews. I've heard her talk badly about them all my life. She's a real bigot!"

My only thought at that moment was, what on earth is

45

there good about the woman? And Alma answered the thought as if I had spoken it.

"She is a good actress. A fine actress. She can pretend anything she wants to. And a professional liar. But when she gets what she wants, she can't pretend to like it."

What was left?

"What will you do now?"

"I'm working for Todd, now. I represent his company in Europe. But it's not much of anything. Just public relations. I'm the pretty young thing. He says I'm his secret weapon against the suits. I want to pay him back for what he's done for me. But I'd like to do something a little more rewarding."

"Such as?"

"I was a history major at Harvard. I know that's not worth much these days, but I love the facts of things. I love to study. I write pretty well. I was thinking, perhaps, maybe, if I can work it out, I'd like to write something about Europe and why Europeans are so different from Americans. They are so different. Really!"

"I believe you."

"And I just had a thought."

I had to laugh, "I can practically see you working your way there."

"I'm sorry. I'm so obvious. Todd says I am guileless."

This was not my thought at all. It was obvious to me that she probably had Todd wrapped around her finger.

"Funny. I was thinking that you are very cunning. What is it you were thinking of?"

She took a breath. What could be so weighty?

"Would you let me help you? Would you let me help you write about Otto?"

I was not expecting that. "I don't think you understand. I'm writing for a newspaper. There's very little payback. But I'm only doing it because I want to revise my book on Otto. Bring it up to date. It's a university press. There is very little in that either."

"It's not the pay! It's the experience! I'll do it for free! I can do research. I'm very good at it. I promise."

For a very brief moment I wished I was twenty years younger and single.

"I don't know what to say. If you want to try your hand at it, go ahead. You have a vested interest. You might find things I can't. But don't involve yourself with the murder. That's a much darker business."

"I think I would like to know more about the man."

"But you're going back to Paris."

"Yes. I have to. But I can work from there."

And another thought passed—it was good that she would be so far away.

Filmmaker Otto Biedermeier buried

October 26th, 2016; A *Hollywood Tab* exclusive by Thomas Lenz

Otto Biedermeier, 76, director of more than thirty films, including *Lost Circus*, *Fowl Play*, and *The Drool*, was buried this week in a small family service at Woodlawn Cemetery, in Santa Monica. In attendance were his daughters, Audrey and Alma Biedermeier, long time family friend Tamara, his attorney Truman Donitz, and several close associates.

In a surprising development, Mysterious Circumstances, Biedermeier's presumed wife of the past twenty years, is currently being held by the Malibu Sheriff's Office in connection with the October 16th murder of Mr. Biedermeier at the beachfront home they shared. It is now believed by authorities that Ms. Circumstances, a former circus performer, is still legally married to Wallace Martin of Oxnard, formerly of Detroit Michigan, from whom she separated in 1990.

Attorney George Peal, of Gregory and Peal, counsel for Miss Circumstances, has said she is innocent of all charges and eager for a speedy trial to clear her name. It is noteworthy that Mr. Martin is now represented by Truman Donitz, previously the legal council for Otto Biedermeier.

Though no motive for the murder has yet been announced, it is also believed that an engagement ring of substantial value as well as legal documents are currently missing from the Biedermeier home.

Mr. Biedermeier is survived by his daughters, Audrey

and Alma. Two sons, Jason and Kenneth, predeceased their father. Jason, a Marine Corps Lieutenant, was killed in action in Anbar Province, Iraq in 2004. Kenneth died in the same car crash in 1987 that killed his mother, Jessie Fleming. Miss Fleming, Otto Biedermeier's first wife, had previously been assistant director on all the Biedermeier films up until the time of her death.

Miss Circumstances, better known now simply as Mysty, married Mr. Biedermeier in 1995. She has vehemently denied killing her husband.

Sheriff Donald Gluck has issued the following statement:

'Mysterious Circumstances, aka Dolly Dare, aka Georgia Martin, aka Georgia Whitehouse, has been arrested on suspicion of the murder of her husband, Otto Biedermeier at their home in Malibu, in the early hours of October 16th. Mr. Biedermeier was stabbed in the chest and found lying on his bed. The weapon used was a modified switchblade, with a retractable blade, previously used as a prop in several of Mr. Biedermeier's movies. The motive may have been a dispute over money. Arraignment was held this morning in the County court. Anyone having further knowledge of this case should direct their inquires to our office.'

Miss Circumstances is represented by well known attorney George Peal, who has also requested that anyone having further information concerning the case call his office as soon as possible.

As reported previously, Mysty called the police after coming home from a party early Sunday morning, October 16th, to find her husband's bloodied body. She has since told this reporter that she did not kill her husband and that she had no idea who might have done it, but confirmed the addition information that private papers and a valuable ring had been stolen from a safe. In addition, a larger safe at their second home near Red Rock Canyon, Nevada, has also been found to be empty.

In light of a recent scandal concerning George Rooney, it is noteworthy that the second safe reportedly contained an accumulation of as many as forty 16-millimeter film reels taken by the director at various movie locations to test exterior lighting, frame selected scenes, and maintain continuity during filming. However, it was one of these reels that included the footage taken by Mr. Rooney himself during an attempted seduction of an underage co-star during the filming of *Apples for Oranges* and clearly shows the unexpected interruption of the events by the director. This oversize safe, and its ornate 'Wells Fargo' emblem, may be remembered from several western movies, including Otto Biedermeier's *The Cattle and the Cowed*.

George Rooney recently sued the *Enquirer* for an alleged slander contained in a lengthy report concerning his extramarital affairs and seductions. In response the *Enquirer* released a copy of the self-made film taken by Mr. Rooney of himself during the earlier tryst. It has been confirmed that this film was taken with the same 16-millimeter camera used by Mr. Biedermeier for his test shots and apparently kept with the others by Mr. Biedermeier in the safe at Red Rock.

In other developments, reliable sources say that Miss Circumstances may indeed not have been legally married to Mr. Biedermeier after all. Her first husband, Wallace Martin, recently of Oxnard and formerly of Detroit, Michigan, has been taken into custody. Mr. Martin has not been officially charged with any involvement with the Biedermeier murder. No further statement was issued concerning the cause of his arrest, but sources have suggested that he may have been working with Miss Circumstances in an attempt to defraud Mr. Biedermeier. Mr. Martin's Lawyer, Truman Donitz, has refused comment.

To further complicate this already muddied picture, it is noteworthy that Mr. Donitz was, for many years, the personal lawyer of Otto Biedermeier.

Miss Circumstances, who was Biedermeier's third wife, is the former Dolly Dare, known to many from the Barnum & Bailey circus circuit during the early 1990's. Hoping to establish her act in Las Vegas, she changed her name to that of the lead character of *The Drool*, following the surprise success of that film, and just prior to her marriage to the filmmaker. Her specialty as a circus performer—an unusual combination of stage magic while walking a tightrope—caught the filmmaker's eye when he discovered the actress while scouting locations for *Three Rings, but one Wife* in 1993.

Dolly Dare was only the second of the former circus performer's several name changes. Mysterious Circumstances, known to friends today as Mysty, was born Georgia Whitehouse, in Detroit, in 1970. In 1988 she married Wallace Martin, a magician with the Shriner's Circus, and became Georgia Martin. It was following the collapse of that marriage that she was able to join the Barnum & Bailey Circus using the name Dolly Dare, working with them until an unfortunate accident sidelined her act in Denver, Colorado, in 1994.

Mr. Biedermeier's oldest daughter, Audrey, a Santa Monica architect, had been hiking in the Carpathian mountains of Slovakia in recent weeks and was at first unaware of her father's death but managed to attend the services.

An initial court hearing of charges is scheduled for November 9th.

For further developments, keep your eyes every week on the *Tab*.

Notes: Audrey Biedermeier
at the heart of it

Audrey Biedermeier, 47, born in 1969, was the second child of Mr. Biedermeier and his first wife, Jessie Fleming. She graduated with a masters from the UCLA School of Arts

and Architecture in 1993. She is an architect today in Santa Monica, and it was she who designed Otto Biedermeier's home in Malibu. She is divorced and has no children. She is just under six feet tall, and thin, as her mother was, with the same green eyes, and the walnut brown hair of her father.

My guess was she must be thinking about her father's murder and have her own ideas. The fact that she'd been horseback riding in Slovakia at the time of her father's death was confirmed by her current boyfriend, Jioi Medved, and placed her outside the immediate investigation.

Dirkson/Biedermeier architectural consultants is located in Santa Monica. Assuming the worst, I showed up on Monday at the office, a small cube of copper colored glass deceptively hiding two floors and asked to see Miss Biedermeier. It's hard to hide in a glass house. I could see her there on the floor above when I entered. I think she saw me as well. She showed up in the lobby downstairs before I could finish making my pitch to the secretary.

"What do you want?"

"Hello. I had a thought and wondered if you could help

me with it."

"I told you on the phone that I don't want you writing about my family."

"Stories will be written. I try to get mine essentially correct. That's why I'm here."

"I don't want you here. I want you to leave."

"Okay. But as I do, please think about this one thing. I think you like Mysty at least as much as I do. And I've been trying to figure how someone might have entered that house without using the front door. Is it possible you designed a safety exit or something of the sort, other than the collapsible fire ladder on the balcony side?"

"Please leave."

I left.

On Tuesday she called me. I'd neglected to leave my number, but she had called the *Tab,* and somebody there was sharp. She asked me to come by again, if I would. I did.

She met me in the lobby again, but this time she asked me to take a walk with her. We walked the block to the beach and sat on a bench. Traffic behind us was constant and took what little pleasantness there was. A chilly breeze swept up from the water. With water so close, Arty was not satisfied with the idea of sitting. I promised him his turn would come.

She says, "Do you take him with you for defense?"

"Yes. I find tall women intimidating. That and I can't afford a dog sitter."

She did not smile. "What did you want to talk with me about?"

"A bucket-load. But tell me first why you changed your mind?"

"About talking to you? Jioi suggested I do it. He's a good friend."

53

Santa Monica beach is broad and flat and boring and at that hour, despite the breeze, it was fairly busy with kite flyers and small groups, mostly kids, playing ball. No one was in the water. I watched this a moment, hoping she would add something more, but she didn't, so I set about doing my job.

"I take it from what you said at your father's funeral that you like Mysty. I want you to understand that I'm here on her behalf as well as my own. I think she's innocent."

She shook her head with the thought. "I hope so. But sometimes people do things they normally wouldn't. I've never seen her angry. I don't think she angers easily. God knows there've been times I have wanted to strangle my father for one thing or another. He's very stubborn . . . Was. But she was in charge. He let her run things. At least anything that didn't involve his films. The films were all his. That was really his private world."

I had a more specific aim.

"What do you think of Truman Donitz."

She laughed. "He's a lawyer. Way back before he was a criminal lawyer, he was our family lawyer all through my childhood. Dad was always going into one deal or another and Truman would be up at the house to get papers signed. We lived at the bungalow then. Up at Red Rock. Truman would show up in the evening and stay the night. He usually slept on the living room couch. He seemed to like it. Closer to the kitchen and no stairs."

"A long way to get papers signed. Why didn't they just mail them."

"Vegas. Truman enjoys the tables. Always has."

"Did your mother like him?"

Audrey looked at me oddly.

"Why are you asking about Truman?"

"Because he is defending Wallace Martin, not Mysty. I

find that very odd."

She grimaced. "That's probably because Mysty never liked him either. And to answer your question, I'm not sure."

"So why was he still your father's lawyer?"

"You don't know my father. Not really, or you wouldn't even bother to ask. Dad was fiercely loyal. He stood by anyone who was a friend. Sometime—years ago, Truman was a real friend. That was all it took. That was it."

"Do you know if there was anything special about that? Had Truman gotten your father out of some sort of jam?"

She looked at me quizzically again.

"Yes. I think so. But I don't know what. . . . You know, Dad was an orphan after the war. I don't think any of us can understand what that was like—having absolutely everything taken away. The American soldiers fed him from their own rations. He's loved the Army ever since. The Red Cross sheltered him. He used to go down to the bloodmobile as often as he could. I went with him a couple of times. They knew him there as just 'Otto.'" She shrugged at something. "And he loved the Kellys. They're the family that adopted him. They're mostly gone now except for Minna. You saw her. She was at the funeral. They had a son of their own, but he was killed in the war. But when we were growing up, we used to drive all the way out to the farm in Illinois, nearly every Christmas, and visit them. Dad always wanted there to be snow on the ground at Christmas. It was cold but it didn't snow a lot at Red Rock."

I had a passing thought.

"Did he ever wish he'd stayed on the farm?"

"No. Not even a little bit. He told us many times that farming was real work. What he did for a living was play. He thought he was the luckiest man in the world to be able to earn a living making films."

"What do you think of Alma?"

55

The change of direction caught her off-guard. I was still more interested more in Donitz, but I didn't think I should press that too hard.

"I like her."

"Did you know her mother?"

"Briefly."

"Did you like her?"

"No."

"By all accounts she was not a very likable woman. What do you think your father saw in her?"

Audrey backed up on the bench.

"These are things I can't really talk to you about."

"Alright."

"There's little enough privacy in the world. I thought you wanted to know about any special entrances to the house."

"Actually, I really only wanted to know about Truman Donitz. There's something about him that bothers me. You're just about the only one I can ask."

She nodded at that. "You don't understand Truman. No reason you should, I suppose. He can be difficult. But there was a time when he was almost a second father to me. Dad was always going off on a shoot or spending the night at a film lab in L.A., and Tru and his wife, Myra, would be up at Red Rock overnight with Mom trying to hold the fort with us kids. Truman wasn't nearly as heavy then. I'm pretty sure Mom must have liked him too. At least she was very sympathetic later on when things went bad for him. They had a child of their own before the marriage fell apart. And Mom used to take care of little Judy, their daughter, whenever Truman would stay at the bungalow and he was 'hitting the strip,' as he used to call his gambling binges. But that all happened later. After Myra left."

"You trust him?"

"I always have. Dad did. I suppose that was the

important thing. Myra was rather flamboyant. She drank too much and liked to gamble as much as Truman did. He was actually the sober one. She was rather beautiful, and I suppose he was mad for her."

"Did Truman have any other kids?"

"Why do you ask?"

"Because it matters."

"Why? I've never had kids."

"And it matters, don't you think?"

That gave her pause.

"And you don't know me, either."

There was an edge in her vice again.

It was a clumsy question. I had to get it right. "No. That's not what I'm saying. I have to judge you whether I know you or not, the same way you have to judge me. And I may actually never know why you didn't have kids, but it matters because people live their lives differently if they do. Even if they're bad parents. For instance, how far would Truman take his gambling 'binges?' Would he risk the security of his own children?"

At least she considered this a moment before rejecting it, as many would.

"No. He didn't. Just the one girl. Myra wouldn't have any more. He wanted a boy. I can remember him saying that he wanted a boy just like Jason. But she didn't want to spoil her figure. 'One mistake was enough,' she said. Really! I heard her say it, and she wasn't joking. . . . So you're right. She was all about herself. She had an affair and then divorced Tru for some gigolo who left her even before the divorce was final. Tru was devastated. I actually saw him crying. I'd never seen a man cry before that. But it was after that, when the food and the gambling took on a lot more importance in his life. He lost just about everything, I think. . . . The last I knew, his girl was in college." Her eyes followed one group of kids playing with a frisbee on the sand before she turned back. "My own reason for not having children was less interesting, perhaps. I was in love with a guy who was not about to settle down. Does that reflect badly on me, Mr. Lenz?"

"Josh?"

Another pause. A frown. I suppose she didn't really understand what I was after.

But she answered. "Yes."

"Don't worry. You won't read about it in the newspapers."

"Why are you asking all this? What does it have to do with Mysty?"

"Call it a narrative. I'm trying to understand what happened. I'm really just trying to piece together a story that might make some sense—trying to get a picture of things and the way they were. Stories should make sense. I don't have the convenience of a police lab and a bunch of detectives. Maybe I'm just looking for the thing that doesn't fit." I could see she was giving that some thought. "But I'd really like to know more about your mother. Can you tell me about her?"

"No. I really don't want to talk about her. That's not important, is it? She had nothing to do with why someone killed my father. And while I'm there, I should also tell you there are no special entrances or exits to the house." The tone of her voice rose, and she spoke faster. "And except for the fact that he was a terrific father and a good husband and a good friend, and a hell of a film maker, I don't think I can tell you much more about Otto Biedermeier either."

By her posture, she was ready to leave. I felt stymied. I should have backed off sooner and left something for another time. My own impatience had the better of me.

"You're one of the few who knew them both well.

You're the only one who knew them the way you did. And you should know that I'm not just reporting about the murder. I'm revising my book about your dad. He was the one who let me write that in the first place. He helped me write it. But it's not really about his personal life. It's about the filmmaker. I'm just looking for some detail that would help me tell his story. Something to fill out the picture."

With the breeze, it was not the sort of day to be sitting still. Audrey stared again at the scattering of people seemingly moving in every direction on the beach. From the side, the green of her eyes had darkened. Then, for a moment, she rested back on the bench again.

"My mother told me once that she married Dad just to make him stand in one place long enough to kiss him. Dad was always busy. Even when he wasn't. The morning after a film was finished, he'd be at the door of my room and say 'Hey, girl! Fabulous blue-sky day out there. Let's go to the mountains!' Or if we were in the mountains, it would be 'Lets go to the beach.'' He never stopped. Mom gave up trying or trying to keep up. She did the things she liked with him and made us go with him for the rest of it. He tried to teach us everything he knew, and if he didn't know anything about it, he learned right along with us. He loved to ride, and he was the one who taught us how to handle horses. He told me once he felt like he knew how to ride before he could walk. We would prowl the canyons out at Red Rock until it was too dark to turn back, and then we'd just make camp on the spot. . . . Poor Mysty. She tried to keep up. She learned to ride pretty well before her horse stumbled up near Mt. Charleston and she broke the same ankle she'd hurt when she was in the circus. . . . Dad had to walk her out. . . . But that was the sort of man he was."

She was tearing up and stopped then and simply stood and ran back toward her office through a break in the traffic.

I walked Arty down the beach to the water until some busybody told me I was breaking the law. Dogs were not permitted on that stretch—a fact I actually knew. But breaking the law has its degrees. At least Arty got his dip.

Tamara
What this was about

Tamara was staying at the Beverly Hills Hotel. This place is easy to find. However, it is not so easy to get into. You can't just call and ask to speak to the movie star of your choice. They are very good at keeping the paparazzi out. And I could not afford to take a room. But I'd been inside a couple of times before, as a visitor, and knew something of the routine, so I called the front desk and told them that Mysty Biedermeier had asked that I speak with Tamara for her.

The clerk seemed to be up on his scandals.

"Is she still in jail?"

"Yes. That's why she's asked me to call. Can you tell Tamara that I'm the fellow she met at the funeral?" And I left my number.

An hour later I got a call back. The voice is unmistakable. Better than Garbo.

"What is it that you want?"

"I'd like to speak with you, if I can."

"I am listening."

"In person, if possible. Mysty thought I should."

"You are a reporter."

"Yes. But this is more as a friend. I'm trying to understand what happened."

She was silent then for nearly a minute. I waited. She has been a life-long smoker and I could hear her breathing, so I knew she was still there. I was thinking that she is well acquainted with Hollywood 'friends.' But I keep that to myself.

Finally, "I am leaving tomorrow for Italy. Can you come this afternoon? At three? I will tell the desk."

"I'm sorry. I have a dog. I couldn't find anyone to look after him."

"I love dogs. I will tell them. We can meet on the patio."

When I get there, Tamara is dressed to the teeth. These duds are billowy, cream white and dark green, lush, and likely to hide any imperfections of age, but I already know she is not in need of such discretion. Apparently, she is going out later and I'm already aware from Laura that she has found a whole new clientele for her fashions with the aging baby boomers. Then again, I suppose, they were always her clientele. I simply still think of her as the willowy model who had shaped my libido when I was twelve.

She did not stand as I approached, ignoring me as she had at the funeral. But she nearly dove on Arty. It is an incongruous sight. The elegant beauty is on her knees, with the fabric of her dress wafting and Arty's dark brown tale wagging. The makeup on her face must be saliva resistant.

"This is unfair. Mysty told you that I had one weakness."

She has a treat and a bowl of water waiting on the small table beside her and she reaches up for that.

"I didn't know. But I'll keep it in mind."

She looks up from her mauling as she says, "My dogs are at home in Gaeta. In Italy. Molly and Malone. I miss them so."

I barely remembered where it was. "That's off the beaten path."

"I grow olives. I am a farmer! Like my father was in Slovenia. But he raised pigs. Olives are easier."

When you are interviewing a subject, you have to grab at any fabric that comes near to your purpose.

"Growing up, were you close to Trieste in Slovenia?"

"Yes. Nearly on the border. Why do you ask?"

"Because of Otto's interest in that city."

"Hah! Exactly! I saw *Lost Circus* when I was eight. No! Don't tell anyone that! But I was that young. It changed my life. I was not ready to fully understand, but that little boy was me for a time. At least until I discovered that I wasn't a boy. And I always wanted to meet Otto. It was a most important motivation that brought me to America. I loved him before I met him." She sat again with Arty close at her legs. "How could anybody . . ." She looked away.

I was hoping to avoid any crying.

"I'm trying to figure that out. For Mysty's sake more than my own. I'm hoping to revise the book I wrote about Otto, but--"

"There must have been a robbery." Her voice was suddenly insistent. "It must have been a robbery. Mysty has told me that her ring is missing. It is a beautiful ring. No one has ever given me such a ring; I can tell you! I have always been jealous of it."

"Is there anyone else who might have had a reason?"

That brought a tilt to her head.

"You sound like the cops."

"I'm trying to help Mysty. The cops have her in jail."

"Of course. So you say. Yes. I understand. But as you say, you are writing a book—"

"It's how I try to pay my rent, so to speak. I have to earn my living, same as you. I may not do it well, but I think I do it honorably."

She lifted her chin toward me. She does not have the neck of a sixty-year-old woman.

"Otto was very keen on honor. Tell me, did you know him well?"

I suspect she knew that answer.

"No. I met him only once. I stayed at the house for a few days and interviewed him."

"He must have liked you. Only his friends stayed at the house."

"Mysty says that he did, but I don't know exactly why. I was a bit raw then and too young to know to ask the right questions."

"Otto was very kind, and very generous, but very determined. When he wanted something, he got it. That made some enemies, I suppose."

She had turned the interview around. I was happy to take it back.

"Any that you are aware of?"

"I probably know many of them. One or two might be in this hotel at the very moment. Otto made money when most of these clowns had to use accounting tricks and tax write-offs. But murder is something else. I do not understand that. And I cannot imagine anyone hating him. That is why I think it must be robbery. An old knife cannot be an easy weapon."

I wanted an indirection.

"Tell me, many of Otto's friends appeared in more than one of his films. You were in just the one. *The Thrum*. And yet you continued to be a friend afterward."

Eyes arched. Her eyebrows were real and not drawn.

"Ah. You are very observant. Yes. But that would be me. He wanted me for another. I declined. More than that. I begged him. I couldn't do it. I needed to be away from him. Jessie was his woman. Period. That was his way. That's how I ended up with my second husband, you know. Jack! Jack was not a bad fellow. Boring. Terribly normal. But he was no Otto, and that was both Jack's main appeal at first and then his primary deficit. I was stronger after that. Otto and I were friends then. That was all. And no more. Well. After I had my own problems, it was Otto to the rescue. He let me stay at Red Rock when they were away on location. I couldn't have survived without him."

"Was Jessie ever there, then?"

"Yes. She knew. And she knew she had no worries. Not with me, and not with Otto. And I loved his children. They were like my own family."

"And Josh."

Eyes wide. "You know too much!"

"I'm sorry. It is not something I need to write about."

"It doesn't matter now. There is no one left to care. Yes. I loved Josh. This is an empty place within me I cannot describe. But it was Jessie who helped me through that, as well. Always the mother. Always the strong one, and she understood."

"I'm sorry."

"What for? For love? I'm not. You must believe me when I say I would have been happier if Jessie had lived and Otto was happy. It nearly killed him when she died. And Ken. Little Kenneth."

Arty wanted more attention and we spoke about dogs, and she told me about pigs and said that they were smarter than dogs but lacked the appeal. She thought it was the fur. Women liked furs, she said. Most women. I told her Laura won't wear fur, even though she sells them in her shop.

"Tell me about Laura."

"I'm supposed to be interviewing you."

"Tit for tat, then. I tell you something and then you tell me. It's the children's game, isn't it? I show you mine if you show me yours?"

She was a woman of her own means.

"She has a clothing shop in Santa Barbara."

"No! Really? What kind?"

"She makes them herself, based on clothes worn in movies."

"You mean that Laura! 'The' Laura! My God. She's famous! I have sent people to her myself!"

At first I thought she was kidding. Actually putting me on. And then I realized her sudden enthusiasm was genuine.

"She is very good. People say that. But I'm not good talking about fashion. Please, tell me more about Otto. What happened after his wife's death? He didn't make any films for a couple of years."

She composed herself, visibly, setting both her feet out on the yellow tiles and placing her hands on the sheer fabric over her knees. Arty watched this attentively.

"You are very determined aren't you? Very determined. But I suppose you have to be."

"I'm trying."

"In 1989, I was the one who took Otto to Europe. It was to escape his ghosts. It's true, he loved me, but not to be his wife. In fact, it's a joke—was—was a joke between us. His greatest satisfaction on that journey was Bosch!"

"Bosh?"

"Jheronimus Bosch. At the Rijksmuseum in Amsterdam, he saw one of the Bosch paintings that he was completely fascinated with, and he started tracking other versions of it down, all over. Bosch had painted several. It was a mission. And Otto succeeded. He dragged me all the way to Paris! I hate Paris! It's full of Parisians, for God's sake. And he finally bought one. Mortgaged his house at Red Rock to do it. I said he had rocks in his head not to marry me. But he bought 'Removing Rocks from the Head,' by Bosch, instead." She tried to

66

laugh but the sound was weak. She was clearly breathless from the account of that time, and I waited a moment. When she had calmed again, she asked, "You have been to the beach house. You've seen it? He has several fine copies there as well as the one I am speaking of. If you are writing again about Otto, you should know this. He told me that this painting gave him a new lease on life."

I had not looked closely at the paintings in the house. I had assumed they were all copies. But now she looked very sad at realizing his loss again and I was afraid she would cry as she did at the funeral. I had to keep some momentum going in the conversation.

"Tell me, please. What is your opinion of Truman Donitz?"

A long breath. She patted her knees. Artery took this as some sort of signal and nuzzled her hands. She smiled again.

"Truman is difficult to like. We get along. I have never understood him. But he was there. From the beginning, I think. He and the little fellow, Philip Reeves. I used to see them around the big table at Red Rock, plotting their battles beneath that big brass shade. They were part of Otto's crew. His generals. They put together the financing for his films. That is not a small matter, you understand. Otto did not want to be beholden to any other production company or studio. He often used Universal, but not always. Not for everything. It was a trick. Distribution contracts are very sticky. But they did it. They always found the money, because they would never take too much from any one source. That way they couldn't be taken advantage of. Philip, especially, was a master at this. I don't know what has happened to him lately. He looks so spent. But then he was very ambitious. He would make deals directly with the movie chains. You could never do that today. They are all the same. But then there were still hundreds of exhibitors that ran six or a dozen theaters each. All across the country. And Otto wanted his movies in every one. He wouldn't let the distributors tie him up. If they wanted his films, they had to come to him."

"And Donitz?"

"He is a very sad man, I think. An unhappy man."

"Why?"

"I truly don't know. He never took me into his confidence. I never wanted it, anyway. But he bothers me."

"Why?"

"Just a feeling."

She was avoiding telling me more of what she knew.

"Do you think he might have killed Otto?"

"No! Otto was his best client! Without Otto, he would have nothing!"

This appeared to be a compelling fact with many of Otto's friends.

"I'm just trying to imagine who might have killed him."

"Well then, I would say what you need to do is look for a midget."

"What?"

"You know! Otto's expression. He often used it on the set. If things were not working out as planned, he would just rewrite the scene to use what we could. He would say, 'If all else fails, we'll bring on the midget! Because every Hollywood production has a midget, or a pair of twins and a case of mistaken identity, or a dream sequence that explains a questionable plot point, or a cliff hanger. We've already used the dark and stormy night.' I put it in my book! . . . But you did not read my book, did you? That's okay. Nobody did."

"Sorry. I thought it was just about fashion."

Tamara forced a smile. "It should have been. But I wrote too much about myself. Now! Tell me how you met

Laura!"

"At a film festival. We both like the same old films."

"God, yes! The clothes alone. It is so hard, today. There is so little fashion sense!"

But I did not want to talk about fashion.

"What do you think of Josh, now?"

"Josh. Josh. My gosh. Every woman who meets him thinks of Josh, at least for a awhile. He has that . . . appeal. I can't tell you. I suppose it's because he knows who he is, inside and out. Most men don't. No pretense. Just a cowboy. And good looking! Oh, my God! And funny! But totally irresponsible. I have been with him at the tables in Vegas and seen him put down his last thousand dollars in chips. I said, you can't afford that! We were going to Italy the next day! And he laughed. And then he borrowed the money from Otto to go with me to Italy, anyway. Just like that. He was always working off one debt or another with Otto. And so unlike Otto. Even so, when I fell in love with Josh, I thought I had found my answer. But no. He is just Josh."

"Do you think there is any way he might have hurt Otto, even by accident? You know, the knife was—"

"Stop it! That is totally stupid! Even drunk, Josh would catch a fly in the air with his hand and let it go. What's the expression?"

"Couldn't kill a fly."

"Yes. Or need to."

Josh Green
What brothers are for

'The Bungalow' had once been a stagecoach stop on the Old Spanish Trail. The high dry air of the northern Mohave is a preservative and most of the original timbers are still in place, but the additions somehow appear just as gray and weathered. The stopover there was originally chosen for a permanent sweet spring that percolates out of the orange, gold, and red sandstone cliffs of the canyon that forms the northern boundary of the property. This life source can be easily followed from there with the eye through the dun-colored chaparral by the green of the cottonwoods, ash and live oak that make a natural fence down to the barn and corral. None of the wood of the buildings appears to have been painted but the metal roof of the barn is a brilliant orange red. The corrals are empty, but the gates are closed.

I noted immediately that, unlike the view from the balcony in Malibu, there was no horizon here. This was a world contained.

Josh Green has been temporarily living in the bungalow at Red Rock since 1987, following the deaths of Otto's wife and son. Otto did not like going back and it is Josh's hand that has kept the place looking good since that time. He replaced the cedar roof shingles on the house with the metal last year. He replaced the old plumbing with PVC the year before, and prior to that, the wiring that Otto and his son Jason had done years ago that was never up to snuff in the first place. Josh rented a backhoe and dug a new septic system when the requirements for that were changed. He leveled the grade of the old stagecoach road up to the bungalow and paved it with three layers of gravel. He told me all of this when asked but offered nothing without direct inquiry.

There are five bedrooms, and he has taken the one at the back, off the kitchen, known as the bunk room. This is the same one that was once used by the boys, Jason and Kenneth. The bunk beds are gone now, and that room is spare but neat with furnishings.

According to Mysty, Otto had put the ranch at Red Rock in the same trust that owned the rights to his films. A provision of this made Josh a trustee and stated that he could continue living there as long as he wished.

I showed up at Red Rock about 11 o'clock on a splendid blue-sky morning, having set out from Santa Barbara well before sunrise. The sound of the tires on the gravel of the driveway echoed on the face of the sandstone cliffs close to the north and announced my arrived. Josh appeared on the porch barefoot, in shorts and t-shirt, rubbing the sleep from his eyes.

"Is it today, already?"

The question seemed to answer itself. I had called him to make the appointment. Behind him the shadow of a woman, apparently wearing only Josh's shirt, stood back in the doorway.

"Should I go back down to Blue Diamond and get myself a cup of coffee?"

"No. No. It's okay. Their coffee is crap anyway. I can make you a real cup of coffee."

Arty got himself up behind the steering wheel at my open door as we spoke.

"Is there some shade where I can hook up my dog?"

"Bring him in. Does he catch mice? We have mice."

Crossing the wide porch had the nice drum of many movie westerns in it. I wished I had spurs.

While I waited, and Josh disappeared into the back, I toured the large front room. It's a living room now, but still identifiable from the scenes in the many films shot there. With the shielding of the wide porch, and the small windows, the room was fairly dark, but I did not turn on the lights. It was easier to imagine its many past incarnations that way. The windows at the front were narrow and could be shuttered from the inside. The board walls were thick with photos and memorabilia. The famous Wells Fargo safe stood like the baby elephant in the room at one side. A pool table balanced that presence at the other. The back wall between the main room and the kitchen had been removed and the gleam of stainless-steel appliances there looked professional. Josh puttered with a coffee maker in one corner before disappearing. In the other corner, by a window, I could see the large round oak table where Otto and Jessie and Truman and Philip had once plotted their battles. The brass shade above the table had turned dark and somehow confirmed the end of those better times.

Suddenly, my eyes fixed on a small and simple dark wood frame, not more than eight by nine inches. And there it was, the yellowed and dampstained program which had been printed seventy years before, using type that was itself already broken and worn, and with inking clearly inadequate to begin with. At the top, the image surrounded by the name, a woodblock illustrated horse, with feather headdress, stands on its hind legs. Beneath, 'Bohemian Circus Fantastisch!' was 'Zirkusdirector und Stallmeister, Carroll Desmond,' and then, in 24-point gothic letters no less bold, the 'Unglaublich Josef Biedermeier, Zaubererr,' and the 'Fabelhaft,' Alma Klage 'Zauberer Assistent.' There were only seven other names given, all in smaller type: the 'Wagemut Arial Kunstler' named Walter

Zurbe,' and his 'Shatten,' Greta Muller, 'Konig der Clowns, Herman Fischer,' trapeze artist Carl Koch, 'Meister der Hunde, Werner Wolf' and his assistant 'Irma Lange,' and lastly, the single name 'Isabella,' whose specialty was not given and could only be guessed at. Just nine names. I wondered once again how Otto had determined who his parents had been from such a clan.

As if at home, Arty took immediate possession of the couch. I examined the circus program and then the clutter of framed photographs, using the light from my cellphone.

Before Josh returned, the woman I had seen on the porch came back. Dressed in jeans and her own blue plaid shirt, she was rather stunning. Another tall woman on a growing roster. She had turned her black hair into a quick bun with rubber bands.

"I'm Marcie," she said, extending a hand.

I introduced myself. Arty was up again and pushed his nose between us while she patted his head uncertainly.

"Josh didn't tell me, or I would have been up earlier. He loses track of time out here."

My guess was that she was a young-looking forty or an old thirty-five.

There were three vehicles parked in an open garage beneath a rusting corrugated roof at the far side of the gravel drive. One was a battered Ford pickup that I guessed, according to its square profile, to be at least twenty years old. One was an open jeep, mud splattered and with a prominent roll bar. The third was a Porsche convertible. I figured Marcie for the Porsche.

"Do you live here with Josh?"

"Ah! Right to the questions. He just managed to tell me you were a reporter."

Well drawn eyebrows arched. "Not exactly. I do some

reporting. I'm a writer. And I'm a friend of Mysty's."

"Ah! Then you would be Mr. Lenz."

"Tom. Yes. How do you know that?"

"I read your pieces in the Tab. Are you writing a book about the whole thing?"

"I might. This is all very interesting stuff to me."

"It should make a terrific book! Murder! Malibu! Hollywood! Just tell me what I have to do to get some ink without becoming a cadaver!"

"You're being sarcastic, I understand. I'm sorry if my coming here is intruding. A writer is always writing a book. But that's not what's important here. Not now. I'm trying to understand what's happened for Mysty's sake."

She gave that a nod and went into the kitchen, speaking through the opened wall as she did.

"How do you take yours?"

"Lots of cream and sugar."

"Better to. Josh makes it strong. He was in Italy once and it spoiled him."

"How long have you known each other?"

"A while. Ten years. Eleven in October."

"What do you do?"

The eyebrows arched again, visibly, even at the distance. "Ah! I'm the show girl! Doesn't every book about murder need a show girl?"

"You work in Vegas"

"Yes. At the Grand."

"How did you meet?"

"At the pool. Josh was the best-looking man there . . . No. It was before that. My last name is White. Josh and I had met at the bar the night before and we compared the colors in our names, and other such small talk, but I never go with guys I meet in a bar so that ended there."

74

Josh had entered the room at this last statement, shaved and dressed in a clean pair of jeans and the shirt Marcie had been wearing before. His boots looked as battered as the truck outside.

He winked. "You are going to give this fella the right idea. I told you it was best to mislead him a little so we could get a chuckle out of whatever he wrote up on us."

I hadn't seen anyone wink convincingly in years. I told him, "I make enough mistakes on my own without any help."

The ice was broken at that point. They asked me about myself. I kept it brief except for Marcie's questions. Arty gathered himself on the couch again, as close to Marcie as he could get without being on her lap. Before long she was stroking him the way he likes.

She says, "You boys are all the same."

I went back to the main line of inquiry.

"What do you think happened to Otto?"

Josh looked at the floor. "I don't know. But Mysty couldn't have done it, I'll tell you that. It's not in her. I think it's what she said. A robbery. Something gone wrong. That knife is the matter, you see. It's not the knife Otto's been using lately. It can't be. I told the cops that. And then I remembered there was another one just like it in that safe there." Josh pointed at the hulking presence across the room. "It must be the one he put away years ago. He always gets two of everything made up. Saves time when things break. They always break. One of Otto's boys had gotten ahold of it one time and played with it and then left it outside somewhere. The way a boy will do. Otto found it and put it away. Even with the blade retracting on itself, it was dangerous. It was that sharp. So I looked in the safe when I got back from the funeral, and it wasn't in the drawer there. But I'd seen it there myself a dozen times over the years. When we're on a shoot, we keep the petty cash in those drawers. I guess Otto just couldn't bring himself to take it out again after the boys were both gone."

This led in a more obvious direction.

"Did you notice that the test films were gone too?"

"Yeah. I did, but I didn't have an idea then that it was a matter. I don't go in the safe much. Usually just when Otto asks me to. Before that, I don't think I've looked in there for a year or more."

"What did you think?"

"Well, I was trying to think how that knife got gone. My only guess is that Otto finally took it out of there himself. Maybe the same time as he took the films."

"Could anyone else have done it?"

"Nah. I'm here most of the time. There's only four or five of us with the combination that I know of."

"Who else?"

"That's what the cops asked. I told them. Beside me, and Mysty, there was his daughter, Audrey, and his lawyer, Truman Donitz."

"Any thought at all about why Otto might have moved the films?"

"No. Not really. Go back a few years and he talked about it once. He had an idea they might be a good item for the University archives."

"University of Southern California?"

"Right. The film school there. But I never heard his talk about that again and those films were still in that safe along about last summer when we shot some scenes for *The Big Cheese* because our petty cash payroll was in there with them."

"When was Otto here last?"

"A month back. He stayed overnight. I was busy with scouting out a location for the next project and he called me where I was in New Orleans about the propane delivery.

Paradise Propane screws the delivery up as often as they get it right. The driver does not like to come all the way out here. Problem is, the driver's the owner's brother.. Never hire your brother, I say."

"So you do go away for short periods of time. When's the last time you were away?"

Josh looked at Marcie. Marcie shrugged and nodded.

"We went up to Canada for a couple of weeks. . . . Marcie and me. Marcie was raised up there in Manitoba. She's a regular farm girl. She wanted me to meet her family."

Marcie rolled her eyes.

"Yeah. Yeah!" She appears to have heard a note of regret in Josh's admission. "I just wanted to get married, you dumb ass!"

He looks sheepish.

I asked, "Did you?"

Josh gives me the wink again like 'mission accomplished.' "Yeah," and pulled the ring out of the watch pocket of his jeans.

Marcie produced her ring simultaneously and wagged it between two fingers.

"You have to believe I am the first woman that ever got Josh Green to marry her!"

"Congratulations."

But suddenly Josh did not look happy. "We come home to tell everyone and get slapped in the face with Otto's murder. Timing on that was not so good. So we've been pretty quiet about it so far."

I'm not a great believer in coincidence.

"Why now? Why get married just now?"

Marcie seemed surprised by that. "Why not! *Jubilee* has closed. There're no big floor show productions left. Just side shows. The writing is on the wall. And there's the matter that the Grand doesn't want their girls married. Some do but they don't last so long. It's sort of an unwritten rule. They'd get themselves sued if they ever tried to enforce it out loud. That and the invisible age limit. But I'm already well beyond that. Thirty-six is long behind me."

The coincidence might be coming from a different angle.

"Did anyone else know you were going away?"

"No. I only knew it was time when she kicked my dumb rear-end and told me to fish or cut bait. After that I just packed my bags. I thought I could surprise Otto pretty good afterward."

Frowning, Marcie shook her head.

"You called Truman that morning. What did you say to him?"

"Yeah. Well." He looked away at the window.

I asked, "Why did you call Truman?"

"That's complicated."

Marcie was sitting up at the edge of the couch by then and Arty was alert and up right next to her. "Why. What's complicated about it?"

Josh pulled a deep breath and looked up at the rafters for help.

"I'd got myself married once before."

This brought Marcie to her feet, looking down at Josh's slumped figure in the chair.

"What?!"

He shook his head for pity. "It was annulled. We had it annulled. It never happened. But I didn't have the papers on it. That was back in '83 and it was all foolishness. Truman handled the annulment. But I wanted to have a copy of the papers just in case. You know. So, I called him. He had it right there and sent them out."

Marcie appeared dumbstruck.

I said, "And you told him why you wanted them."

"Yes."

"And that you were going to Canada?"

"Yeah. I guess I did."

Probably wanting to get some space between himself and Marcie, Josh walked me around the immediate property and told me bits and piece about that. But it wasn't until I was driving away that I thought to ask who it was he had been so briefly married to.

Notes: Point Doom
The topography of the past

I remembered well that Otto called Point Dume, the famous coastal promontory of Malibu, Point 'Doom,' rather than the fey Point 'Dumay.' He said it to me more than once as if playing with the name as an idea for something more. I have often wondered what might have been in his mind. And now, with his death, I can hear his voice say the word again, very clearly. It lingers easily on the lips.

This morning I used the emergency key to enter the beach house. There is a large healthy key lime tree, maybe eight feet tall, on the street side there, where the sun shines most through the day. The base of the tree is framed in irregular stones, one of which looks longer than the others—Mysty had described the stone as looking like Italy, but I did not quite see that, the key was indeed beneath it, nonetheless. The idea of using the key lime as the hiding place struck me as just the sort of whimsy that Otto would have loved. Mysty had confirmed this, telling me Otto had the tree planted there especially, against his daughter's wishes. She'd been very particular about the tight landscaping around the house, butting up as it did against property on both sides. He had won the argument by insisting on his love of limes, and limeys, as well as reminding her that he often lost track his keys.

I walked the house through several times. It is small, with two bedrooms, the larger of which shares the expanse of the balcony, with one very large living room next to that. The kitchen, which is on the street side, opens onto the living room and a dining area. The windows on the street side, for both the kitchen and second bedroom, are primarily purposed to catch light, and are well above the eye and public view. There is an interior stairwell, locked at the bottom, that leads down to the beach level, but even that feeds up to the foyer and the one main entry. On the side opposite the key lime there is a narrow gravel path, terraced into broad steps, which also leads down to the beach. There is no window on that side that's reachable without a ladder.

The main bedroom had been straightened and cleaned, but the beige carpet is permanently darkened at one side of the bed and there are no sheets on the mattress, which is also darkly stained at one edge.

Walls and flat surfaces throughout the house are decorated in the sort of family photos and assorted artwork and nicknacks I have in my own home. The presence of several Jheronimus Bosch paintings in the entry, with their stark mix of reality and the absurd, are in keeping with Otto's sensibilities. *Removing Rocks from the Head* is the third of these and the smallest. I could not tell the difference between the copies and the original. Other paintings, mostly seascapes and flowers, I laid to Mysty's hand. The collections of small shells and sea glass was impressive, filling at least a dozen wide-bodied jars. These are Mysty's 'little treasures.'

The photos present on almost every flat surface are distinctive for the way Otto holds Mysty, and though he was several inches taller, always found some way to get his face close to hers, creating the sort of contrast of dark and light that a director can love.

The wall shelves closest to the second bedroom were filled with books. I had remembered those being half empty on my first visit years ago, with the open spaces taken then by nicknacks. Now they are full and overflowing with the novels and the historical reference of two distinct reading habits. Mysty apparently loves novels of almost any genre. Many of these titles were classics, though a few more recent authors showed up repeatedly, and there was no order I could immediately detect, alphabetical or otherwise. Otto loved history, mostly twentieth-century history, primarily European.

A patrol car arrived about fifteen minutes after I did, and I showed the officer Mysty's note. The officer's name is Rebecca Ortiz. To me she seems an unlikely cop. Too pretty, perhaps. Other than the stern look she managed; she did not seem fierce enough. I took the opportunity to speak to her as well. Though half a foot shorter than me, she acted as if she were intimidating—feet planted apart, thumbs in her belt where the paraphernalia of mayhem bulked close at hand. I wonder if I was misjudging her.

"Did you know Otto or Mysty?"

"Both."

"I realize that you wouldn't break a confidence, but does any of this make sense you."

"No."

"I promise not to report anything you say, but I'd like to know if you think Mysty killed her husband."

"No."

It didn't appear she was going to give me more than one-word answers, before I asked, "How did you get to know them?"

"They had us all in for the Fourth of July and Christmas every year, if they weren't out on location. A nice little party. The fireworks are great from the balcony. My kids loved it."

She was a cop and she had kids.

Enough said. But I wondered if her husband was charged with taking care of the kids.

Standing on the balcony, there is a great view down the coast in both directions. At that moment, Point Dume stood alone, as if it were an enormous ship, plowing an ocean mist.

In 1996 Otto had taken me there. He had said then that despite its previous use in other movies, there was another film to be made at 'Point Doom.' All he needed was the right story . . . Yet another opportunity lost. I don't remember asking what sort of story it might be. Perhaps I should have tried to write one for him. At least I might have had an appreciative audience of one.

In that remembered time, we stood there on the top of Point Doom at sunset and watched a swollen tongue of red sun melt between an orange sky and a blackening ocean. Otto told me that sometimes, if things were just right, there would be a flash of green just as the last of the sunfire winked out. We had waited for that but there was none that evening and we'd stumbled down the path afterward to our car in the lot below, with Otto recalling all the places he had seen that phenomenon through the years—Spain, Cornwall, Key West. He told me then that this wink of green was often the exact color of Jesse's eyes, and it had been right there on Point Dume that he had proven it to her. And that his daughter Audrey had those same eyes today.

Notes: Leo Carrillo to the rescue
and the past is always with us

I had not made an actual appointment to speak with Otto Biedermeier when I first arrived in California; afraid, I suppose, of the cold reality that his offer to meet me was only a polite answer to my letter of gushing admiration. But I'd borrowed a little money from various friends and relatives and taken the bus from New York to L.A. on the double pretext that I wanted to see Hollywood first-hand and get some hard facts for my Ph.D. thesis. That, at least, was true enough.

My notes from those first few days are sketchy and difficult to read—written as they were on the bus, and in various cars and on odd benches.

At the Greyhound bus terminal in L. A. there was a fellow with a large aluminum frame pack on his back. Knowing too well what my resources were, I asked him where the best camping was. I remember he looked down at the small beaten aluminum suitcase in my hand and must have thought I was nuts. I was, of course. But he directed me to Leo Carrillo State Park, just up the coast about 40 miles. 40 miles! 40 miles struck me as being in another state. But I knew who Leo Carrillo was, at least.

On the way I bought a backpack of my own and a small blue nylon tent, a sleeping bag, a blow-up air mattress, and a cooking kit (this last item is still in its original cardboard box, never used, and sitting at the back of a shelf in the garage, having been rescued from several yard sales and Laura's ongoing attempts to clean things up over the years). There were a couple of other odds and ends, all of it bought on the recommendation of a cute but skeptical young woman in an Army surplus store who wore a denim jacket with the sleeves cut off to display her tattooed shoulders. Her sales advice was not dubious, but the expression on her face was all of that.

She asked, "Have you ever camped before?"

I admitted the sad truth, "In the back yard once on Long Island. For a few hours. I remember it got very dark that night."

What didn't fit in my new backpack I put in my suitcase.

She also confirmed my choice of Leo Carrillo State Park. If I kept on the same street going toward Marina Del Rey I could pick up 'The One' and maybe hitch a ride the rest of the way from there. I bought a map and she marked it for me. I noticed later that she had also put a phone number on the bottom margin. I still have the map too, tattered and rippled with sea moisture, and that phone number has always struck me as a portal to another life. One that I didn't live.

My second ride, caught around Pacific Palisades, was from a Pepperdine student who took me all the way, 'just for the heck of it.' He'd never seen where the park was before and was curious for himself.

I paid for a campsite immediately but stashed my stuff with the Park official (I remember him being unhappy at the idea) and went right down to the ocean. I had several days of sweat and grime on me. Unfortunately, the water was about the same temperature as Long Island's Jones Beach on a hot day in May. That is, not warm enough to swim. I settled for a cold shower.

After eating a prepackaged sandwich at the Park store, I finally worked up my courage and made the phone call to Otto early that evening.

Mysty answered, "You're the boy in New York who's writing something?"

"Yes. Only, I'm here now. I'm in L. A."

She held her hand over the mouthpiece but spoke loudly enough that I could hear.

"It's the boy you talked to about Warren William . . . I don't know!" And then she asked, "Where are you?"

"Leo Carrillo State Park."

She repeated that. There was a pause. And then she asked, "Are you camping?"

"Yes."

"Are you alone?"

"Yes."

"Why don't you stay here?"

And that was it. Half an hour later Otto picked me up at the camp entrance. I slept in the second bedroom with the high window at the back. For three days.

This is an easy thing to recall now. I take Arty down to Leo Carrillo to swim about once week. It's only an hour down the coast from Santa Barbara and one of the few good beaches where dogs are allowed. We stay in the shallows, and I throw the tennis ball until he's pretty much exhausted, or I am, whichever comes first.

Before Arty, this was where the kids and I used to take Fritz. Fritz was not so fond of the water, but he'd go in after a ball if he had to. One of the best beaches in the world. Never too busy. Just a little expensive, even then. But still.

I sat up on a rock there on Tuesday afternoon, thinking about that first meeting with Otto and Mysty, when I was on top of the world. The world always seemed to be at my feet in those days.

In retrospect, that was just a matter of luck. Otto could

have been away on a location shoot, or busy with some other details. Instead, he was reading scripts and on a break.

I sometimes think that if he had not been there, after a couple days on the hardpack earth at the campsite I might have made my way home again to New York instead of staying in L. A. It could have gone that way. I am not easily discouraged but reality can too easily sober you from the intoxication of dreams. After four days in the thickened air of a bus, my head was not so clear. I remember thinking, 'What the hell am I doing here?' And that was probably thought of in my Dad's voice.

Or maybe I would have ended up with some tattoos of my own.

It was on the second day that Otto and I drove up to Point Dume to see where they filmed the last scene of *Planet of the Apes*. Don't know how that subject came up. We'd been talking about Warren William. After all, it was Otto who wrote the essay on William for *Film Quarterly* that had sparked my interest. But Mysty stayed at home that afternoon and Otto and I went over to the relative isolation of Pirate's Cove beach, beneath the cliffs, and talked about films and filmmaking before going up the sandy paths to the top of Point Dume.

The park was as run down then as it is now. Maybe there were fewer houses in the neighborhood across the street. I remember it looking somehow tawdry and unkempt. Abused by feet and small bits of trash caught in the scrabble of desiccated growth. There was more of the low chain link fencing then, rusting along the paths in the park, and fewer of the metal lines on spindly posts that have been installed since. It was summer and busy with visitors.

I remember some fool climbed over to an edge and couldn't make his way back on the loose sand. You could see he had one hand on a root that did not look all that substantial and the panic on his face was memorable. A couple of the lifeguards came up from the beach and threw him a life preserver on a rope. Very undignified to be hauled out of thin air that way. But then, a hundred-foot fall will kill you as sure as a thousand.

Which brings another memory to mind.

Earlier that day, Otto stood by the water's edge on Pirate's Cove Beach, at the very bottom of the cliff, and just stared at the bluff above. You can't see any of the houses from below and it appears much as it always has in paintings and old photographs. At that point, I might have been doing most of the talking. Too bad. He was fascinated with the place, and I should have done more listening while I had the chance.

I remember his saying that in filmmaking it was all a matter of short cuts to get to what was important. I didn't have my notebook with me, like a fool, so I can't tell you his exact words now, but he went on a little about John Ford filming at Monument Valley. In *The Searchers*, Ford knew everyone would recognize the place from his previous films. It was a sort of permanent establishing shot. It was a visual coming home. That was the West. As if saying, now, for Christ's sake, pay attention to the story! I believe Otto thought of Point Dume in that way.

He'd said something like, "But on my smaller budget, I can afford only the one bluff."

I believe it was there that I decided my thesis would be about Otto Biedermeier and not Warren William. William would have to wait.

But was he egging me on?

He had asked why I was working on a doctorate. I didn't have a good answer. Did I want to teach? No, I didn't. What was the good of it then? I should be writing my own screenplays. Write what you've got. Write it down or it's lost. At least get it down in black and white. 'Technicolor won't fade but memories will.'

I remember that. I told Laura that.

"Write until you die!" he said. "What good is living otherwise? What else you ever thought or felt will molder with your bones. All that's left are your children, and your work. Make good on them both."

Yes, he was egging me on. But I took no notes on that. I think I was embarrassed by his interest. Who was I, after all?

My first significant verbatim quote from Otto Biedermeier is this: "People in Hollywood are the same as people everywhere. Some are smart. Some are stupid. Most are in-between. The trouble is, Hollywood people are more often cursed by arrogance and egotism. You can see that anywhere else as well, but you see it more here. They may think of themselves as exceptionally beautiful, but you can find more beauty in any small town in America. They may think they are exceptionally smart, but their lives tell a different tale. They think they are liberal because they espouse liberal causes, but they drive their Porsches and their Mercedes to the charity events and take the tax right-off on their generosity at the end of the year. They live in gated communities and think they know what poverty is. They fly their jets to conferences about saving the planet. It's always been that way. During the Second World War they went to bond rallies while the rest of America worked in factories and died on the battle fields. It'll never change. I think that has a lot to do with the limelight and being told they are more important. It has to do with being applauded for successful pretense. For what? Acting like someone who actually did something? For pretending to be a murderer, without the balls to do the job? Pretending they're Howard Hughes or Mozart but never learning to fly a plane, much less design one, or write a musical note, much less a symphony? What happens in the chemistry of the mind when someone pretends that they are someone else and then assumes that they know what that other person knew? It is a sort of madness, isn't it? A schizophrenia."

And then this: "On one level, Hollywood is a terrific concentration of talent focused on a single craft, film-making. On another level, it's shillsville: home of canned laughter and false promises, treacle and cocaine, arsenic and old lace. It's the reason I've always liked working with younger actors before they lose their minds to it, and with the old ones who are in recovery."

Gloriosky George!
Rooney Tooney

George Rooney is famous for being one of the best-looking men in Hollywood; square jawed, a full head of naturally dark hair, piercing blue eyes. He is also a jerk. Just as beauty often overcomes intelligence in women, a man who has inherited too many good genes can rot from the inside out like an apple in cold storage.

This is not to say that the women Rooney has seduced are innocent of bad behavior. They bare themselves and bear their own burden of stupidity, but I suppose some greater blame must be placed on the male in our society, the expected predator, for lying his way into bed and then not being willing to lie in the mess he has made. Rooney was a 'child actor' on the successful western TV series, 'Farnum,' and still 15 years old when he had shared responsibility for his first abortion—this time with a 'sister' on the series who was four years his senior. That particular scandal had been the ultimate cause of cancellation for the show, but he had not been held responsible then due to his age. Interestingly, fifty years after Fatty Arbuckle was pilloried for less, the career of Rooney's 'sister' on the series, Morgan Jones, was not immediately damaged either—an unremarkable feat that was finally accomplished by the half dozen bad film choices she subsequently made.

Rooney was just eighteen when he had attempted to film his own seduction of co-star Sylvia Place during the making of *Apples for Oranges,* a Biedermeier 'beach party' film made in Ft. Lauderdale in 1978. His real mistake was in borrowing the 16mm camera Biedermeier kept at hand on the set. Too soon, the director noticed it missing and went looking. And this then was the short 16mm film clip, purchased by *The Enquirer* from a still unknown source, which had previously been kept in Otto Biedermeier's safe at Red Rock.

I had called George Rooney half a dozen times at various numbers wheedled from contacts. When I finally reached him, it was late on a weekday morning and he was not alone.

I told him who I was. He hung up, but not before a women's voice had asked, "Is that my agent?"

I called him again that evening. It sounded as if he were out someplace—maybe a restaurant—but he loudly told me to do something anatomically impossible.

When I called the third time, on the following day, the number had been blocked. That was when I decided to go to his home. He lives in Malibu, only a quarter mile away from where Otto Biedermeier was murdered.

The gate there is locked. I decided on a D-Day approach. But this landing was greatly simplified by the fact that the man himself was already on the beach along with a friend. It's still morning and the sun is in his eyes as I come up.

His first words as he rises from his beach chair are direct. "This is a private beach."

I said, "We're below the high-water mark."

"I don't give a fuck if you're in the water. Move along."

Rooney is wearing loose blue trunks. The ample hair on his chest is littered with gray. He was already thickening in the middle and there is a visible paunch. He is also a lot shorter than I thought he was—probably five foot ten. Thankfully, Arty was not with me. He would not have liked the tone.

"I'm the fellow who called you from the *Tab*. Why are you begging for bad publicity?"

He shakes his head dismissively, "Every knock a boost, as the man says."

"I believe it was Elbert Hubbard."

"Who?" The frown on his face deepened. And then "I don't give a damn."

"Clark Gable."

He moved forward at me before realizing that might not have been the best direction.

"Wise guy. You wrote that shit in the *Tab*, didn't you? There I am reading the obit for an old friend and suddenly I'm in the middle of it with *Apples for Oranges* and that childish mistake that happened thirty years ago."

"37 years, I think. But who's counting. I was writing about Otto's career. You were involved. Hard to miss. And now he's been murdered and the best I can determine, you were not an old friend."

He looked me up and down. I was in my jeans and Nikes. The woman on the beach chair next to his was looking directly up at us with her hand shielding the sun from her eyes. She might as well have been naked given the shear fabric of her pale-yellow bikini. An old song came to mind. Her skin was as tight as the fabric. I figured her for twenty.

Rooney finally says, "So, what do you want from me?"

I made my decision. "I'd like to sit down and chat with you when you're free. That's all."

He lets this thought stir. What wile is he conjuring in this consideration?

"Later. Lunch? How about 2?" He looks quickly down at the woman reclined below us with a grimace as if to apologize for something. "Abalone Joe's?"

"Good!"

Frankly, I didn't expect him to be there. He had gotten rid of me by suddenly going along with my request. But when I arrived, he was already at a table on the far side of the dining room by the windows.

He smiles and says, "I told them this is on your ticket. Make your paper pay for it."

I'll try. I'm thinking it would be a first if they did.

I ask, "What do you know about me?"

He shrugs. "Enough. You wrote the book on Otto. I know that."

"I was a friend of his as well as Mysty's."

"Everybody was his fucking friend. Except me, it seems."

"But that was on you."

"I suppose. To start. I was young and randy. But why the fuck did he keep that film? And why did he give it to the fucking *Enquirer*? Do you know?"

A waiter showed up and I got the cheapest bourbon on the list. I decided I needed it. Rooney was already nursing a Bloody Mary.

"No." I'd already decided to keep my approach direct and to the point. "If he was so well liked, who do you think would murder him?"

Rooney looks at me with a blank stare.

"If you're thinking I did, you're fucking bananas."

"I'm thinking that someone who was not Otto's friend might have some insight that his friends do not."

He bounces his head up and down on the thought. I let that sit.

Finally, he says, "I saw her that night, you know."

I know immediately who he's talking about.

"Where."

"At Denny's party. I'm just two doors away. She was there alone. She doesn't really know me, I suppose. Maybe Otto never told her about our fracas. Anyway, I spoke to her. She seemed flattered by it. I think she's a fan. I asked her how Otto was. I was expecting some usual answer. You know. Instead, she says he's fine. He was feeling fine but he had something on his mind and needed some time to himself to think. Very serious. Like a confidence. I was a little embarrassed. You know? She thought I was another one of his friends. She thought I was really concerned that he wasn't there. But I'd been drinking. So, I got a little smart. I told her to tell him I said hello and give my regards. I was thinking she would tell him in the morning, and it might spoil his day."

"She didn't look upset to you?"

"No. She looked like she was enjoying herself. She was talking to everybody."

"Who else was there that knew her?"

"Everybody. Everybody knows them both."

"Was anyone there you wouldn't expect to see?"

"No. The usual crowd. Even Otto's lawyer, Donitz. He's always trying to drum up business. But he doesn't talk to me because he was part of the deal back when—when I promised not to say anything about Sylvia. But he was there. I suppose I don't see him around very often these days."

"Can you tell me about that? No reason you should, I realize. I'd just like to understand it all from Otto's perspective."

"What's to tell? Sylvia was like a nymphomaniac bunny back then. After, she blabbed to the press about it herself. She'd tell anyone who'd ask. She saw it as her conquest. She'd slept with George Rooney! Who, ha! I was barely a name then, but she thought it was a big deal. She may have been fifteen, but I certainly wasn't her first. You've got to see that. She was already being considered for a remake of the *Wizard of Oz*, for Christ's sake. Can you believe? Dorothy blowing the Munchkins? Her big mouth cost her."

This was not the direction I wanted.

"What actually happened that night?"

His eyes brightened. He was probably thinking I wanted prurient detail.

"She'd gotten her roommate to sleep in one of the other rooms. But we never got a chance to sleep, I'll tell you. Otto came in on us before anything actually happened. Like gangbusters. Otto was generally a very calm guy. He got excited about a shot or a bit of acting or something, but I'd never heard him yell before. He looked like he wanted to kill me. Jessie had given us all the big lecture before filming started. We'd promised not to get involved in any hanky-panky during filming. Most of the kids were underage. Otto didn't want a bunch of twenty-something professionals just pretending they were newbies. He had us all bunked up, guys apart from girls, two by two, in separate rooms. What we did after was our own business. And Jessie was the chaperone. She's signed off on that with all the parents. It was a big deal to her. You know? 'Mother Superior' we called her."

"You liked Jessie?"

"She was the best!" He emptied his glass and held it up for a refill. "I never got to apologize, you know. She was the one who was hurt by it, I think. Actually, a nice lady. But I never saw her again after that. Instead, Otto slapped me pretty good and told me to get out. I could hear him talking to Sylvia from the breezeway. It sounded like he wasn't going easy on her either. Whatever he said, it sounded to me like he already knew that she had her own ways."

"But you finished the film?"

"Yeah. But not with Otto. He didn't want to see my face after that. He had Josh do all the final shots with me. We were nearly ready to wrap anyway. That's kind of the way it happened. We both knew—I mean Sylvia and I both knew the shooting was nearly over. We were only in Ft. Lauderdale for two weeks and we'd been rubbing up against each other pretty much the whole time. It was Sylvia who'd seen Otto's little camera around and it was her idea to do a scene. What was I going to say? No? So I got hold of a light rig. She wanted to do one of the scenes from the movie but without the bathing suits. The volleyball scene. Pretty nice. She even got some unused stock. Sounded good to me. I was young and stupid. Any sex at all was fair back then. It's all hormones when you're that age."

I was thinking that he was telling me more than he had to in order to come across as forthright. He is not all that bad an actor. At least he's been doing it long enough. But it was time to get back to the main event and he had a fresh drink in his hand.

"So when you talk to other people, and they talk to you, what do they think happened the night of the murder?"

The change of direction had him taking a loud breath.

"I'll tell you the truth. Anybody that knows them thinks it was an accident of some kind. It's crazy to think Mysty would be doing anything nasty. It's just not in her. You can see that! Listen. I know women. I know what I'm saying here. There are women you can't turn your back on. Missionary position only. Mysty was the type of woman who might get in trouble for trusting someone, but nothing else. I think that's the way everyone feels about it. I've even heard speculation that Otto might have caused it. Somehow. I think he had more of a temper. And she might have done something in self defense. But I don't see that. I think it was just some kind of accident. The *Times* said she didn't remember a thing. That's shock, isn't it? Shock, right? That's all. Listen. Don't write this. It's personal. But my mother died when I was a kid. Right in front of me.

Bad heart valve. I don't remember a thing about it, but I was right there. I was holding her hand at the hospital. I know what that kind of shock is. They had to take my hand away from hers, because I wouldn't let go. They told me about it later. I couldn't remember a thing. But I wouldn't let go."

I believed him.

Wallace Martin

the unknown unknown

Wallace Martin, 46, formerly of Detroit, Michigan, currently occupies a weekly rental in Oxnard. Apparently, he is still legally married to Mysty Circumstances. Both are former circus performers. They separated in 1990.

George Peal told me this: "It seems Wallace Martin moved out to California specifically to extort Mysty. He's had a 'run of bad luck' you might say, and, like the more colorful George Washington Plunkitt, he's seen his opportunities and he took'em. Mr. Martin was aware that his divorce from Mysty had never been completed. Likely as not, he purposely made that not happen. But, according to the laws of Michigan in 1990, when they officially separated, the divorce was never finalized. Therefore, as a matter of law, Mysty was not, in fact, legally married to Otto Biedermeier."

I'd asked, "Why did he wait so long to show up?"

Peal had no idea. "Maybe his luck had just taken a turn for the worse. Who knows?"

It seemed to me that Peal ought to find that out. He didn't seem all that interested.

A cold gray mist had moved in off the water during the night and was still thick enough when I drove down to Oxnard in the morning that the sun was illuminating just the tops of things from above and transforming the top wisps of the mist into a pink meringue amidst the cars on the Ventura Freeway.

In spite of the traffic, I saw smiles on the faces in other cars. But there was something ominous about plunging from that heavenly topography on the coast into the singular gray fog that occupied the lower reaches of Oxnard.

Martin lives in a low two-level complex of apartments just outside of the Port Hueneme neighborhood that might have once been built for the Navy or Coast Guard—or at least had that military base look to them. The mist did not help the appearance. Not all the doors have numbers, but most had Halloween decorations on the windows or a pumpkin on the stoop. I rang the one that had nothing at all. He didn't answer his door at first, but I had a feeling and waited. After a moment, the shade on a window went up as someone looked out to see who it was. I waved.

He opened the door abruptly then. "What do you want?"

He was dressed in wrinkled slacks but only an undershirt and he had not yet shaved. He is about my height and still a very muscular looking fellow for a man who must be at least fifty. My guess is that he still works out.

I said hello, told him who I was, and immediately added, "I thought you might want to give me your side of the story."

The laugh is loud and the gestures broad.

"Ha! I'd like to do that! You don't know all of it, I'll tell you, man! But Mr. Donitz has told me not to talk to you, or anyone else."

"I can understand that. He's keeping a firm hand on things. As he should. But I can't figure something. Who's paying his fees?"

"I am!"

"Five hundred dollars an hour, or what?"

"He's doing it as a favor. In trade. I've been working for

him."

"Great! That's a deal. You couldn't turn that down. Only, I can't help but think he's probably working something out for himself in all this."

"Sure. Every man for himself."

Then the door closed on my face.

The newish looking Toyota Corolla parked in the space closest to his door didn't seem like Wallace Martin's sort of car. Besides, it had California plates. So, I took a stroll around the corner of the building. There was a ten or twelve-year-old Ford Explorer with Michigan plates and rust on all the under panels and I guessed that would be more his style. I took a couple of pictures with my phone for details.

It was just about then that Wallace Martin sucker punched me from the back. Whether on purpose or not, he had missed my kidney, but I didn't know that for a while. The pain in my ribs took the air out of my lungs and I hit the sidewalk with my head.

He says, "I told you to leave me alone!"

He hadn't said exactly that, but I wasn't arguing. I did note, looking up the way I was, that the pink of the mist had dropped down and offered a rather nice frame to the dark bulk of his figure.

He then got in his car and pulled away hastily enough to leave a bit of rubber behind.

I did not really want to follow any police procedure in all this. But that could work two ways, so I drove down to the Oxnard police station and reported the attack. Filing a complaint took another half an hour of my life. Trying to sit upright on a plastic chair, so as to keep my back away from the hard surfaces, was difficult. I paced a little, trying to stand upright against the contraction of muscle. But I was already running late for an appointment in Malibu to see Mysty at the jail.

At least Mysty seemed happy to see me. A real smile.

"You've been busy," she says. "I was right to talk to you. George Peal has been over here several times, now."

The table between us is broad and she has her hands up on it and fingers spread. When I told her about being attacked by Wallace, she closed her eyes for a moment and her hands folded into fists. Obviously, she had some memories in that regard to deal with. A female officer who brought Mysty to the room to speak with me stood guard, and she is suddenly frowning with some real concern over my story as well.

I told Mysty "I can't help thinking Wallace is a good possibility for a murderer. He's vicious enough."

She opened her eyes. "That's what I told George. But he's not so sure. He said that it's on record now that Wallace has been working for Truman. The connection is there. That wouldn't be very smart."

All I could say to that was, "People who think they're smart are usually mistaken."

She shook her head at me,

"Truman is very smart. Otto always depended on him to cover all the bases."

"Maybe Truman and Wallace were working together."

"To kill Otto? Why?"

"I don't know. Maybe something went wrong. I don't think killing Otto was part of any plan. Not the way it was done."

Her eyes turned briefly to the guard.

"Can't the police see that?"

The guard was stone-faced now.

I said, "I think they can see a lot more than I can. But I have a question for you. Given the sort of fellow Martin is, why do you think it took him so long to come looking for you?"

It was the way I phrased it that caught her off-guard. She blinked.

"Did you guess that, or did Wally tell you?"

Sitting straight with a pain in your back is sobering. But I knew exactly what she was asking. Of course, Wallace Martin had come to her first. Then, realizing she didn't have much money at her disposal and not wanting to waste the opportunity, he had gone to Otto Biedermeier.

"I'm not so smart but it wasn't a hard guess."

She is the sort who likes to study you when she talks to you. Now she had her eyes down on the table and the hands were locked together.

"He showed up back in February. I didn't tell Otto. I was ashamed of the whole thing. I thought it was over. Long past. So long ago. And then one morning, after Otto had left, there Wallace was at the door."

"You let him in?"

"No. He forced his way in."

"What happened?"

Her eyes were closed.

"He raped me."

Hearing it said all of a sudden is hard enough for any guy to deal with, I suppose. If you're a father, you think about what you'd do if your daughter ever said something like that to you.

"What did you do?"

"He wanted money. He said he was on his way to Hawaii, and he needed money. And that's when he told me that we were still married. He said he was just taking his rights. Long overdue, he said."

I guessed.

"Did you give him your engagement ring then?"

"No. He didn't know about the safe. He only wanted

money and I didn't have much. A couple hundred dollars. He took the jewelry on my dresser. Just some silver. My turquoise ring that Charlie Parrot gave me. I loved that ring. I wore it all the time. Otto asked me what happened to it and I told him I lost it. But I don't think he believed me. He could always look right through me."

"And you didn't tell the police?"

"No. Wally said he would go away. He said I was fat. I was too fat for him, anyway. And I thought I could finally get the divorce without him, now that I knew what had happened."

"And you never told Otto."

"No . . . I was going to. I would have, I think. I wanted to. But I never could."

"I think you should tell George Peal."

"What can he do?"

"I think the police should know. They probably already know something. They'll know everything eventually."

She shrugged and looked away.

"I don't care now. Otto is gone."

"What about Wallace? Don't you want him punished?"

She did not hesitate at that. "No! I want him dead! But I don't know that he killed Otto. I want to know who did it."

I said, "You won't be able to see to that if you're in prison for Otto's murder."

"I didn't do it. Someone will figure that out."

"How? Why do you think that?"

Misty shrugged again and spoke in a smaller voice, "It's what Otto always said. 'Someone will figure it out.'"

This didn't sound like Otto Biedermeier. Otto was the sort to do the figuring.

"In the mean time Wallace Martin may hurt someone else."

"No. It was only me he wanted to hurt. Because I left

him. Because his life went bad after I left."

"I thought he left you."

"I said he left me with the bills. He went off on the Shriner Circus Tour."

"What happened to him after that?"

"They let him go. He wasn't even good enough for them. After that he robbed a couple of stores, I think. He didn't say much about it. But I know, he shot someone."

Another guess.

"Was he in prison?"

"Yes. For second degree murder."

"I suppose the cops must know all about that too. But still, they think you killed Otto. Why?"

"I don't know."

"I'm going to speak with George Peal about this."

She nodded and stood for the guard to take her back.

I sat there a moment and tried to understand.

An injustice served

November 3, 2016; A *Hollywood Tab* exclusive by Thomas Lenz

The argument in favor of Mysterious Circumstances, generally known now as Mysty, and the ostensible wife of Otto Biedermeier, is compelling. That she loved Otto Biedermeier was well understood by those who knew the couple well. That he loved her is inarguable. By all accounts, they had been living happily together as man and wife for twenty years.

In the early hours of Sunday morning, October 16th, the well-known independent film producer and director Otto Biedermeier was murdered, and Mysty has been charged by the District Attorney with this seemingly senseless and bloody act. That Mysty denies this, and is devastated as a consequence, is of no matter to the authorities. That she is now incarcerated in the County jail, suffering the deprivations of imprisonment and must face such charges, is a truly unkind and cruel punishment.

In the meanwhile, other and more blatant possibilities are apparently ignored.

A multi-jeweled engagement ring of great value, given to Mysty by Otto Biedermeier, is allegedly missing. The theft of this object alone would be the cause of murder.

At present, it appears that Otto Biedermeier was being blackmailed by Wallace Martin for the fact that the director and the former circus performer were not, in point of fact, legally married. A previous marriage between Mr. Martin and Mysty, aka Georgia Whitehouse, was still in effect. In the 21st century, such a point of law could not be worth a great deal, but it is believed that Otto Biedermeier had already put together $20,000 to keep the matter quiet. This information is contained in a legal complaint of extortion against Mr. Martin and now filed with the court by George Peal, Miss Circumstances' attorney.

Importantly, this charge was not made by Otto Biedermeier's attorney at the time of his death, even though Truman Donitz was apparently aware of the transaction. Even more significantly, Truman Donitz is now the attorney for Wallace Martin.

It is also noteworthy that independent sources, including those on the other side of this argument, confirm that Mysty most likely knew nothing of this transaction.

However, it is a truism that blackmailers are seldom satisfied.

The actor George Rooney has recently sued the *National Enquirer* concerning a short film clip which allegedly shows the film star, then eighteen, seducing actress Sylvia Place, then fifteen years old. It is known that Rooney holds Mr. Biedermeier responsible for this disclosure.

The District Attorney for Los Angeles County assigned to this case, Helen Wright, has filed her charges in the case, and those include one count of first-degree murder. This is important at least for the assumption of premeditation.

However, the assumed motive for this homicide is still a matter of dispute.

Perhaps the couple had been in a heated argument? Friends have said they never heard Otto's voice raised toward his wife. However, immediate neighbors have told reliable sources that they heard the couple arguing earlier in the day. Even so, a death resulting from such a confrontation would not constitute first degree murder.

In the interim, Wallace Martin has been charged with one count of extortion. This is, essentially, a charge of blackmail. At his own hearing, Wallace Martin has stated that Mysty Circumstances knew he was in the vicinity, and that she had met with him to discuss his own plans.

The assumption of motive on the part of the District Attorney, based no doubt on the full police report currently unavailable to the press, might be that the defendant had acted in anger. It is suggested that she may have taken the engagement ring, estimated to be worth as much as a quarter million dollars, and given it to Wallace Martin, herself, or that he may have been blackmailing her as well. Still, these are insufficient reasons for a charge of premeditated murder. The engagement ring in question was hers and apparently already missing on the night Otto Biedermeier died.

Mysty is charged with killing the director with malice and forethought.

What had she done prior to the incident that might make this charge stick?

The police have discovered that an additional life insurance policy had recently been taken out by Otto Biedermeier. But that is common enough prior to the start of a new project such as the making of a film that would require greater temporary expense and financial risk.

What else?

For the time being we must await a full explication of the charges.

My own theory is that Wallace Martin has told the police that Mysty had conspired against Otto Biedermeier, perhaps with the intention of leaving the director for her former husband. This makes no sense. Mysty already had a very fine lifestyle, a loving husband, and good friends. Why would she leave that to return to the arms of a thug.

But this last paragraph did not make it into the *Tab*.

Jheronimus Bosch
and old keys in a box

What a difference a day can make. I have a letter this morning from the University of California Press. They're interested in my proposed revision and updating of the *Biedermeier* monograph. They are offering me the expected $3000. I rejected it immediately. After all, I have Laura at my back. Though I won't tell her that I've rejected the offer just yet. I told them I would consider $10,000 if they would add more photographs. I'd forgotten about the additional photographs in my original proposal. You can't sell anything these days without photographs and Otto's movies are loaded with memorable moments.

On top of that, I was just thinking that Jheronimus Bosch was my 'key lime' to all of this.

This came to me in a dream. Bosch paintings are dreamscapes but that was not what was in my little night terror. What was there is vague, but when I awoke, I was remembering talking to Otto about those paintings years ago, when I stayed at the house. He told me then that they were 'authentic reproductions,' a term of art he found funny, and made by some outfit associated with the Getty Museum. I have the notes for that conversation from 1996.

But Tamara had now reminded me that in his *Ottobiography* he talks about going to Europe in 1989 to get away from himself following the death of his wife and son. He writes, 'Up until that time, before going to the Rijksmuseum in Amsterdam, I had never seen an original by Jheronimus Bosch. I went there to see Rembrandt and instead I found '*Removing the Rocks in the Head.*' In that small painting, which is about a foot and a half high and a foot wide, the outrageous figure of a surgeon in a pink robe is standing behind a highchair where the patient, dressed in white, is bound while sitting up. Oddly, the surgeon's robe is open to a bare leg, and he is standing in a pair of high wooden shoes. This was intended to be ridiculous, of course, and typical of visual satire. But with the trepanning in progress, the patient is looking at the viewer and appears unconcerned at the surgeon slicing open the top of his head. Meanwhile, three men at a table in the foreground appear more interested in a small stone that one of them is holding in his open hand, and a woman behind them is in obvious distress over the operation in progress. At the rear of this tight cluster of people, a fellow is having his own head bandaged by another member of the party. Clearly, this is an ongoing process. I remember that I almost immediately laughed. Several people who were there in that large museum room at the time must have been startled and moved away from me.

'This subject is known by several titles. *Cutting the Stone*, *The Extraction of the Stone of Madness*, and *The Cure of Folly*. The brochure explanation of the satire in English did not seem to address all that I was seeing. But what I saw then was myself and how I had allowed calamity to steal what life I had left to me.

'Soon afterward, at the Prado in Madrid, I encountered a similar painting, also attributed to Bosch. This work, considered by some to be the original, is only slightly larger and surrounded by a gilt Fraktur typeface that I could not decipher. In this version, the surgeon was also wearing a pink robe, but it is not open at the leg, and he has a black shoulder cape.

However, here he's also wearing a strange funnel hat, something like the one worn by the Tin Man in the movie *Wizard of Oz*—a symbol of the fool, or of complete insanity. The patient here is in a loose white shirt but wears tight blood-red leggings and is also bound in the chair but he is staring dumbly back at the viewer, mouth agape and perhaps drunk. With them is a priest in black robes gesturing as if to comment on the proceeding, and a woman leans forward at a table, her face unperturbed, while she balances a large red book on her head. We are talking full visual absurdity here! There is a small object on the table which is explained in the museum brochure to be a tulip flower, with the suggestion that the surgeon was removing a tulip bulb instead of a stone. And in this version, there is a name given to the patient, Lubbert Das. So you know now where I got the name of the wise madman in my movie, *The Drool*.

'I understood that it was common for painters to make copies of works that were popular. They were trying to make a living before the age of the photocopier. But the second was so unlike the first, especially with the woman balancing the book on her head highlighting the absurdity, that it drew my attention to the singular relationship between the surgeon and the nonsense. Obviously, the doctor was the greater fool. This seemed so close to the very thing I play with in my films! But what I take twenty-four frames a second to say this guy has said with one!

'Now, several weeks later, in Paris, I was in a gallery where they actually had a Bosch for sale. At least it was attributed to him and painted in that time and place. It looks like Bosch to me. And incredibly it is yet a third version of the same subject I had seen in Amsterdam and Madrid. But here, the surgeon was in a red robe and skull cap, with a bit of red tongue showing at his lips as he concentrated on his task. There was more red blood visible at the wound, but this patient appeared to be speaking casually to his wife as the operation progressed. A priest, again in black, stood behind the table, hands together, praying. A woman, likely the patient's wife, wearing a head scarf, prays with him. Here the red book is open on the table, with a stone holding the page. In this rendition the satire is suppressed. Not quite subtle, but at least with more allowance for reality. Trepanning was a common method for relieving certain illnesses then. Hell, they still do it!

'I wondered which version had come first! Had he realized this interpretation failed to make his point and done the others, or had he thought to make his statement here a little more clever? The Inquisition was in full force at the time, remember, and Spanish Habsburgs ruled much of the Netherlands during his life.

'Totally intrigued, I bought this third version on the spot. How could I not? This one was only attributed to Bosch and not confirmed, but it was that very doubt that made it affordable.'

These were Otto's words. In fact I had seen this same painting at the house in 1996. I remembered it well. Otto might even have spoken to me about it, but I had no notes for that, just the memory of seeing it. But something else was the matter.

I called the jail immediately after eight and made an appointment to see Mysty. Then I went to the house. Arty was confused by the hour. He had just eaten and was looking for his morning walk.

All four paintings were there in the foyer, away from sunlight, high on the wall, at eye level. The one I wanted was the third. They are all clearly hand painted. But *Removing Rocks from the Head*, did not seem to be painted quite like the others. It looked to be newer. And in this copy, the priest is not praying, but holding an object, much like the one at the Prado, and the red book is on the woman's head. And there is no bit of red tongue at the surgeon's lips.

At the jail, I left Arty in the car in the shade with the windows cracked and told the officer at the front desk I would not be long.

Mysty was looking like she'd lost some sleep. I felt for her.

I asked her about the paintings and *Removing Rocks from the Head* in particular.

"Yes, it's there. It was Otto's favorite but it's a copy, like all the others."

"Are you sure?"

"Sure. I don't know anything about it but what Otto told me. He would have told me if it was original. They're all just painted copies from the originals. Otto never told me it wasn't."

"I think it was an original."

"Why?"

"Because of what he says in his *Ottobiography*. He says he bought an original. Don't you remember? And the problem is, it's not there now. I just checked. It's gone. There is a copy in its place."

The distress on Mysty's face was disturbing. Perhaps it was made worse by exhaustion.

"No. It wasn't. I know that. It couldn't be. He would have told me."

The sound of her voice had become higher pitched. The guard frowned at me.

"What about what he says in the book?"

"I don't remember that."

I pulled my phone from my pocket and went to the notes.

"Page 344. You can—"

"I can't!"

"What do you mean, you can't?"

"I can't read it! Damn you!"

She got up. What she was saying finally sank in.

"You can't read?"

"No!"

"But what about all the books?"

"For show, dammit! That's all! I grew up in Detroit, don't you know?!"

She had already turned her back on me and was at the door by the guard.

"But Otto knew, didn't he?"

Almost through the door with the guard behind her she turned.

"Yes! Oh dear, yes. He tried to teach me. He read to me. I loved when he read to me." Her arm flared as if she were in her home again, but her knuckles hit the mental frame, and she flinched. "He read all those books to me. Everyone!" And then she began to weep.

I went home then and called George Peal from there.

"There was an original Jheronimus Bosch painting at the house. It's gone."

"Since when? I saw several there when I went to look things over, didn't I?"

"There are four copies of other painting by Bosch. Otto loved the guy. But one was real. And that one is missing. The four there are painted copies."

"And you're sure? You saw it?"

"I saw where it was. And I remember seeing it twenty years ago."

"Maybe he got rid of it."

"Maybe."

"You think it might've been stolen?"

"Yes. Very recently. Probably sometime after Mysty was arrested. She might have noticed otherwise."

"What would it be worth?"

"Hard to say. A hundred thousand—half a million. It's only attributed, but still."

"That ought to be in his records. How much did he pay for it?"

'I don't know. Maybe Philip Reeves would know."

"I'll call him."

It was not until the next day that Mysty had calmed enough to speak with me on the phone about it.

Yes, she had gone to special classes. Yes, she could read signs. She got along fine. But she had done all that she could. She'd always just believed that something was wrong with her. They called it dyslexia. Otto didn't. He simply believed that she was different. But, because he knew it upset her, Otto never told anyone.

I wondered if anyone else knew.

And Mysty confirmed one other point. She had looked at those paintings many times. Every day. In the original, the book was not on the woman's head. Definitely not. The priest was praying. And she had always thought that bit of tongue was funny, and it always made her smile.

Kill all the lawyers
again

As established, Truman Donitz is a very dislikable man. He was clearly my primary suspect in all of this—along with Wallace Martin, who was likely his partner in crime and more likely the one who actually killed Otto Biedermeier.

So, when Donitz texted me saying he wanted to talk, I said yes.

He said, leave the dog at home.

I was at his office that afternoon. The dog is at Laura's shop. But women love him, and he gets all the attention, and they forget to buy any clothes.

At Donitz's office, there was a new-looking mud-colored Land Rover outside. The secretary was not at her desk, but I only knocked once. Donitz simply opened the door and waved me through. Thankfully, he stepped back from the door sufficiently for me to get by. There was no attempted handshake. He quickly settled himself in the well-padded chair behind the desk that looked like it was more than capable of holding his weight.

Right off he says, "You understand I don't really want to speak with you. I certainly don't have to. But I think I do have an obligation to Otto. He was always square with me. He was a friend. He was my best client for forty years. I knew him and all his family very well. I cared for them and I cared for him. What has happened is a tragedy, and I have thought long

117

and hard about what I might have done to bring it about. And yes, I do think I bear some responsibility."

This was a good beginning.

I said, "I'm listening."

He straightens a sheet of paper filled with copy and notes. I wonder if this is a script for our meeting. He doesn't seem like the sort who leaves a lot to chance except when he's in Vegas.

He sighs. "Mysty never liked me. She might have told you that much."

"Yes."

"The chemistry there is hard to guess. The feeling was mutual from the very start. Twenty years ago, Otto came to me with the idea that he wanted to marry her. I told him he should just live with her. He didn't need another marriage. As it is, I guess that's what actually happened, given Wallace Martin's testimony. But at the time Otto said it was important to him and to her. We came up with a prenup agreement to cover the situation and that was it. I hadn't met her yet. I didn't even know she was black."

Donitz finished with a shrug and raised both eyes as if to say, 'What can you do?'

I said, "Why do you think you bear any responsibility?"

His jowls quivered with a negative.

"It's problematic, you might say. There were several things involved. But the worst of that was my very stupid idea of employing Wallace Martin."

He paused. I was sure now this was an attorney doing his thing before the jury of one.

He held up a hand. "This part of our discussion is just between you and me, you understand. If you have any kind of recording device on you, I will sue you for the rest of your life —or my life, in that you're likely to live longer."

He could not sue me for my memory. It was likely my only real asse, and I wasn't going to give it up for his benefit. But my phone was on in any case.

"Understood."

"Good. Listen, I knew from the first that Wallace Martin was a head case. He's a nut. And he has a fixation on Mysty. When Otto married her, Martin was still trying to get her back. He'd even contacted her. Even gotten her mother to write her. Otto had me write back. That was twenty years ago. But I knew he was not going to leave her alone without a good reason." Donitz studied his notes and took a breath. "I think we both know, with Martin, money is the only reason. It's all he knows. As it happens, I have a lot of very unsavory clients. Gangbangers. You name it. It can be very lucrative, but I've been roughed up on a number of occasions. I used to hire a guy name Philips. He was kind of my Paul Drake, if you know what I mean. He did all the footwork for me. He was an ex-Marine, and he could handle himself. But he lives in Hawaii now. The jerk got married himself and had a kid. So, I needed somebody else. At least for awhile." Again, he looked at the sheet of paper. "I've been thinking about retiring, you understand. Anyway, there's always that adage, keep your friends close, but your enemies closer."

"So you hired Wallace Martin."

"Yeah. Well. He showed up looking for money. He knew he was setting himself up for an extortion charge. But he was taking the odds. And he also knew if I paid him a dime, I could get slapped too. So I hired the sonofabitch. It was the best I could do. If he was on my payroll, I could pay him anything I wanted."

"When was that?"

"About four—five months ago."

"So that's when Otto found out his marriage to Mysty

was not legal?"

"Yes."

"What did you do about that?"

"Otto asked me to contact the State of Michigan and see what I could find out. I did. I found out that, legally, Mysty and Wallace were still married. So Otto came up with the $20,000 that Martin wanted to keep things quiet, but Otto asked me to look into the thing in the meantime and see if there was any way around it."

"Is there?"

There are moments in any conversation, even ones as scripted as this, when there is a change. Usually, it's when you know things are done and you have to wrap it up. Nothing is said, exactly. It's just the temperature of the thing. The tone. And at that moment there was a change just like that. Donitz looked down at the papers on his desk and I knew he had not already planned an answer to this question. He had to wing it.

"No. Nothing."

And I knew immediately then that he had in fact found something. But I had to keep up my own questioning so that he might not realize he'd given anything away.

"How exactly did you contribute to the death of Otto Biedermeier?"

"I'm not sure I did, exactly. I mean, the cops have Mysty dead to rights—so to speak. She still had the knife in her hand when they got there. There was no one else there." He shrugged. The wattle shivered and he leaned forward in the chair with his desk pressing at his belly. "She did it! Even so, the cops had me down to the station the next day! They gave me a good grilling. I don't know why, but they were sure I was involved. But I wasn't. And I couldn't exactly come to Mysty's defense, given that I was a suspect too."

"Why do you think they suspected you?"

"I have problems of my own, you might say . . . I've got a monkey on my back." With that word, I knew he was back on script again. This was his pitch. This was his attempt to humanize himself. He shrugged. "I gamble. Too much. If I could, I'd live in Vegas." Now Donitz leaned back again, comfortable with what he had left to say. "That same night they picked up Wallace Martin speeding down the Ventura Freeway through Thousand Oaks with a $1000 cash in his pocket and what's the first thing he says? 'I want my lawyer.' Naturally. He wants me! The cops had the particulars on him in a minute. They know he'd been married to Mysty even before they have me in for questioning. And there is Mysty with the bloody knife. The whole thing looked too ripe. I thought my goose was about cooked."

"How did they think you were involved?"

"I don't know, but you can guess. Otto's safe was evidently robbed. I needed money. Martin works for me. Nobody really wanted to think Mysty did it, did they? Why not the shyster lawyer. Why not the bully ex-husband. Right? But then the cops had me pegged for being right here, at the office, when the murder happened. And Martin too. As coincidence would have it, he wanted more money that very night. His landlord was going to kick him out of his place in Oxnard, and his cell phone was already cut off. He called me. I told him I was just about crapped out. He wanted me to get something more out of Otto. I told him I had a couple of bucks I was going to spend in Vegas the next night. I'd give him that if he would just back off. He said he would."

I said it out loud. "I don't believe in coincidence."

The face altered slightly. I'd seen this look once before, on the morning of our first meeting.

"I don't give a fuck what you believe! You could be a Mormon for all I care. That's what happened. And the cops confirmed it. They even have footage on some of their traffic cameras."

That last detail was something I hadn't thought much about. But there were other things I had missed. He stood then and called our meeting to an end.

After speaking with Donitz, I went to see Mysty. She had called that morning and left a message. I called back and asked to see her. I thought it would be a good opportunity to compare notes about Donitz.

What Mysty wanted was a favor. Would I go to the apartment where she had been staying when she was arrested and get her things.? Her friend Doris would be there that evening cleaning up so it could be rented again. Mysty's car was still there as well and if I could drive that back to the house, Doris would give me a lift one way or the other.

I filled Mysty in on my meeting with Truman.

At the apartment, there is Doris, a middle-aged woman in jeans, flannel shirt rolled up to the elbows, a bandana on her hair, and looking like the lady on a package of cleaning soap. She's already sitting on the bumper of Mysty's Ford Explorer, waiting. She gives me a very suspicious look. I tried to be friendly. Her suspicions did not appear to be allayed.

So I asked, "What's the matter?"

She had not moved from the bumper of Mysty's car.

"Why does she trust you?"

"I don't know. I've wondered about that myself."

"You know she's innocent."

"Yes."

"Why don't you just say that?"

"I think I'm getting quite a lot of opinion in the pieces as it is. But the situation has to be reported as it stands. It's a legal matter."

"They should just kill the lawyers and have done with

it."

"That's a thought."

"I was up there to see Mysty yesterday. She's a wreck."

"It's a difficult situation."

As it was, Doris drove Mysty's car and I followed her back to the house. I parked alongside the lime tree and tried to remove the key as surreptitiously as possible.

She says, "Don't worry. I'm the one who waters the plants when they're away."

We both took Mysty's things inside.

It was only when we were outside again and standing on the gravel with both cars there, that it finally occurs to me.

"But where's Otto's car?"

Doris rolls her eyes. "The Land Rover? I think Truman has it. Otto loaned it to him a couple of months ago. Truman's car was a lease and it got repossessed. But I don't know why. I mean, why Otto did stuff like that. Truman Donitz was no friend. He hasn't done anything to help Mysty."

"No. He hasn't."

In addition to that thought I had to wonder just how many people knew the key was under the rock at the lime tree. Enough to keep my mind busy all the way back to Santa Barbara in traffic.

Philip Reeves
in accounting

Philip Reeves has an office on the second floor of a newish little stucco building just around the corner from Wilshire Boulevard in the middle of Santa Monica, and only a few blocks from Truman Donitz in one direction and Audrey Biedermeier in the other. The glass in the lobby is lined with large decorative pots where cactus are trapped in gravel, a different sort incarcerated in each. There is a cosmetologist and a dentist on either side of the stairs at the first floor. There is a psychiatrist across the hall from him on the second. It occurs to me that the landlord has most of the human condition well covered.

Truman Donitz and Philip Reeves are two very different looking people. 'Phenotype' is the word for that, but it's an antiseptic word. 'Constitution' is the old word you see in books, but that's not used in the same way these days. And this difference was especially true of their physiognomies. Reeves is thin, the way a lot of heavy drinkers are. Smaller, if not exactly short. Desiccated looking. His face is hawkish, with no jowls. But he is well tanned and wearing a loose Hawaiian shirt, light blue pants, tennis shoes. Regular California office attire for the retired. I figure him at about five foot six if he didn't slump as much as he does. His thinning hair is combed back with something in it and it takes me a minute to realize the smell is Brylcreem. I didn't even know the stuff was made anymore.

Even so, I had the feeling the two men, Donitz and Reeves, were brothers.

Reeves has no secretary. Without a divider, his office looks enormous, especially in that his desk is over by the window in the corner. There are two extra chairs. Against one wall there is a small sofa that looks like the convertible kind. Several piles of folders lean against a wall near one tall file cabinet. Two other short metal files are over next to the sofa. I'm guessing those are for his clothes. On another wall, in a cheap chrome-plastic frame, there is a clipping from a magazine that refers to him as 'The accountant to the stars.' This decoration was hung up in the same way Donitz hangs his law degree. I looked for some equivalent accounting certificate, but there was none visible.

He greets me at the door when I ring the buzzer. He doesn't ask me my name or offer to shake my hand. Another characteristic in common with Donitz. Unlike Donitz, he doesn't seem to mind Arty, and doesn't give him a second look.

He says, "I have an appointment in a few minutes. What can I do for you?"

I'd called for this appointment and waited more than a week for it. That made me testy.

"My name is Thomas Lenz. I'm writing—"

"I know who you are. You called. I met you at the funeral."

"Yes. Well, I do have a few questions."

"I'll answer what I can. Most of what I know is confidential. You should know that. I can't speak to anything private."

"I understand. Can I sit?"

He looked toward the two chairs as if he was surprised they were still there.

"Sure."

I slipped Arty's leash over the doorknob and decided to dispense with any preliminaries.

"Mysty has asked me to look into what's going on. As you likely know, she says she didn't kill Otto. I believe her. But it appears someone wants it to appear that she did. In the course of looking into things I've been coming across a number of financial matters that don't add up and you're the one person I can ask about those."

"Ask if you like. I may not be able to answer. I keep my client's privacy."

I say, "Did you have the combination to the safe at their home?"

I knew the answer to this, of course. Mysty had told me. But he wasn't ready for it.

"No."

So the lie begins there. Reeves had often been charged with the responsibility to take care of financial details while Otto was away on a shoot.

"Do you want to think about that?"

He returns my challenge. "Why?"

"You've been handling financial matters for Otto for what—-thirty years? Wasn't going to the house when he was away one of your responsibilities?"

He stared at me a moment, blank-faced.

"You're going to write all this up in the *Tab*?"

"No."

He rocks in his chair.

"Okay, then. Alright. What I do for clients is nobody's business. Yes, I know the combination."

"When was the last time you were there?"

"What are you, her lawyer? I already spoke with George Peal."

"Do you recall?"

"Sure. Seven or eight months ago. When they were wrapping up on *The Big Cheese*."

"What did you see in that safe then?"

"What do you mean, what did I see?"

"What did you see?"

"I opened up the file drawer and took out a couple of contracts. That was it. It's a small safe. There's not a lot to look at."

"Was Mysty's ring in there?"

"That was kept in one of the little drawers I think. I didn't look. I didn't see it."

"Didn't you take some cash out of one of those drawers?"

"How do you know that?"

"I was told."

"Donitz? He doesn't know shit."

"So, you didn't take the cash out?"

"I did. It was an emergency."

"Wallace Martin is an emergency?"

"You know about that?"

"At this point I know a whole lot of things that I wish I didn't."

"So stop asking questions."

"Mysty is charged with murder."

"She shouldn't have killed him."

"She didn't"

"I guess we'll find that out."

"I already have."

This exchange went very quickly. I got up at that point. It seemed like a nice dramatic exit line.

Reeves remained sitting, but his hands are no longer folded together. It looks as if he's holding an invisible beach ball but with his wrists attached to the desk. They shake a few times before he gets to his words.

"Who did it, then?"

"I think you know."

"I know a lot of things, too. I know that Otto was my friend. And I know that Mysty was taking advantage of him."

"How do you figure that?"

"None of your business."

"Then I guess you know about as much Truman Donitz knows."

Arty was happy to leave.

Laura is happy to hear all the details. The kids are bored by it and leave the table as soon as possible. But they missed the best part.

For many years, beginning with our courtship, Laura and I had a dog named Fritz. He was mostly German Shepard. A good dog in every way. Great with kids. But Fritz didn't quite make it to his eighteenth birthday. Laura was heartbroken. Shortly after that, there was a French silent film that was very popular, called *The Artist*. We saw it several times. Laura liked the fashions, and the popularity of the film gave a boost to her business, but she was especially taken with the dog, Uggie. Laura told me she wanted a Jack Russell terrier like that.

Now, I have a problem with small dogs. They're cute. But I've never been into 'cute.' They are nippy and nervous. I don't like nippy and nervous. So I took matters into my own hands. I went down to the Animal Rescue League and got the cutest puppy I could find—mostly chocolate lab. I knew he wouldn't be cute for long. And he wouldn't be nippy or nervous. And I also knew as soon as Laura laid eyes on him it would be a done deal, and it was. The deal was this: it was now my responsibility to feed him and to walk him. No need to expect the kids to do that. They were busy—unlike me? They have school.

Nevertheless, Laura named him Arty, after the cause of my endeavor, *The Artist*. Unlike some women, Laura has a sense of humor. Mostly sarcasm. And 'Arty' fit her sense of irony.

Arty is purely artless. He is blatant, in your face, no holds barred, and either enthusiastic or asleep.

Thankfully, I had cause to be happy with the name. Back in Levittown, New York, I used to know a fellow name Arthur Burgess. Arty Burgess was an old soldier and of the special sort who used to show up for any community function, whether it was a blood drive, or a parade, or a Boy Scout clean-up. Enthusiasm was Arty's whole attitude toward life.

Suffice it to say, I have become very fond of the dog, even if he is diffident to me. Of course, I'm the wrong gender.

I had always assumed gangbangers used guns. I suppose it's the 'bang,' that misled me. When I left Reeves' office and walked the half block to my car, I find three fellows hanging on the fenders. They don't have a guns. They are dressed in cut-off sleeveless shirts, tattoos that appear to stretch from their knuckles to their necks, and baggy black jeans.

The smallest of the three, a fellow with a shaved head tattooed like a Maori warrior but without a discernible sense of design, uses a line I haven't heard outside of a movie theatre since I left New York. Guys are always bumming cigarettes in New York, especially now that they cost a buck apiece.

"Gotta smoke?"

At that point, Arty has gone stiff legged behind me, and the leash is taut.

My answer, something smart-ass left over from New York, is "No thanks."

Arty growled.

The little fellow points down in mock fear and says, "He's dangerous, man. He should be put away."

I pulled Arty out into the street and around to the driver's side to get in. One of the other fellows is leaning there.

Remember, this is Santa Monica. Things happen, but it is a relatively safe neighborhood. There are houses close on both sides of the street where people may be watching. Seemingly safe enough.

I say, "Excuse me."

This guy is almost my height but has a better build. He has creatively limited his tattoos to the right side of his face and his left arm.

He says, "Why? Whad'ya do?"

His sarcasm is appreciated.

"I'd like to get in my car."

"This yours? Really? You oughta get it fixed."

I can see then that the back tire on that side is flat. Completely.

I pulled out my phone—maybe to call the AAA, maybe to call the police. But this fellow leans out from the car and takes a swipe at my hand. My guess is, this was to knock my phone away, but he misses because Arty has his mouth clamped on the guy's bare arm tight enough to see the teeth embedded. The third guy at the other side of the car is suddenly coming around and has something in his hand that looks like a short black metal machete with a curved hook at the end—very likely what was used to slash the tire. At this point I am not at all sure what I'm going to do, but I guessed Arty was in the greater danger, so I jerked him away with a couple of hasty 'down' commands.

Just then there was a car coming up the street, and I backed up there into the middle. The woman driving, who has likely seen some of what was happening, tries to swerve around me, but I was not about to let her get away, and I end up practically sitting on her bumper when she brakes to avoid running me over. I'm thinking she was more worried about Arty than me when she stopped. I can see she has her phone on her ear.

The three gangbangers disappeared.

Now, this might be a coincidence. But I don't think so.

Charlie Parrot

a fishing expedition

He is a crusty looking fellow. Maybe an inch shorter than me but almost twice my weight. Most of that is muscle. He is wearing a Hawaiian shirt that has lost a lot of color. He has on a misshapen panama hat stained through at the brim by sweat and the crown pinched by greasy fingers. Wide suspenders that might once have been tan and were now stained variously in shades of gray, grab at a pair of cargo shorts with every pocket lumpy with one thing or another. He has rubber sandals on his feet and his toenails are stubby and white.

He corrects me when I introduce myself and call him 'Mr. Parrot.'

"Here they call me 'Papa.' I was born a 'Papagayo.' But my father was not a good man. He had a bad reputation around San Carlos. It is a small place, and everyone knew him."

"Why was that?"

"He liked guns, and he used to say, 'A gun only has two reasons, bad and worse.' He often proved it."

"Papa, then."

Charlie pulled a clear plastic food bag from his pocket and cut a plug of tobacco with his fishing knife before offering some to me. I declined. "It was Otto who gave me the name, Charlie Parrot. I guess it rang right to Anglo ears. My business took a jump after that. But ask for Carlo Papagayo today and you'll still hear some dark stories about my old man. He and Tio Frederico ran drugs and women to Los Angeles in the 50s and '60s. Probably still would be doing it if one of the local gangs hadn't buried him." He spat toward the water but hit the already stained dock. "Eh. Maybe not. He'd have to be a hundred. But maybe so. He was a hard prick to the end. Papagayo wasn't even his real name. He never told us what that was. Likely as not, he had killed someone and had to change it to avoid retribution. But with Carlos Papagayo, everyone knew where he was from. No more questions asked. Even my brother left the name behind."

"You chose not to go into the family business."

"Chose? Not exactly. Life chose for me. My mother and my sisters needed someone to take care. My brother was off in Tijuana selling hierba to the rich kids. And then I met Teresa." He shrugged at the necessities of life. "You see, my father had three boats. One for Frederico. One for himself. One for emergency." He pointed down to the deck with his finger, "You're standing on the emergency boat." I looked down at the deep honey shine on the wood at my feet. Charlie shook his head at me. "The deck is new. I put that down last winter after Odile. But the hull is quarter-inch steel. Or at least it was, sixty years ago. Likely it's lost a little to rust since then. It's World War Two surplus. My father bought all three for $150 and towing fees at San Diego in 1949. They were all a little small for trawler yachts. Barely 36 feet. The engines were too big. Used for unloading in shallow harbors. But he knew what he wanted them for. If he hadn't become what he became, he could have earned a good living just repairing boats. Tio Frederico could make any engine run. This one still has the diesel he put in it back around 1976. But all of that wasn't good enough. They wanted more."

"How did you meet Otto?"

133

"He met me. He came looking. He was making *Storm Warnings*, and he wanted someone who knew a little about the drug trade, but he didn't want to deal with any of the bad guys. That's what he always called them. 'The bad guys.' Someone put him on to me. My father was just dead a year or so then. Frederico was laid up with a bullet in his lung. And Teresa was pregnant. Otto walked right down the pier like you just did and says, 'I need some help.' Charlie spat directly into the pale green water below the dock. "Like he needed my help. I was busy trying to feed six mouths, and he needed help. I took that as a laugh. He says, 'I'll pay you fifty dollars just to hear me out.' I never stopped listening after that."

"What happened after that?"

"Well, I was a little famous after that. I was in a moving picture, you see. My face was as big as a house on the screen. Otto said it made me look more dangerous. Eli Wallach looked like a used car salesmen when he was standing next to you, but when Leone did that close-up in *The Good, The Bad, and The Ugly*, you thought twice about it. And I have the shoulders for a heavy. So then I took Otto out fishing after *Storm Warning* was in the can and he loved it. He came down every year after that."

I'd made the phone call first, of course. He did not want to talk on the phone, but he said, sure, come down. The whales were gone for the season and the fishing business was still slow after the big hurricanes. So, I'd taken five hundred bucks out of the family savings account, bought a $300 round trip to Loreto in Baja, rented a $60 Ford Escape with broken air conditioning and driven the three hours down to Puerto San Carlos from there. The hotel was clean and $35 a night. With the cost of chewing gum and what passed for fast food, I had under $100 in my pocket. Like Papa's father and uncle, I was hoping for more.

"How much do you charge to take people out on the

boat for a day?"

"You wanna fish?"

"No. Just to look."

"Fifty bucks."

"Great! Done."

"But for you, nothing. You were square with Otto. I'll be square with you. I went to see Mysty when I was up at the funeral. She told me you were a friend."

"Thanks! Thank you. But how about I cover the gas?"

"Bien."

There was much to write about after the fact. We were alone on the boat for the day, and it seemed to free him up a little. Boat rides bore me, so I paid my attention to him.

At one point I asked, "Forgive me, but things seem a little worse for wear. Has business been that bad?"

"The money? Yeah. But life has been very good to me. My wife still listens. My oldest son has a farm near Loretto. He hates the ocean. My daughters are married. One, not so well, but I have seven grandchildren. What's to complain about?"

"We have some of that in common then. But I have three boys and a girl. No grandchildren yet—that I know of. They are still a little young."

"You have it easy. Boys are easy."

I could have disagreed and talked about family matters. As usual, I was impatient, even while sitting in the middle of the Pacific Ocean.

"But what happened to the money? You made six films, by my count. You said yourself—you were famous."

"That was before Odile. And before that, Jimena. The hurricanes took everything except for the boat. The boat ended up on a sand bar down below San Buto. The steel hull took a beating, but there wasn't a leak. Not one. You see, I had stupidly used a good piece of my money on a splendid house

135

right up against the ocean in San Carlos. Big man that I was. With my face eight feet tall. I tried to copy what Otto had done up in Malibu but with more rooms and without the cliffs. I used pilings. Very High. Very grand. You can still see the rubble from all that on the channel now. 'Charlie's Folly,' they call it. Now we live in a little house that Teresa chose that befits my actual size."

"Is your brother still selling hierba?"

"No. Now, heroin."

"Sorry."

"Why? It's his life. Not mine. The only difficulty is when someone comes looking for him. We are twins. This is known, but people are often surprised. He tells them, my brother is the one who wears the funny shirts."

"I bet."

"There was one time—I'll tell you the story—there was this one fellow from L. A. who made the mistake and came here looking for my brother. Someway, he found my home and disturbed Teresa. My brother found out and shot him. I said, 'Isn't that bad for business?' He says, 'Are you kidding? There are more Anglos looking for gato than I can supply. I told the guy to wait, and I would get back to him. But he didn't, and I don't need the trouble.'"

"But you didn't turn in the same direction?"

"That was for Teresa. But if I had, my brother would have shot me first. He always loved her, himself."

"But you were close. That must have been difficult."

"No. That life never appealed to me. My grandfather was a fisherman. But my father did not want that. He wanted the easy way. I went fishing with my grandfather when I was too young to hold a net. He taught me to mend them instead. My brother went with my father. From the beginning."

"What made the difference do you think?"

The answers had been quick until then. This one he studied for a moment in the glyphs on the chop of the water.

"I think it was because my grandfather told us stories. Nothing much. An incident here, and something there. People he had known. Things that marked his life. He had known a fellow who lived on a raft of debris for forty days and forty nights after his boat sank. There was a story for each that kept the fellow from going crazy. And a roosterfish that used to steal his lines and come to the surface to crow about it. And he told us often of a whale he said he knew, named Percebe. Percebe was my favorite. He was King of the Whales, but none of the others listened to him, especially his wife. He was always getting them out of shallow waters."

"Your brother didn't like the stories?"

"Not so much. When we were growing up, my father used to tell us stories too, but all of them were to his benefit, and about what an important man he was. Pepe liked those. But when our father died, he was nothing. The papers included his name in with all the others that were murdered that day. Nothing more. I pointed this out to my brother. Pepe said— Pepe is his name, you understand. He took the name Don Carlos because he thought it made him sound stronger—Pepe said that they did it to belittle him. He would show them. But in truth, he was a little man. So is my brother, I guess."

Mid-day he pulled us into a narrow cove on Isla Santa Margarita, announced, "Time for a swim," and went in first, naked off the side of the boat. I know water that is so deep it appears depthless, but here it was so bright with the white sand beneath, it appeared to have no depth at all. It was colder than I expected but soon felt near perfect.

He flashed an arm across the arena of the shore. "You recognize this?"

Ragged cliffs arose around us, not high but forbidding.

I admitted that I didn't.

"This is where we filmed, 'The Oddissey.' Not one of Otto's more successful films, they say."

"I liked it. I think Homer would have understood the script changes."

I laughed at my own attempted humor. Papa turned away to scan the shore.

"But it was a failure, even if it made money and got a couple of prizes. The prizes are all phony. Self-promotion. Party-time. Ha! You know, I even went to one of those parties. In Cannes. Teresa was embarrassed. She was right. A lot of under dressed women and over dressed men doesn't make something important."

"What did Otto think?"

"He was unhappy. He told me, he was trying too hard to say something. It was better for the story to speak for itself."

"That was a rule with him."

"But he broke the rules. Even his own."

But impatience was ruling me.

"So, who do you think killed him?"

Papa looked back at me to be sure I knew he was saying the truth. "I don't know. Otto was down here with Mysty and Audrey last October. We got to talking about my old man. How bad he was. And about my brother. Pepe runs all of that trade now himself. Mostly on the roads. Boats were too much trouble for him, so he let me be." Treading water, Papa shook his head. "Otto said there were bad guys in every family. I asked him who the bad guys were in his. He said he wasn't sure. He had an idea, but he wasn't sure. And he didn't say."

"Any guesses about who he meant?"

"Yes. But I can't tell you that. He didn't say, and you don't play with such guesses. Not unless you must. The police detective who came to see me, Jones, said not to make guesses.

138

People could be hurt. Let him do his job. I guess I'm okay with that."

"You don't think Mysty is in danger?"

Charlie turned in the water, weaving his hands out to the sides as if to calm the waves.

"She didn't do it. They'll figure that out."

There was that phrase again. I was not reassured.

"I hope you're right. But they don't arrest people without evidence."

"No?"

His answer was too quick. There was more to this.

"What do you mean?"

He shook his head and squinted away. "We all have our own experience. You understand? But that's just Hollywood, I suppose. Speculation is half the game."

"Why do you trust Detective Jones?"

"I don't. I trust God. And Jones will do his job."

Some people are better at sublimating their worries about the things they cannot control. I understood this, coming from a man too far away from the center of things to affect the outcome—especially one whose life had been overturned more than once by forces beyond his control, like hurricanes, and drug cartels, and Otto Biedermeier. But I felt as if I were in the middle of it and responsible for doing anything I could.

"What do you think of Josh?"

A quick smile at that.

"He was like Otto's brother. Everybody likes Josh. Some too much. Keep him away from your daughter. But he didn't kill Otto, if that's what you're thinking."

"You're sure of that?"

"As sure as I am of myself, or of Mysty. I know about brothers."

"That's good, because I'm not blessed with your

equanimity. I need someone to talk to who can tell me the way of things without breaking confidences. And I think I have to do what I can to make sure of God's trust. I'm talking about his trust in me, you understand."

"I understand. You talk to Josh. You talk to Tamara. You talk to Audrey. Then you will know what you can."

"What do you know about brothers?"

He smiled.

"I'll tell you. Mine is a very bad guy. But I can trust him with my life."

Biedermeier killer still at large

November 16th, 2016; the figments of my delusion

Charlie Morris is managing editor at the *Hollywood Tab*. He's a reasonable fellow. If you've got the goods, he pays the price. If not, he doesn't. I went to him this morning with the lede, 'The murderer of Otto Biedermeier is still at large.' I sent the story to him by email with some notes, but that was the first sentence. He sent back the response it deserved: 'Really?'

I have now been taken off the Biedermeier story and will no longer be getting the two hundred bucks a week stipend plus expenses plus whatever else for each story filed. I just don't have 'the goods.' Five weeks in and I have earned just under three thousand dollars, of which half was spent getting the other half.

Sure, I can hope for a new revised edition of my Biedermeier book, but that will probably get me little more than another three thousand or so. Reporting is not an eleemosynary enterprise. The job is to sell papers or get clicks on the *Tab* website. Even 'Biedermeier Killer Still at Large' will not sell papers. Not with Mysty already charged and sitting at the county jail waiting for a court date and the DA making it clear they have a solid case against her. Not with most *Tab* readers wondering who will be playing Spock in the next *Star Trek* reboot.

This morning, with a nice fog hovering over Malibu and the Pacific Ocean nicely still—even dampened, if water can be that—or at least quieted to the whispering of small swells playing out on the beach, I was standing at the water's edge there in front of Otto's house and pondering the facts: i.e., I was pounding sand. Arty is in love with water of any sort. He stands chest deep and stares out into the mist as if something else is moving there. Maybe a seal or an otter. But to my eye, there is nothing. At least there was no one around to tell us dogs were not permitted.

There was more of the story that I might cover, but it was all looking very much like sidebar. The presence of Charlie Parrot at the funeral had suggested to one online wag that there was a possible link to the drug trade. Certainly, Otto himself had suggested such dark elements in his film, *Storm Warnings*. A short treatise on the Hollywood/Mexico drug trade might sell a few papers, but I was not an authority on the subject and Charlie Morris had better people to do that. People who had done more than smoke a couple of joints in their youth.

True, Otto's next film was to be about a Jihadi who had gotten lost on her way to a suicide bombing. According to the script, the knife that was used to kill Otto had been intended to be the confused suicide bomber's last defense against her fate. Was there a radical Muslim connection? I could easily put together more of such speculations on the murder, but the *Tab* doesn't publish fiction. Not knowingly.

Funny how something like this can draw contrast and definition.

I married Laura in 1997. I was on top the world. A book published. Another proposal accepted. Two published articles and three more in the pipeline. They even did a feature on me at KNBC that year. I was almost a celebrity.

Laura and I had just met at the L.A. Sound Film Festival. It was the 70th anniversary of the *Jazz Singer*, and thus of synchronized dialogue in film, and I couldn't stop talking.

She was nuts for old films. I was just a nut. We were married about five weeks after we met—just about the same amount of time I have been working now on the story of Otto Biedermeier's murder.

In my car, back then, I had a CD of Johnny Cash and June Carter singing *Jackson*, which was already a thirty-year-old song at the time, older in fact than either of us, but we felt like we had no time to waste. I remember us singing it at the top of our lungs with the windows down and practically gliding through the curves on Route One. You want the whole world to know when you're in love.

Laura already had her idea about a dress shop. At our wedding, she was wearing something copied from *The Philadelphia Story* that she'd made herself. But she was prettier than Katherine Hepburn. I wore a rented tux and definitely looked more like Jimmy Stewart than Cary Grant. With both of us being raised Catholic, it meant the wedding was a necessity as far as our parents were concerned. Our first child, Benjamin, wasn't interested in waiting an extra four weeks to make it a proper nine months from the date on the certificate.

That first year I made twelve thousand dollars. We required a little assistance from our families. The next year I made eight thousand and we required more assistance. The third year, between Benjamin and Alice, Laura managed to get her shop open. Her dad put in about fifty thousand on that. I made almost nine thousand. Only open for four months, Laura made twenty something—after expenses! It's been that way ever since, except she usually nets between seventy and eighty thousand a year now. I have rarely managed more than ten.

I've had job offers. There were other opportunities. But my plan was to write the screenplay that would change everything. I've written a dozen or more of those now. More, because every one of them has been rewritten a dozen times.

I've come close to getting a couple of them optioned. But that's as close as I get.

No. The closest I've come is with *Fitz-James*. That is a lovely piece of work, if I do say so myself.

Let me remind you.

In March, 1862. Fitz-James O'Brien, 33 years old, Irish poet, dramatist, storyteller extraordinaire, and emigre, who has sold his body for a pittance so that a rich Yankee could avoid the draft, is in a field hospital in Maryland dying of the tetanus that is deep in his battlefield wounds, and the stories are spilling out of him in a rage of delirium. For brief moments of clarity, as the tent sides billow in the weather like the struggling of his own lungs, he knows he's dying, though the nurse tries to make him believe he'll recover. To please her, he lets her think she has convinced him. She becomes his last object of affection and the heroine of his final imaginings. Oddly, she calls him Georgy, just as his mother once did. But she too is in fact a creature of his own fabrication. The actual nurse is a clean shaved young man, wholly bewildered by the onslaught, who does not even know the author's name, anymore than the dozens of others needing attention.

This was a screenplay about a self-made character, larger than the life around him. The scenes were his delusions as he rages and cajoles his muse and the fates, writing his last letters to anyone he can think of, including President Lincoln, whom he images comes to his bedside in response.

Yes. It was never made—but you remember it! That's because, after I'd submitted it to an unethical producer (excuse the redundancy), those thieves took the story, gave it the old 'Hollywood haircut,' called it *Cumberland,* and made it at Paramount. It was, after all, an historical incident and free for the taking. Except it wasn't. It was mine—at least for the most part. They even used the name 'Georgy,' which was entirely my own fabrication. I was advised by an attorney not to waste my time and money on a plagiarism suit. Besides, the studio had screwed the delusions into a homoerotic wet dream. I really didn't want any association with that, did I?

So, now, what do I do. The mist is impenetrable. The house is at my back and a chill from there makes me turn. It's a twenty-foot drop from the balcony to the sand, and with the rails of the balcony above like spindle teeth, and the gaped rocks below, the darkened space beneath the house appears to be more of a maw than it should. I'm being swallowed. I am delusional. I have no excuse. My battlefield wounds are not life-threatening.

Is Walmart hiring?

The sun above bores a white hole there, and the filigree of gray that drifts at the edges makes it moonlike.

Arty rips a nice bark into the fog that strangely echoes into the maw behind us.

Arty wags his tale. He doesn't care if I can't see what is obvious to him in the mist. He is simply pleased to be a witness. He fears nothing but an empty bowl. Maybe, not even that.

This evening Laura gave me the long look. I told her everything. Almost everything. She is my mainstay.

At least she will bear with me.

I sat down after our talk and wrote the following to Charlie: 'Mysty Biedermeier is innocent of her husband's murder. The circumstantial evidence that is being used against her is real enough, but it is only a portion of all that matters. You want that story! I'm telling you, that story is the real McCoy!"

I used 'McCoy' instead of something else, like 'the real deal' because I'm being smart. I know he loves old television shows. Charlie is not quite so forbearing. But he's managing. He has been a managing editor for twenty-four years. Likely he is sitting in front of his computer right now trying to make copy ends meet. He will not pay a stipend or expenses, but if I want to continue to submit my delusions to him on a weekly basis, he will run them as sidebars where he can and pay me for those.

Minna Kelly
The good sister

My success with the expedition to see Charlie Parrot likely made me overconfident about going to Illinois to see Minna Kelly—Minna Kelly Whitlock. But this in turn was likely more a reaction to the wasted hours spent on the phone with several dozen other possible key sources. Those calls included the Los Angeles County Clerk's office (they have about 200 million records, but they are not on-line and they are not all accessible at any one time, either by an self-important *Tab* reporter or a research assistant for a defense attorney), and the Sheriff's Office Record's Department (they are happy to assist you, please hold), as well as Universal Studios (the primary distributor for M-16, Otto's production company). The names of friends, acquaintances, neighbors, former business associates and the like, which I have accumulated the notes for, were as frustrating in their own ways as the electronic menus which have replaced flesh and blood human beings almost everywhere.

But there is also something about getting out and around that gives you a sense of physical accomplishment that cannot be duplicated sitting at a desk.

This bit of exercise cost me another $300 for a round trip ticket plus $300 expenses out of the family savings account. Laura told me she would likely lose that much from sales by keeping Arty at the shop during the day. I thought this was an unnecessary exaggeration, all things considered. All things considered she didn't want to discuss the matter.

I got off the connecting flight at General Wayne A. Downing International Airport in Peoria. I suppose if they had wanted to honor the man they could not have simply called it 'Downing' International because that has the wrong ring to it. But everybody seemed to call it that anyway.

Long Island, New York, is relatively flat. But growing up there, I can say your horizon is generally defined by the neighbor's back door, or trees. I used to get a great and magical sense of distance when we went to Jones Beach, but an ocean horizon is nothing like the rim of the Earth seen from the middle of Illinois. An ocean begs only for the voyage. An earth horizon takes your breath away for all the places in-between. I rented a car and found myself stopping on the infrequent overpasses just to look at it in every direction. The time of year meant I didn't even have to rise above an elephant's eye to see all the way to the end of things by simply standing beside the car.

Minna Kelly Whitlock still lives in the same house where Otto grew up when he was between the ages of eight and eighteen.   Yellow with green trim. Something different than the usual white in that neighborhood. From the gate on County Road 2300 N you can see six grain elevators at different distances in all directions—four white, one blue and one yellow. As the highest and most massive objects on the plain, these are the primary perspective points, and the gray clusters of trees that flag the locations of houses are usually not far removed. From where I stood, each of those farmsteads is an island on a sea that is flatter than the ocean, as far as the eye can see, with nary an amber wave of grain. Even the sky above must curve to the will of the earth here. This was Otto's boyhood world. The one he left behind.

When I took the bus from New York to L.A. in 1996, there was little chance to step out onto that solid sea. Now, I had done this more than once just to feel what it was like. And I wondered what such a sense might have done to the mind of a boy who had never known permanence before. At the gate I stood long enough in awe at the thought to have roused some concern. Minna came out on the porch and called to me.

She treated me immediately as a friend. I did not understand this at first, but I did not question it. Frankly, her friendliness was a little overwhelming. I had failed to speak with her at the funeral and I was surprised that she remembered me at all.

She stands very straight for a woman in her late seventies, and she is not thin or frail. The white hair is like cotton, not silver. As I had seen before, her skin is a permanent pink. I was soon treated to a lunch of fried baloney on toast with mayonnaise—something I had never thought to eat before.

"Most the farms are owned by corporations now. Co-ops." She told me, "I'm very lucky to be here. And the Kelly Family Trust will keep it here for the grandchildren." Later, she told me "He was a trustee, you understand. It was Linc who helped us set up the family trust in the first place, after Daddy passed. Momma certainly couldn't have handled it alone. But Linc did not want a share in it. He left that to me and my boys, Will and Garth."

"Where are your boys now?"

"Oh, they're both married and have their own places closer to town. Closer to the schools. It's better that the children aren't on the bus for an hour each way, like we all had to do in the day. They both still work here, but it's slow season now and there's a little less to do."

Interestingly, she speaks as fast as my daughters, with

one thought running into the next. I took out my phone and she didn't mind, so I started recording because I knew I wouldn't remember it all.

When I asked her what she thought about Mysty, she did not hesitate. "We didn't know why he married her. We didn't know what came over him. We thought he'd gone crazy. After Jessie and Kenneth died, he must have been broken. We didn't see him much for a while. I was married then myself, of course, and had my own concerns. And then he married that French actress. He never even brought her here to visit, you know. We never saw her. None of us. It just suddenly happened, and then that was over. And we never got to see little Alma, either. She is such a sweetheart, isn't she? Not so little, any longer. I was very happy to finally meet her. A fine young woman . . . But then there was Mysty. We called it 'Mysty madness!' What was he doing! What could he possibly have in common with a black girl nearly half his age! He'd lost his mind! We all predicted it wouldn't last a year. No one thought it would. A middle-aged man like that! With all those Hollywood women prancing about. With that Tamara there just waiting. What was he thinking? . . . But of course, we were wrong. Terribly wrong. Mysty was a real woman. She understood him. She set him straight. I would never have believed the change in him. He settled down. It was as if he'd been going a mile a minute after Jessie died. He just didn't want to stop and think. And then suddenly he did. He sat himself down in the house there by the ocean. And everything was okay. Everything was good again . . . And I'll tell you this, whatever happened the night he died was an accident. I am sure of it. I went to see her, you know. I talked to her. Mysty told me what she remembers. Whatever happened, her mind has put it away. We can't know, can we? I knew a fellow once, Burt Riggins, who managed the Food Co-op in Macomb. As nice a fella as you would ever meet. But Burt went crazy one night and killed all his chickens. A hundred and fifty chickens. He shot them, every one. Bam. Bam. Just like that! Lucky he didn't turn the gun on himself. He woke up in the morning and found them all dead. Couldn't remember a thing."

"Did Burt recover?"

"Yes. Just like Lincoln did—Otto, I mean. He met a good lady. It was what he needed. And he stopped drinking."

"Did Lincoln drink?"

"Nooooo. Burt did, though. I'll tell you what. Linc always had his head on. I never saw him drunk once in his life. Maybe after Jessie died. I don't know. Linc was happy enough with just a pack of beer after a long day. And he had reason to drink, I know. What Linc did was work. The harder it got, the harder he worked. You couldn't stop him." She took a breath. " Daddy had 120 acres in corn one year and the combine busted. It was old. As old as daddy. His grandpa bought it new in Springfield at the fair one year and had a tractor pull it all the way over here. That would have been a hundred miles on the old road across the Havana bridge. And the roads were not paved back then. Mostly gravel pack. Well, that old Harvester finally gave out in 1959 and every other machine for a hundred miles was busy, given the time of year. Linc wouldn't wait for chance. He went out there and started taking those ears off by hand, husking right in the field, like the farmers used to do it. One ear at a time. Daddy was too old for that then, but Linc went out and Connie and I followed him and did what we could. Linc was a young man possessed. Momma drove the tractor with the wagon. You know, we often got a hundred and fifty bushels of corn per acre at that time. Linc was husking way over a hundred and fifty bushels a day. Between us Connie and I pulled maybe half that. We took almost 1500 bushels of corn in four days. He was just sixteen. There wasn't nobody could get in his way after that!"

"What happened to the rest of the corn?"

"Oh, Daddy got Nathan Stiles down from Pekin and he got that Harvester fixed up again and they did the rest. But even then, Linc sat by Nathan while he fixed it, so he would know how to handle it the next time. I dated Nathan for a while after that. But it didn't work out."

"So, why do you think Linc wanted to be a filmmaker?"

"He didn't at first. He wanted to be a photographer, I think. Momma bought him a camera, an SLR—a good one—for his birthday. Japanese. Daddy just stared at it like it was a bug. Daddy had killed a few of those people during the war, you know. But that got Linc to taking pictures. I guess one thing led to the other. I still have that very camera in the other room. I can show it to you."

I spent several hours with her looking through a photo album that was mostly pictures Lincoln Kelly had taken when he was fifteen years old. These were the first ones. He had thrown them all away, but Minna had retrieved them. It was clear to me that he already had the eye a filmmaker needed. And it was plain to me that he must have already had film making in his mind. Every shot begged for movement. Something was about to happen or had just occurred. A spill of grain on a barn floor glistened in a late sun, but the blur of a leg and hand at the edge told you an accident had occurred. The weight of a horse bowed the planking of a stall. Did the horse break free? A tractor and harrow moved into a dry field leaving dark soil behind. The imperfections were difficult to see. A blur here or there that maybe should not have been. Not good enough, I suppose, to the eye of the photographer. To me they added the 'newsreel' quality he often developed later on to give his stories verisimilitude.

"Did he ever talk about when he was a boy in Europe?"

"There were times. We had an old horse back then named Jester. He was already too old to work but Daddy kept him on. Linc took good care of him. He knew something about horses, and he told me once that was his job when he was little—to calm the horses. I asked how. He didn't know. He only remembered that he was told to stand by them, and he did. I asked him about where that was, but he wasn't sure. They moved a lot, I believe. He already knew it was a circus but not much more. "

Finally, I asked, "What did you mean at the funeral when you said, 'The truth is, I loved him more than a brother. God forgive me for the thoughts I once had?'

Old women blush oddly. But Minna could not have added color—it was a tilt of the head and a purse of the lips.

"It's a fact. When he was sixteen, I was already twenty-one. I had had a boyfriend or two. And I had thoughts about Linc . . . I can tell you now that I wanted Linc in the worst way, brother or not. God is my witness. I couldn't help myself. But he could, and did. He wouldn't do anything to hurt Momma or Daddy, whether we were blood relations or not. Period. He fended me off. I was the wild one back then, and I can tell you I was a farm girl and a lot to be fending off. You know, my older brother Stanly had died in the Korean War. I loved Stan like a brother, so I knew what that was. I just could not learn to love Linc in the same way. I married Delroy Simms soon after that. I thought it might cure me. But I didn't stop thinking about Linc until he'd been gone to school in New York for a couple of years and I had met Jason Whitlock. Delroy and I got divorced and I married Jason. And he was a good man too. Linc liked him. They got along. Linc even named his younger son after my Jason."

"Can you think of anything else Linc said to you about his early childhood?"

153

"No. There wasn't much he could recall, I guess. Just the horses. Standing by the horses to keep them calm. I read his book. It was amazing to me how he managed to follow his parents all the way to Prague. But that's Linc. You couldn't stop him if he wanted something. Jason and I went out and stayed at the bungalow in Red Rock more than once and I saw that little circus program there on the wall. It wasn't much to go on, was it?"

"No."

I slept that night in Otto's room—Linc's room—what had in turn been her son Will's room, under the eves of the attic with a single window facing north. At that great height of about fifteen feet or so, it appeared to me that I could even see the cloud of soiled air that hovered over Chicago. But then, that might have been my imagination.

A wrong turn at Albuquerque
and no place like home

Sylvia Place was in rehab again and I read a story in the *Times* that made me think she might want more publicity. I called the Ryson Clinic and left a message. There were no direct lines. A couple of hours later there was a message waiting for me. She would be available for an hour at three that afternoon, if I wanted to come over. I said yes.

The Pet Place where I left Arty is probably not as expensive as the Ryson Clinic, but I'm not so sure. I scheduled Arty for a grooming, which is only twenty-five dollars more than the day boarding rate, and went down to Pasadena to see Miss Place.

With the hills as markers, it's hard to get lost in Pasadena until you do. The Clinic is over near Mt. Wilson, and, except for the observatory, the roads are not well marked because they don't want just anybody driving around. The GPS had me at a dead end, facing a rock wall covered with vines. I called the clinic again. The young voice who answered told me she didn't drive and couldn't help me with directions. I asked her how she got to work everyday. She told me she got a lift with a friend. Where was the friend? He was in the kitchen, and he was busy getting the dinners ready. Was there anyone else around who could help? Maria was at the front desk, and I explained it all again to her, but she didn't know how to help me either. Her boyfriend drops her off.

I started driving in widening circles. About 3:15 a cop in a car spots me and assumes I'm a thief in a mini-van looking for likely opportunities. He literally drove me to the front door of the clinic.

Miss Place was waiting in a domed solarium, sitting on a white wooden bench with various and sundry orchids at either side of a gravel path around her and misting machines going on and off like rattlesnakes in the bushes. She was reading a book. I figured this for a prop, but this is not the most surprising thing. That shock was that she looked like an old woman.

The *Times* interview had called her 'middle aged.' I thought she looked elderly. I'm pretty sure she's not even ten years older than me.

The first thing she says is, "Here at the Clinic they're very big on punctuality."

"I'm sorry. I got lost. I had to get a police escort."

At least she laughed, "Well, I'm used to that. But I got here in a cab."

"The woman at the desk told me I only had twenty-eight minutes left and the fact is I have to pick my dog up at four thirty so I'd better get right to business if you'd let me."

I said this while looking for a chair of some sort to pull over. Miss Place smiles again and pats the space on the bench right beside her.

"That's okay. I'm used to fellows who want to get right to business."

I smiled and knew right then that dinner tonight would be like a confessional with me retelling every detail to Laura.

"Can I use my phone to record?"

"Fine with me. You want to talk about Otto's murder, right? I don't know a damn thing about that. I just wanted a little company. It gets pretty boring here." She flicked her wrist at the foliage. "These are Hollywood orchids, pretty but dumb."

I sat. There was less than four inches between us. I reset my priorities.

"What are you reading?"

"George Eliot. *Middlemarch*. I had to read it in high school but I never finished it because I had to go on location to Ft. Lauderdale. The whole thing with Otto's murder reminded me. It took them a week to find me a copy. Nobody reads the classics anymore."

This was an unexpected statement and I believed it was just a bit of Hollywood colorization, so I asked, "What's your favorite?"

"Classics? God. I don't know. I like Trollope a lot. He understands women better than Dickens or just about anyone else. He treats them more like his men than the others. But there's no sex! Not even an intimation of sex. I like Austen, of course. Everyone likes Austen. You might have seen that terrible version of *Northanger Abby* that I did. I wanted to do *Emma*. I so wanted to do *Persuasion*. But my age got me *Northanger Abby*. Unfortunately for me, those other roles are not in my wheelhouse anymore. But if they would do some Trollope again, I could play Mrs. Proudie in *Barchester Towers*. I always wanted to do Mary Scratcherd in *Doctor Thorne*, but now I suppose I could still handle Countess de Courcy. Anyway. None of it matters anymore. Not really. I haven't had a decent offer in a couple of years. It's all behind me, I suppose."

She had put me in my place.

"The woman at the *Times* thought you had something else in the works."

"Oh, I lied to her. It was the *Times*, for Christ's sake. You can't tell the truth to the *Times*. They'd just screw it up and you'd never get a correction. Besides, they were only here because of Otto. Same as you. They're putting their pieces together for Mysty's trial."

"What do you think about all that?"

"Stupid. Mysty didn't kill anyone. Ridiculous. Everyone knows it. Some smarty is going to have to put two and two together. That's how things get made. You know that." She turned and leaned toward me. She had no makeup on. The fine hair on her upper lip darkened the wrinkles. "Are you that smarty?"

"I hope so. I'm trying."

"Who have you talked to?"

"Quite a few, now. Did you know Mysty?"

"Sure. I was out there for dinner a number of times. Usually when things got a little rough. Otto always knew when I needed some comfort food. Mysty can make ham and green beans like no one else. I'd stay over in the spare room there and have yellow grits for breakfast. Where in the hell can you get good grits in L.A.?"

I recalled now that Sylvia Place had been a teenage beauty queen in Savannah, Georgia when Jessie had spotted her for the role in *Apples for Oranges*. There was only a hint of that remaining in her voice.

"So Otto didn't bare a grudge for what happened during the filming back then?"

"Otto? No. The only grudge there was with George. He's a jerk."

"Do you see George very often?"

"Unfortunately, yes. He's very good in bed. He has a well-earned reputation. We've hooked up a number of times over the years."

This was the plain-spoken Miss Place who was well known to the supermarket tabs.

"Why was he still angry at Otto?"

"Billing. He gave Otto a lot of lip after our little tryst was broken up. It upset Jessie pretty badly. I feel bad about that,

158

but what can you do. You don't win any beauty contests on your feet. Otto put him lower down in the credits and wouldn't give him back that little film we made. There wasn't anything on it, really. Except that I was underage. And then there was that whole thing with the *Enquirer* last month. George called ME up to squeal. Like I had anything to do with it. But he was pissed, I'll tell you. I told him, he should he glad. Publicity is hard to buy these days."

"Do you think George could have killed Otto?"

She leaned back to emphasize her answer and let a frown pucker all the wrinkles on that once pretty face.

"Are you kidding? George is a coward. George gives the lie to the whole thing about balls and courage. Balls have nothing to do with it, I'll tell you! And George is living proof."

"Who do you think might have done it?"

"Loan me a couple bucks and I'd put it on Truman. I don't know who this other guy Wallace Martin is that I've read about. Maybe they're in it together."

A young woman from the clinic was hovering over us at that point, and I left.

A school for scoundrels
The U. S. C. School for Cinematic Arts

I have the habit of deleting most of my emails—those that are not filtered out first as spam. The kids are more into texting. Laura calls. My relatives send emails and I watch for those. But nine out of ten are promotions related to one site or another that I visit regularly for information. I am on the U. S. C. School of Cinematic Arts mailing list because I go to the film series as often as I can—lately only a couple times a year. So I almost threw the note from an 'A. C. Evans' away. Whoever that is, the note was badly labeled. The word, 'opportunity' is almost a guarantee of spam. Why did 'A. C. Evans' think a word so abused would catch my eye? It didn't. What did was the part of the address line that read 'filmarchive.'

The rivalry between the film schools at U.S.C. and my own alma mater N.Y.U. used to be something. Since George Lucas dumped a load of cash on the one place, not so much. But on the other hand, the downtown campus for U.S.C. has none of the authentic grime you'd see in Manhattan. Maybe that's why they can still do realism a little better back East. And the halls are wide. Not so much of the clutter and no boxes or equipment to step over. Or perhaps it's the more constant sun, but there is a cheerfulness present that is just a little off putting. Don't these kids know the world is falling apart at the seams and their future is bleak? The gray of New York granite is replaced here by a pleasant yellow stucco veneer.

It's the sort of place that wants to colorize film noir.

A. C. Evans was writing to inform me that the school had recently come into possession of a small trove of 16-millimeter film donated by Otto Biedermeier before his 'untimely' death. I reacted to the word 'untimely' the way I always do: in whose opinion?

A. C. Evans was suggesting that, given my previous experience with Mr. Biedermeier, that I might want to participate in the archiving of this collection and perhaps write some of the descriptive catalog. Importantly, she added "there is no current budget for this opportunity, but for the benefit of the school, it was our thought that you might want to see such a project go forward while public interest is high."

My first thought was that A. C. Evans should work with one of the larger movie studio publicity departments. She was master of nouns like 'opportunity' as well as the adjective. There had to be something more lucrative than 'administrative assistant to Professor James Jackson, Curator.'

Funny thing is, I was not surprised. This was the answer to what happened to all those films in the Wells Fargo safe at Red Rock. Somehow, I expected an answer like that. The films had little value on the market. But what hit me most was that Otto has been dead for less than two months and the school was already jumping on the opportunity to make something out of it. But then again, what could I expect. This was Hollywood.

I finally met A. C. Evans in a small windowless anteroom to the corner office occupied by Professor James Jackson on the third floor. Evidently, he was just between other appointments. Or so I was told. At least Ms. Evans was very pleasing to look at as I waited, even though she did not look much older than my neighbor's kid, with hair dyed black and cut short to her ears, and skin white enough to be untouched by sun.

"He's very busy," she said, a second time, as if to reassure me.

I'd called that morning after reading the email and then grabbing the neighbor's kid as he skulked around his back yard, pretending to mow the grass, and forced a ten-dollar bill into his hand to take care of Arty. Arty was none too pleased.

Jackson is both an instructor at the school and curator at the library (not a mere librarian, mind you). He had little time to spare and mentioned the fact to me again, perhaps thinking I had not heard him before because I kept asking him questions. His office is very neat, with his own authored or edited books gathered, out of the larger alphabetical order, at the center of the shelf behind his head where he sits in a reproduction 1930s oak office chair that I immediately envied. My guess was that this juxtaposition of volumes was for the standard head shot that anyone doing a filmed interview might want. I have no idea why anyone would want to interview the man. He has no opinions more complex than a preference for green tea and bow ties. Even his mustache lacks substance, creeping across his lip in a thin line that barely moves when he speaks.

I asked, "How did you come by these films?"

"I am not at liberty to discuss University business with you Mr. Lenz."

"That's okay. I really just want to know if you helped Otto move his films. Was it all four hundred?"

"Yes. Approximately. But that is not my department."

"Do you know who did?"

"I'm not sure."

"I'm sorry. I thought you were in charge of *this* department?"

This caused a slight spasm in his Adam's apple.

"Are you being impertinent?"

"I'm just trying to find out how Otto's films got through your doors. He didn't move them by himself."

"I do have to get to another appointment."

"So the lede on my story is that Professor James Jackson, Curator at the USC School of Cinematic Arts Library has no knowledge concerning over 40 canisters of film from Otto Biedermeier that were smuggled into the library archives about the time of the director's murder."

"That's not what I said."

"I asked. But you didn't say anything. That's either because you're hiding something, or you don't know. If it's the former, I am going to find out what you're hiding. If it's the later, then someone else ought to know about that."

"Who are you? What right do you have?"

He knew who I was. I had used that small wedge of credibility associated with the publication of my monograph on Otto to ask for his time. What was he was hiding? I suppose it was the publicity value of announcing the bequest of films, given the public attention to the murder.

"You don't have to answer. But I have the right to ask, and to make assumptions based on what answers I get."

"I have another appointment."

"So do I. I thought this would be brief. I just wanted to know who helped Otto bring the films in."

The man winced. This was a full squeeze of his facial muscles that brought the hair on his top lip up to the tip of his nose and his eyebrows down to the bridge. What his mind was doing behind this grimace is anybody's guess.

"Joshua Havens."

"Does he work for the department or the University?"

"The film school is independent. He works here."

"Do you know where I can find him?"

"Why? What would he know? He just helped move the

films from the truck."

"A beat-up old white Ford pick-up?"

"Yes."

"You were there?"

"I had to supervise. Of course."

"Where were the films moved?"

He sighed. It was a weak exhalation of breath, but likely all that was in him.

"To receiving, in the basement initially. But now they're right here in the closet outside my office. The door is locked. They're safe. We were expecting Otto to bring over some descriptive material for each of the films, and then Annie was going to archive them."

"But you weren't going to make the gift public."

"Not until—the agreement was that he would tell us when it was appropriate—either that or, in the event of his death, they were ours to do with as we saw fit."

"Is that why they're in the closet? Now that he's dead, you were getting ready to archive them and make the gift public?"

"Yes."

"On the shelf there, to your right, is a book, *Biedermeier, the filmmaker and his films.*"

"Yes. Your book. I know. We were going to use it for the cataloging even if you didn't volunteer."

"I warn you, there is a mistake on page 87. The assistant director on *Apples for Oranges* was Jessie Fleming. But thanks for your time."

I went downstairs immediately in search of Joshua Havens.

Right off I see that Mr. Havens is the sort of young fellow you wouldn't mind your daughter dating. No tattoos. No baggy shorts. A little shaggy but that is more likely a matter of saving his money, I suppose. There are fewer than a thousand students registered at the school and he is already a junior.

I introduced myself. He didn't seem impressed. I told him why I was there. He shrugged.

"Did you and Otto get a chance talk much?"

"A little. Mostly he was interested in what I was doing. He never went to film school, and he was curious about what I was studying. I asked his advice, but he said I was doing fine without it. I'm in a work-study program to help with the bills. He liked that. He said he'd worked his way through at NYU in New York. That was before Tisch, you understand. I didn't know that."

"What are you studying?"

"Documentary."

"So you knew a little about him?"

"Pretty much. I've seen a few of his things. I'm not a fan of 'horror,' but you can't help but laugh. He did his own thing. Pretty impressive. And I saw the first—*Lost Circus*. That's classic."

'Did he seem upset the day he was here?"

"No. A little tired. I think he'd been up early to drive down here from someplace in Nevada."

"Do you know what was in those canisters?"

"Yeah. He told me. I was going to take a peek when I got the chance. But then Mr. Jackson had me move them upstairs."

"There was no one else with him?

"No. He was alone."

"What day was it?"

"It was in September."

"Do you remember the day?"

"No. But it's on a receiving manifest. I wrote that up myself. I can get it, for you. I just have to call upstairs first."

"That's okay. You might want to keep it handy for the police, though. They might inquire."

The lamb on Skid Row
Where's the beef

Because the U. S. C. campus downtown is fairly close to the M-16 warehouse anyway, I had gotten another thought that morning and I dropped by the Malibu Sheriff's office for the keys before going all the way in.

My encounter with academia had been brief, so it was still early when I tried to park about two blocks away on East Sixth, over by a Los Angeles Police Department facility. I hoped the car might have a better chance there. But because all the meters were broken, this still seemed like a risk, so I went inside the police station and asked. When I finally got some attention, the fellow told me if the meter was broken, I couldn't use it. They would tow me. And true enough, there was a tow truck practically there when I got back to my car. The fellow in the cab looked disappointed. So I drove back to a garage at least half a mile from San Julian and paid the price for some more reliable protection instead. Five bucks for two hours.

Skid Row is everything you think it is and less. Various attempts to rehabilitate the area have resulted in half-empty semi-high-rises scattered amidst the older buildings, which are generally low, or just a couple of floors. The streets are perpetually littered with trash. The sidewalks are stained in ways you don't notice elsewhere, making you think that blood has been spilled as well as wine. The general smell of the place is filth, rotted garbage, and weed. The darkly soiled bodies of head cases—most of the bums are head cases—as well as the plain unlucky who are there because of the proximity of free meals at the various charities, are scattered along and across the sidewalks, usually gathered in areas of daytime shade and nighttime light, many of them knotted in jury-rigged tents and makeshift cardboard shelters. Occasionally you will see something as elaborate as a small wooden shipping container festooned with scraps of fabric or old carpet, both inside and out. These are all within a block or two, in any given direction, of the charity shelters that are generally not filled at night unless the weather is harsh but do at least offer food and minor medical attention. Makes you wonder what goes on in the shelters.

Sadly, there were more women than I remembered from the last time I was there, which was likely the afternoon Otto had driven me to see his 'garage,' in 1996. These women will stare at you, their expectations only discernible in the level of their attention, and it is somehow more difficult to comprehend their lives in passing—and how much more damning of the political promises over the past twenty years to see than it was to read about them.

Otto had used actual street people in his 1997 film, *Otherwhen*. Barbara Duke, the former child star who had fallen on hard times, had been featured in that, and gained much attention, but she had died the next year of a drug overdose. Though the film did well overseas, winning a Lumieres award in France, it did poor box-office in the US. Between elections, the politicians then were between promises, and the idea in the movie of grinding the homeless up for dog food didn't appeal to pet owners. In his *Ottobiography*, Biedermeier questions his own motivations for making the film and regrets not doing more for Duke. But certainly, the exposure did little good.

Walking through this obstacle course of supermarket

grocery carts, discarded household furniture, and such, I felt conspicuous, which is of course just me being self-conscious. I think I wasn't really noticed all that much. There are a fair number of people who work in the area and you can spot them from the rest. The thing is, because of the street people, the place looks a lot busier than the shuttered buildings with metal grills and graffiti embellishments would indicate.

I found the garage door decorated with the large brown spider right off. It was the roll-up steel type and big enough for a truck to enter, but a smaller windowless metal door at the side was the one I used. This one actually had two keys. One was for a bolt lock and the other for a heavier door lock and both were good. There were no signs of recent breaking-in that I could see. Immediately inside was the keypad for the alarm and I punched in 'B-I-E-D-E-R-M-E-I-E-R' as instructed and waited for the beep.

An unsteady fellow wearing a stained Boston Red Sox cap did try to come in the door with me, but I shook my head at him and gave him a buck, which was all the cash I had remembered to bring with me other than the quarters for the meters that were still in the car. I was reminded just then that the police sergeant who gave me the keys asked me if I was going there alone. He had nothing else to say. Just the unsettling question.

But what I had briefly forgotten is that Otto made horror movies.

Granted, he did not use a lot of props for these, mostly just the insinuation of menace was necessary. But he would often play with a few good visuals. A headless cadaver, for instance. I knew he'd used 'Mr. Bob,' as the rubber cadaver was affectionately known, in several films because he floated very nicely, and I had met him once before. Mr. Bob could be dressed in many ways, but whatever parts of him showed, always looked real. At least, briefly. He was made of high-quality flesh-colored latex, and purchased from the University of Los Angeles Medical School, along with a few other nice items, when they upgraded their equipment over twenty years ago.

As Otto's humor would have it, Mr. Bob met you at the inner door when you opened it, dropping down from above, his removable head in a noose. He scared the living shit out of me once again, and the bum who was at my heels disappeared. I could hear Otto chuckling from somewhere in the heavens. It also occurred to me that the police sergeant who had given me the keys was having his own laugh as well. He had accompanied the lieutenant detective on the case when they had first checked the warehouse out.

Almost windowless except for the skylights, the place was darker than I remembered, but the light switches by the door illuminated things very nicely.

The entry where I stood was now paneled in dark wood and the inner portion of the door was lined with ancient-looking oak boards sporting iron straps. I recognized this instantly as the prison cell door from *The Man Who Laughs* and the secret castle entrance in *Dr. Caligari's Dog*. The idea of hypnotizing pets to make them mind an evil genius had been brilliant, and the foil of American pet obsession had struck a funny bone with the public. But I knew that this had only been Otto's answer to those who had protested his previous device of human dog food in *Otherwhen*.

He had installed high canvas curtains to section the wide-open space that I had seen long ago. These were strung on runners suspended from the ceiling with thin wire. Several large props—a hanging tree used in *The Cattle and the Cowed*, with removable limbs and the noose still attached, a full-size shark with articulating jaw used in *Apples for Oranges*, the front of a Victorian house in movable pieces not quite reassembled from *The Thrum*, and an old corner street lamp with a brownstone stoop used in *Park Slope Adventure*, all lined a center corridor. The rubber suits from *Swamp Monsters in Love* hung from a hook above my head, casting their shadows provocatively against the folds of the curtain to my left. No accident to that.

The space is a little more than a hundred feet across and maybe two hundred feet deep. I had written in my book that Otto had referred to it as 'God's half acre.' It was far smaller than the sort of studio sound stages that were used during the Golden Hollywood days, but as he said then, "still more space than I have the talent to fully use." At the center, the area opens, giving access to the dozen sections walled off from each other by the canvas curtains.

The eaves are about twenty feet high on one side, and drop to about sixteen on the other, with the roof rising to at least twenty-five or thirty at the center ridge, where the skylights peak. On the right are several smaller 'rooms' with no ceilings and movable walls. One is a 'living room' neatly piled with furniture from various eras, one an 'office,' and one is a 'kitchen.' Each of these were there when I first visited and were partly laid out for actual use, but also so that they could be filmed when needed.

The idea Otto had described to me in 1996 was that he would make a contained space that allowed him to use and reuse small sets that he could then easily alter to create different 'looks.' Most of his films were actually shot on location in houses, barns and farmyards in the San Joaquin Valley or higher in the Mohave desert. But every movie required controlled interiors and that was his objective here. It looked to me as if he had achieved most of what he had imagined.

This then was Otto's 'toy,' as Mysty once described it

and I first related in my book. He himself referred to it as his 'workshop,' or just, 'the garage.' It was, by all odds, his refuge. Here he could spend long hours preparing to shoot a particular scene that might last a minute or two. According to Mysty, he liked the time spent alone there and she had learned to get along on her own, learning to paint, collecting her shells and small treasures, and listening to tapes. She had already acquired enough Italian by the time of my first visit to help on their vacation to Italy that year. Understanding now her difficulty with reading made this even more impressive to me.

There are several large mirrors suspended from the ridge of the ceiling above, arranged to direct light to a particular section in use. A shaft of sunlight fell away from one of these and out of little more than curiosity I went back to the area where it shone. Most of what I found there I recognized as the set from *Orphan Andrew*, not one of Otto's most successful films, the premise being perhaps too broad. In that, the young Andrew of the title has killed his parents and then thrown himself on the mercy of the court for being an orphan. The old joke worked well enough but was deemed by audiences as insufficient to carry the ninety-minute running length despite other bits of business. Looking into the pieces of that set now, I was surprised so much of it remained. That picture was made in 2001. I could not recognize any part of what was still in place or stacked there beneath tarps as anything from another film. There is a freestanding bedroom wall and false window at the back of this. The plaster of the wall was marked with pencilled calculations. I recognized Otto's hand. The bed was still made, but now lay beneath a loose clear plastic cover. On a stand beside the bed there was an ashtray. There was a cigarette butt in the ashtray.

I do not remember Orphan Andrew smoking. I do know that Otto smoked, off and on, but most often while filming. I'd seen him smoke while we stood at the top of Point Dume, waiting for the flash of green. I think he told me then that Mysty would not allow it in the house. It was easy enough now to imagine this part of the set had been kept as a refuge.

The plastic containers Mysty had spoken of, all nicely alphabetized, were on metal shelves at the back wall. I found the knives easily. The switchblade was not there.

But I continued to wander. This was a toyshop, and I did not want to leave.

By the time I got back to my car, the parking cost me another five bucks. And when I got home, the neighbor's kid wanted another ten for watching Arty longer than usual.

A police procedural
or Perry Mason defeated

Police procedures can vary from one place to another. It's not at all like what you've likely seen on TV. The coincidence between reality and an episode of *Perry Mason* half a century ago, or more recently *The Good Wife*, is almost accidental. The concern in drama is not just to meet some legal criteria that might convince the viewing audience that the pretend cops and lawyers know what they are doing, but more importantly, to meet the known legal demands of the court, all packaged within a sixty or hundred-and-twenty-minute time frame, allowing for commercials, comic asides, and the domestic issues of principal players, etc. In practice, none of this applies. If they're not plea bargained, as are the majority of cases, most can drag on for months and years, time enough for the average TV show to be cancelled. In reality, Perry Mason almost never gets his chance to interrogate a witness on the stand. The police know all too well how to make things fit the criteria of the court, and they go about their jobs as best they can. 'Speedy' trials are now conducted within two years of the charges being brought. Patience is necessary. Mistakes are made. But guilt or innocence is usually not the matter in dispute. Gaming the law is the larger effort.

I knew all this from having worked on a movie script several years ago. At the time I had the brief opportunity to observe offered by a friend, Derek Hanley, a detective who worked then in the L.A. Police Department Robbery-Homicide Division. A nice guy. But after five years of it he transferred out to a small town in Northern California, where his primary concerns are marijuana growers and traffic tickets. He couldn't take the politics that has come to replace any semblance of justice. It was my friend Derek who first pointed out to me the chasm between the original purpose and the current practice of law.

You may have heard from one public service announcement or another that your help is wanted. Citizens are the eyes and ears of the police department. But this was not what was wanted in this case. In this case, it appeared that my input concerning the murder of Otto Biedermeier was considered 'interference.' My job was to keep Mysty happy, not get involved in the legal proceedings.

As of now, I have no friends in the police department, or friends of friends, which is more often the case for gaining an entree. I did get a traffic ticket a couple of years ago, but I doubted that the cop involved would remember me.

So I called the only police officer who came to mind: Rebecca Ortiz. At least she knew Mysty and liked her. I left a message at the Malibu office of the Los Angeles County Sheriff's Department. She called me back a couple hours later with, "This is Officer Ortiz. What can I do for you?"

I explained who I was. She was still using single word answers.

"Yes?"

"I need your help?"

"Why?"

"Mysty is getting a bad deal. I believe she's innocent. I want to prove that."

"How?"

"I think there are other suspects. I want to at least show

that they had as much motive and opportunity as Mysty did. In fact, I think, a good deal more."

"Who?"

Now, I should be keeping my opinions to myself on this, but I am also aware that if I am too vague, I'll get nowhere.

"For one, Otto's lawyer, Truman Donitz. For another, her former husband, Wallace Martin."

Officer Ortiz was silent for half a minute. I have learned to wait when people are thinking things through. That applies to both spouses and children, as well as cops, and anyone who's likely to have other priorities.

"What do you want?"

That was four words. At least I was moving in the right direction.

"Is there anybody you might know in the department who could help me—or Mysty? I have new information, and I've left messages, but I don't get call-backs. In fact, you're the first police officer to return a call in several weeks."

"What sort of information?"

"Martin attacked me. He punched me from behind."

"You reported that and the police didn't do anything?"

"It was in Oxnard. They filed a report there."

"What did you do?"

"I tried to ask him some questions."

I heard her take a breath.

"Anything else."

"I went to Otto's accountant. While I was there, some thugs slashed my tires."

"That could happen anywhere."

"On a street in Santa Monica in broad daylight?"

She seemed to consider that.

"Anything else?"

"Mysty says she's innocent!"

As I suspected, Officer Ortiz was a woman of strong opinion. There was no hesitation now.

"You want my brother."

"What does he do?"

"He's a cop. He is a detective with L. A. P. D. Robbery and Homicide."

That was promising.

"Should I call him?

"Let me call him. Then he'll call you back."

And that was it. No more. She didn't even say goodbye.

I did receive an unexpected phone call very early on Tuesday morning, however, from Alma Biedermeier. She was in Vienna, on business. She sounded as if she was more excited than her usual, which in itself awakened me from my stupor.

While waiting for an appointment with one of Todd's perspective clients, she had taken the time that morning to "pop into the Österreichische Nationalbibliothek" with the idea of looking into the records there. Evidently, she had written down the several names from the circus program found sewn into Otto's clothing in 1945, and started at the top. Following the lead from what Otto had done fifty years before, she had located the newspaper archives for the *Kronen Zeitung,* one of the largest of the period. But these had been digitalized and the records indexed. "It was simple! And there he was!"

Almost immediately she had found a reference to Carroll Desmond, 'Master of the Horse!'

"You read German?"

"Very well. Three years of it at Harvard and a semester in Heidelberg."

"What does it say about him?"

"That he was famous! Well. The article says he was.

This was from 1938. That might have been puffery. His circus had just arrived from Prague. It says he had already achieved the highest honors from the riding schools in Hanover and Westphalia and was acclaimed since 1934 at the Spanish Riding School right there in Vienna with the Lipizzan horses."

She was actually sitting at a table in the library at that very moment, in front of a computer monitor, and reading the digital copy.

"Anything about Josef Biedermeier?"

I could hear voices in the background

"No! . . . No. That's the thing! There is an advertisement for *Bohemian Circus Fantastisch!* on the very same page! Newspapers were just the same then! Running articles to sell ad space."

"Amazing!" I hoped I did not sound to cynical.

But it appeared that there was more!

"But now, this is a very curious matter. There are names given for the performers, just like the program that Otto had. It even has the very same woodblock print of the horse at the top! But the names are not the same! All of the names are different, except for two, Carroll Desmond, and Isabella"

She was clearly very excited by this. I was disappointed.

But someone had come and told her to stop talking so loudly, and she told me she would call back again.

Truman

Ogres have mothers too

The next time I went to see Truman Donitz, I called first and made an appointment. The secretary I had seen in his office the first time answered by simply saying 'Donitz.' I knew it was her by the tone of voice—disdain. I had also smartly left Arty with Laura at the shop. Laura hates this. Some of her customers are afraid of large dogs but most are nuts for them, and her customers are pretty much all women. I made my case: Tuesdays are slow in Santa Barbara. So she gets her assistant to keep an eye on things and takes Arty over to Elings Park, while I roam. Arty believes he is her protector, so this can be an adventure among the other dogs at the park, as well as their predatory male owners. Parenthetically, I have often wondered what those fellows do for a living, walking around in the middle of the day, walking their dogs—but then again, they might be wondering the same thing about me on occasion.

Traffic was reasonable and I was in Santa Monica by 10 am, the appointed hour, but Donitz made me wait. I sat awhile on a sofa in the former living room. The secretary, the waifish looking woman with the gold ring in her nose, was still in search of a 'q' or a 'z.' I gave her the business card that has 'Thomas Lenz, Author,' on it that my daughter printed up several years ago in a high school shop class. She only made a hundred, and I still have at least fifty of them. The important thing, however, was that this has my phone number on it. Then

I sat down and, after looking for a copy of the *Tab*, pretended to read the latest *The Hollywood Reporter* from the stack.

From down a short hall, I could hear Truman Donitz's voice coming through the door of what I assumed was a bedroom in better times. The door was not thick enough, and the carpet between was not plush, but he was speaking loudly, nonetheless. Someone was not doing what they should have.

When the man finally came out he was flushed and breathing quickly. I was worried that he was going to have a heart attack right in front of me.

But he says, "Why are you here?"

I reminded him, "I called and made an appointment. Yesterday."

He looked puzzled and turns to his secretary. She shrugs without looking up from her alpha search. He says, "Yes. Right. It was a busy day. That's fine. What did you want to see me about?"

He made no move to invite me into the office but looked around the living room instead as if something was amiss.

"I left Arty with my wife."

"Ah! Yes. Alright, come in."

Off the short hall there is also an open door to a bathroom, bright with a display of 1970's pastels and a flowered shower curtain. There's a toothbrush in the porcelain rack. Another door on the hall is closed. The office-bedroom was not large to begin with and there is something oddly intimate about being there, with only the desk between us. The walls are sparsely decorated, but there are a few pictures of various famous film people, including Otto Biedermeier. The leafy plant in the corner is fake and looks like something stolen from a cheap motel lobby. I realized it matches the one in the living room.

This is a man who has been an attorney for fifty years and represented many Hollywood stars in some very high-profile cases. What happened? The office decor strikes me as post-chintzy.

I say, "I'm trying to help Mysty. That's all. This is not an interview for any article. I'm only here to help her."

He shrugs.

"Thou doth protest too much."

I went for a transparent projection and hoped he would see through it. "I'm trying to lay out the grounds for what I'm doing. You seem to have gotten a negative idea about me."

"You're in it for something. A book then. Whatever. So tell me why are you here?"

The wattles below his chin shivered. I felt cold.

"You've known Mysty for twenty years. You know the kind of woman she is. You were a friend to Otto Biedermeier for more than twice that amount of time. Whether she's guilty of stabbing Otto or not, you have to believe that she did not kill him with malice and forethought."

He rested back in his chair.

"Accepting the premise that you're acting on Mysty's behalf and not just looking for a juicy titbit for the *Tab*, I have to make you aware that you are ill informed concerning this case. There are circumstances which confirm the District Attorney's charges. I'm afraid that you'll just have to accept that. George Peal is a good attorney. He will do what he can for her."

"I think you're right about my being ill informed. That's why I'm here. I need some help with that."

"How? I see you listed as an assistant to legal counsel. Are you suggesting collusion?"

"No. Just a last scrap of friendship for Otto."

The man braced himself at the desk edge with fingers

spread.

"I knew Otto for fifty years, at least. I knew him better than almost anyone. He was not an easy friend to have. Especially for a lawyer. But we both did well out of it. Now that things are not as sweet as they once were, losing his business isn't going to help. But there it is." Donitz leaned back. "You understand, we didn't have much back then. Either of us. I couldn't afford an office. He had a trailer. He and Jessie used to live in the trailer, did you know that? Same one they came out here to California with. He used the very same one on locations too. Saved a bundle on rooms. They even lived in it again when they were rebuilding the bungalow at Red Rock. Same damn one. It had a smell I still recall. Smelled like beans. He used it at the State Parks in the beginning. Back then you were lucky if there was a toilet available. I remember once, after *Tryst Trip*, when Otto had lost pretty much everything, he met me in his truck at the parking lot below Point Dume. That was the very beginning for me. He didn't have a lawyer for *Tryst Trip*, and he paid dearly. The distributor kept every dime. I'd worked on a couple other films for a friend of ours, David Nagel. You remember him, right? *Black Day, Blue Night?* David died broke because he wouldn't listen. Anyway, Otto got a hold of me—all I had was an answering service then, you understand. And he wants to come to my office. I say I'm just going out. Actually, I was going to the beach with my wife. He asks if he can meet me at the beach. And that's where it all began. He and Jessie met me and my wife at the beach. No, actually Jessie and Betty did the beach. Otto and I sat in his truck and did business. Right there in the parking lot below Point Dume."

"Can I use that? It's a good story."

"Sure. No problem. That's the way it was. The way it is now, I have a responsibility to another client. By my estimate, you would like to believe Wallace Martin killed Otto. He didn't. But you can make his life a lot more difficult by what you decide to report. He told me you showed up at his house."

"Did he also tell you he sucker punched me in the back?"

"No. But I wouldn't be surprised. Wallace has been in prison for a few years. He has a slightly different perspective on things than you or I. In prison you have to be more proactive."

"Does that include rape?"

"How so?"

"He raped Mysty."

"When was that?"

"A few months ago. Shortly after he arrived in California."

"Can you prove that?"

I let a beat of time pass first.

"Wrong question. But it is an answer of sorts. It tells me that you really don't give a damn about Mysty."

He is sitting up now, high in the chair

"You're wrong about that too. I do. But I have other responsibilities here. Wallace may be a difficult man. But he is not difficult to understand—just to stand by. I suppose Mysty found that out long ago. And I'm sorry if he hurt her. But I can see how he might have thought he had a right to do it."

That statement brought up a sudden ire in me. I had tried to suppress my opinion of Donitz for Mysty's sake, but it just came out.

"You're a sleaze if you think like that."

The wattles froze.

"That's the second time you've insulted me. I'm not interested in a third. Now, get out!"

I wondered what the first insult was.

On the way out again, I looked again at the secretary. I

am pretty sure she's in her thirties, but she's still wearing the mismatched blouse and skirt that passes for young fashion these days. No wonder Laura's fashions do so well. And judging merely by the display of talent, this woman is not a secretary at all. At roughly a quarter of her boss' weight, I suppose she can't be much of a bodyguard either. But she is in a position to know things. Donitz knows that. I figure she's either his girl friend or a relative.

Just guessing, I say, "Your dad is up to something wrong here. I hope you're prepared for the consequences."

She looks back at me with a squint, "I've been prepared all my life. How about you?"

She was right about that. I wasn't. But I didn't answer. She had the last word. Still, I was pretty sure Donitz had heard me from the bedroom.

So, this was what had become of 'little Judy.'

Police Lt. David Ortiz called me while I was driving back to Santa Barbara. He left his number and I called him when I arrived there but got the answering service. He called me again that evening.

His first advice to me was not to get involved.

"I am involved. If I wasn't, Mysty would be sitting in jail for two years or so before being convicted of something she didn't do."

"The system works. You've got to let it work."

"The system doesn't work and I'm not going to let it swallow Mysty."

"She can afford help."

"She doesn't have a dime in her own name."

"Is this your 'do good' for the year? What is it you think you can do that the police can't?"

"For one thing I can investigate what happened. There's

184

been little or none, so far. They have an open and shut case and apparently think they have more important things to attend to."

"I just read the report. It looks open and shut to me. What am I missing?"

"She didn't do it."

Long silence. I thought he had hung up on me. Finally, he says, "I'll call you back."

A reason why
to do or die

The thing of it is, most of what passes for science these days is just paid proof. If Proctor and Gamble wants to say their shampoo is better than Unilever's, they pay some guy in a white lab coat to prove it. He comes back with the sad truth that one soap is as good as another. And it's too cheap. But if they add a little aloe, they have it made. A nickel's worth of aloe will let them add a dollar to the price. Colgate gets wind of this, and they do the same. Suddenly everybody has better soap, all of it 'soothing to the skin'. In the meantime, it takes you twice as long to get the stuff off your hands. But if you want a result, you can buy it. You just don't get a better bar of soap. If you're looking for a cure for cancer, there's billions to be had. So they will keep looking for answers. The pursuit of knowledge is supposed to be the classroom ideal, but most of the teachers I meet just want the answers, not the questions. That's always been the way.

Maybe that's the problem here, looking for answers instead of questions.

For instance: why did Otto stay home that night? On that particular night? Or why did Mysty leave without him?

They had argued. A neighbor heard them. What was that about?

I made a call and went down to the Malibu County jail once again.

Mysty is not looking good. I think she looks sick. She's definitely losing weight.

But I asked my questions.

She looks up at the guard, who is staring off into space. Perhaps my visits were becoming a nuisance?

"George thinks it would only prejudice a jury. When the time comes."

"They will ask that question. You better have an answer."

She breathes a moment for some composure.

"We argued about the ring."

"That day?"

"Yes. A little while before I left."

"Why?"

She let a sigh go, enough for two people.

"I told him we should sell it."

"Why."

"Because he was having trouble raising money for the next picture. He'd lost distribution on the last one and he couldn't find any way to replace it. It's not like it used to be. He couldn't sit down with his buddies and cook something up. You pay for what you get now, in advance, or you don't get it. They want guarantees. Percentages. I told Otto he should sell the ring. It upset him. I felt bad about it, but I thought he should get over that. It was just money. He could always buy another ring. There it was, just sitting in the safe. I only wear it a couple of times a year. I told him. He said it was more than that. You have to see it the way he did. You know? He never bought a ring for Jessie. He always felt guilty about that. He was always spending everything on the next picture. So that was part of it. After *The Drool,* and all the money that made, he suddenly had it, but she was gone. . . . So, I got the ring." She was crying again. "And like he always said, it was for the security."

She wiped her eyes and I waited until she got her breath again. The guard was rocking on her feet.

"Was it insured?"

"Sure. But they won't pay until they know who stole it. You know that. The insurance companies already had someone talking to George. They want to come and talk to me. He's putting them off."

"So that's what the neighbors heard?"

"I guess. We were out on the balcony. They could have heard it. It really wasn't that loud. Mostly me. Otto never raised his voice much."

"But what do you think they actually heard? The police must think it was something."

"George asked me that. But I don't remember what I said, exactly. I got upset. I'm pretty sure, I said I wanted to sell it. We need the money now. We need the security now, so he could make another picture now, not after he's dead."

"The ring was in the safe there. You didn't take it out?"

"No. It was in an envelope in there, with all the papers. It's not that big. It's really the diamond that's worth anything, I'm sure of that. But there are other stones. There're two rubies. It's what they call an Art Nouveau piece. It's very old fashioned. Otto said it was from England sometime in the 1890's. But it really wasn't that big."

"Could Otto have taken it out after you left?"

"Sure he could. Maybe just to think about it. I think he understood. He gave me a kiss when I left. Told me to have a good time, and to tell him all about it after. He apologized for being a sour puss. . . . He said to have a good time for him."

She was crying again.

I went to see the neighbors.

The woman who answered the bell was a housekeeper.

Mrs. Dean wasn't home, she said. But the ghost of Mrs. Dean lingered—-shadow passed on the floor behind, likely from a balcony. Arty was in the car again, and not happy about it. I told the maid who I was, gave her one of the cards my daughter made, and said that I just needed some detail about the events of the night Otto died. I said I would be around for a little while and if Mrs. Dean returned, I'd love to talk to her. I'd be down on the beach. Then I went back out to the car and got Arty.

After awhile, she came out a door below her own balcony and made her way across the sand, carrying two chairs. The maid sat above and watched attentively. Mrs. Dean handed the chairs to me and waited for me to unfold them both before sitting down. She is a thin woman, perhaps eighty years old, and stooped enough now to be about five feet tall at most.

Arty seemed disappointed, sniffed once and then went down to the water's edge. I introduced myself.

She wasn't interested. "We don't like dogs on the beach here. And I know who you are."

This is the second or third time I'd heard this, and it surprised me. I suppose *The Tab* should be informed. It might encourage them to pay me more.

I began my spiel, "I was just talking to Mysty."

She shrugged, bony shoulders lifting thin fabric, and stared out at the horizon. "So! Is Mysty saying she didn't say what she said?"

"No. She doesn't know what she said. She was upset."

"She was that. I could hear that. She told Otto he was being stupid!"

"Anything else that you heard?"

"Just what I told the lawyer."

"What else can you tell me?"

"She said, 'I'll kill you!' I heard that clear as a bell."

"Do you know what they were talking about?"

"A ring! She said, 'It's my ring. I can do what I want with it!' I couldn't hear what Otto said."

"And she said, 'I'll kill you.' Nothing else?"

"Sure. There were other words, but that's what I heard."

"Anything more?"

"They talked a lot. I wasn't listening the whole time. Just when it got loud. They are right there, for God's sake. If they wanted privacy, they could have gone inside!"

"Is there anything else that you remember?"

"Like I said, I couldn't really hear Otto all that much. He talks in that low voice of his. Otto has always been the calm one. Mysty gets all worked up."

"Did you know them well?"

"As well as neighbors do. We were never friends. Before my husband died, he used to talk to Otto more. They were both in the business, you know. Ted was a producer. He made over a dozen films. They had things to talk about."

"Are you retired now?"

"Retired? From what?"

"Do you still work?"

She straightened in her chair. "I never needed to work! You never saw me in my day."

This was one way of putting things into a different perspective. I went in another direction.

"Do you think Mysty killed Otto?"

"Of course she did!"

"Why?"

"Why? She's just the type."

"What type is that?"

Mrs. Dean sat straight again and turned her upper body to give me a fierce look.

"You are not going to get me to say anything. You

understand? All I said was that she's the type. You can interpret that for yourself."

I did.

Before I left I looked again from the balcony and confirmed that Mrs. Dean might have heard something. Then I left a message for Mysty to call me when she could. I heard from her that night and I told her what Mrs. Dean said.

The tone of Mysty's voice turned sharp. "I didn't say anything of the sort. I wouldn't, not even if I was angry."

"What do you think she might have misheard?"

"I don't know. We were arguing about the ring. That's all."

"When you told Otto you didn't want him to have to die before you sold the ring, how did you word that?"

"I don't remember. I told George Peal that."

"Could you have teased him? Like, 'I don't want to kill you just to sell the ring.'"

Silence. Then, "The damned thing! I said, if it would kill him for me to sell the damned thing, I wouldn't do it!' I said that! He kissed me after I said it. He hugged me a good long time after that. Then I didn't want to go. I just wanted to stay there with him. But he said he needed some time to think. And he sent me off."

The prenuptial agreement
a verbal contract worth the paper it's written on.

I spoke to George Peal the next day and described my conversation with Mrs. Dean and with Mysty. He only offered that it would be a difficult testimony to deal with. She had already told the police that she couldn't remember.

"Aren't you allowed to remember something later? She was in shock."

"We can work on that."

After briefly covering a few of my other inquiries and getting the sense from his tone that I was bothering him, I asked if there was any way he might get hold of the prenuptial agreement between Otto and Mysty. I couldn't ask Truman Donitz for it myself.

He says, "Why? They weren't getting a divorce. And they weren't even married."

The fact that he would ask troubled me. It seemed obvious to me that anything with a bearing on their relationship should be looked at.

"Well, just for instance, if she was well provided for in that, she wouldn't have had a reason to kill him."

I suppose he regretted his first reaction.

"All right. Okay."

But I thought the idea deserved more than an 'okay.' My initial worries about George Peal loomed large.

These thoughts were certainly colored by my

appreciation of all attorneys, whether they weighed in north of 300 pounds or spoke in moderated tones like George Peal. I understood that Mysty was charged with a capital crime and could not be released on bail, but I did not understand Peal's willingness to abide. Obviously, the possibility of a two-year incarceration awaiting trial for a crime she did not commit was intolerable! He seemed untroubled.

"There's no rush," were his exact words.

He was eating at his favorite restaurants and taking long walks on the beach with the objects of his romantic intentions, while Mysty sat in a cell, allowed two hours of television per day, and ate institutional food.

The next time I spoke to him, I had to ask, "What exactly are you doing to help her?"

"Whatever I can."

"Have you hired a detective to investigate Wallace Martin?"

"As I believe I told you, detectives cost money. But if I have reason to look into something, I will. Listen. You don't like Truman Donitz and you don't like Wallace Martin. I concur, at least on the latter. Truman is another matter. I think you simply don't understand the law nor, apparently, Truman's unfortunate addiction to food. But Wallace Martin is a thug. I agree. Confidentiality prohibits me from telling you all that I know about that man, but none of it is good. However, he was not at the scene of the crime. He may have indirectly brought about the confrontation between Mysty and Otto Biedermeier, but he cannot be indicted for that. Nevertheless, he is being prosecuted for extortion. It is very likely he will be convicted for that. In the meantime, on Mysty's behalf, I'll see to it that the prosecution jumps through every hoop. If they screw up, fail to cross a single 't' or dot a single 'i,' we will get her charges reduced or dismissed. I'll see to it."

"What confrontation? She's innocent!"

He shook his head at me, "And I have another client to speak with now, so we'll have to continue this discussion at another time."

"Have you found a copy of the will yet?"

"No. As you know, whoever took the ring from the safe probably took that along with the other papers."

"How about the prenuptial agreement?"

"That too."

"Don't lawyers usually keep copies of that kind of thing?"

"Yes. Usually. But Truman has been through some tough times. He even went through a bankruptcy a year or two ago. I'm told his old office was cleaned out into a dumpster."

"Is there anything on file with the County or the State?"

"No. Not that I can find. I filed a request for that stuff a month ago, just in case. But what we want is all from the early '90s or older. Ancient times. Before everything was computerized. Now, I have to take care of other business. Goodbye."

Mysty herself had little memory of the 'prenup.'

Our conversations on the phone were more frequently broken by long silences.

"I think it must have said I don't have a right to the houses or the films. That all belonged to Audrey and Jason. That's the way it should be. That's why Otto gave me the ring."

But Audrey had a slightly different memory of it.

"Dad left a trust. He had a family trust set up after Mom died. Pretty much everything went to that, and Jason and I were trustees. I suppose that would only be me now. But Truman handled all that."

"And you don't remember him saying anything about

the prenuptial agreement?"

"Not really. Mysty was provided for. I know that."

I probably should not have, but I told Mysty that I thought she should look into finding another lawyer. Peal was only doing what fair practice required. She needed more than that. The case against her was substantial. It was my opinion that George Peal thought she was guilty of killing Otto and was acting accordingly.

The next morning, I received a call from George Peal's secretary. I was no longer to associate myself in any way with Gregory and Peal, or the legal defense in the case against Mysterious Circumstances. All verbal agreements with Mr. Peal, assumed or otherwise, were hereby revoked. Access to Miss Circumstances would be limited to normal visiting hours. An email statement and letter to that effect had been sent.

I left a message for Mysty telling her about Peal and then I called Audrey Biedermeier. My guess was that she would continue to have some access to Mysty, if my own visiting privileges were curtailed. She was surprised by Peal's reaction. She agreed that Mysty needed another lawyer but said she would keep that to herself for the moment.

Lt. Ortiz called me again today. He told me that George Peal thinks I'm interfering and ought to be instructed to stay away from any principals in the case.

"I think he's right. I am interfering. He's not doing his job."

"He can file a restraining order."

"I'm a member of the press."

"I told him that. He can still try."

"And I'll keep doing whatever I can."

"I'll call you back."

Judy, Judy, Judy
what was never said

Sometimes driving Route 1, back and forth, can be tiresome. Not the traffic. The process. The act itself. Done one too many times, you don't see what's there, which is pretty grand. It makes me think about what else I was missing.

Why was I even doing this? Not for the money. Was it for Otto? Or for Mysty? That sort of thing? But obviously, it was for me. Because there was nothing better for me to do. And because, ultimately, I had made an agreement with myself a long time ago. I would do what was important.

Back in 1996, I had asked Otto why he made films. . . . No. I was too raw then to ask exactly that. The idea of making films seemed an obviously wonderful thing. I had asked him why he made the films he did. Horror films. Why those? He had been so successful with *Lost Circus*. Why not another documentary?

He said, "Because the holocaust is among us now. The loss of our souls is the real story. That's the true horror. We ignore it. We become numb to it. We stop seeing it. I was looking for a way to open the audience's eyes at first. Then I realized, after *Tryst Trap,* that I could not open other eyes without first opening my own. I was a late comer to the most obvious precept of philosophy."

Still deaf and blind myself, I persisted. "But why horror? Doesn't it trivialize everything?"

He laughed. I remember that, though I did not put it in my book. I thought he might be laughing at me. But I don't think so now. I think it was more his sudden understanding of my simplicity of mind.

"Ah! That! Because I could make them cheaply. Quickly. The way westerns used to be done. The conventions were all set. A couple of new twists each time kept the old tricks going. For the basic magic stuff. I love magic. Special effects aren't necessary if you can do a little smoke and mirrors. Work a sleight of hand. But the key to all that—those tricks and trappings—is the story. The story could be told in the Wild West, or on the planet Mars—it was still the story—mere human beings trying to get along as best they can as human beings, while facing the odds. The conventions of horror let you get down to basics. The universe is mostly cold. Heartless. It's only the friction of life that gives it warmth."

"What did you do for those years after you finished *Lost Circus*? How did you pay the bills?"

"After my hitch in the Army, I came out here to Hollywood. The only thing I could get for work then was a gig as an assistant to the director on *Billy the Kid Versus Dracula*. and *Jesse James meets Frankenstein's Daughter*. Great stuff! I actually got to watch old William Beaudine work. I think I learned a lot there. That was pretty instructive. But there wasn't a lot else going on. Mostly just TV. The worst sort of formula. There were some openings there that I didn't take. But you don't get to work with someone like Beaudine every day."

"When did you realize what you could do?"

"If you said 'no' to them back then, in Hollywood, you were out. So I went back to New York. I did some work on commercials. Jessie got a few things. And then the Public Television thing with *Lost Circus* took off. I used every dime of that and then some to make *Fowl Play*. New York was full of stage actors at the time who were desperate for work. The most expensive part was making copies of the rough cut. Someone at Universal saw one of those. Of course, the Beatles had made a hit by then with *Hard Days Night*. That opened the door. *Fowl Play* was still pretty ragged at that point, but they gave me some money to clean it up and released it. That was it!"

"So why did you go independent?"

"After *Fowl Play*, they wanted me to make it over again. Basically, the same deal with a bigger budget. I said 'no,' again. I showed them my idea for *Tryst Trap*. They said no. No! . . . What they said is, 'It sounds like a French film. We don't make French films here.' So, I took my marbles and went to France. In France they told me it had too many Germans in it. Really! And they didn't make German films. So, I went right to Trieste. The Italians said, how much money do you have? I said, I'm an American! How much do you need? So, we found this crew that were making travelogues in Venice. They were like a family. I hired them all. They didn't know a word of English. The humor went right by them. But they were gung-ho. We shot the whole thing in six weeks. Then Jessie and Kenneth and I went back to Hollywood. It only took me a month to find someone to pick it up. American International was rolling then and Sam Arkoff was the most creative guy in the business. He was familiar with the dubbing techniques we had to use. They took it on. And even though it was a bust after it came out, he came through for the next one, *Blue Magic*. After that, things just kept moving."

"But then you started making your horror films."

"I'd started buying props from other horror movies back in 1968, when I happened to be walking across the old Universal lot and saw a dumpster full of the stuff. Nobody wanted it. I rarely had to build my own from scratch after that. A little paint and a new color, or a couple screws for another arm. The newspapers gave us the material for the stories. If you have a guy like Nixon for president—a guy with two heads, one of them brilliant and the other one stuck up his butthole, how could you go wrong? You can translate that to a dozen different horror sets without breaking a sweat. I've often thought that Doug, the Presidential assistant in *Bethesda Drowning,* should have turned up again in a sequel, as a zombie. There was all that bullshit in Watergate that went unused! But I had other projects to do."

"You make it sound so easy."

"It was. It was a lark. I was young and having too much fun to stop. From that point on, it was all petty theft. If I'd tried to tell any one of those stories as an historical, let's say, I would have needed expensive sets, the right garb, authentic looking weapons, the whole megillah. If I'd made it as science fiction, the same thing—although I admit I didn't see what Sydney Newman and Don Wilson saw when they created *Dr. Who.* That was brilliant! But you can't think of everything. I was stuck with my own concerns. I wondered how people became who they are, and what made them do what they did. I guess I was really just wondering who I was, myself. Everything is identity, you know. How we see ourselves. How we see others."

"So that became your philosophy, then?"

"But, for me, that still doesn't explain what people are willing to do to get along—I mean everyone. The ones who work their lives away on a farm growing corn. The ones who work in coal mines. Especially the ones who want power over other peoples lives and are willing to kill for it. Take two people, one who works the check-out counter at the supermarket and the other who stands by the door and checks off the names on a list of human beings on their way to the gas chambers. What is the difference between them? You can't ask them. They don't know themselves. Most people hate introspection. That was part of the problem with *Tryst Trap*. Hilda, the lady with the clipboard at the door to the showers who has trouble with her math because she is distracted by the naked bodies, just wasn't funny, after all. And you can't ask others to express their opinions because it would be mere gratuitous speculation. Usually, it's self-defensive.

"Besides, there's no time. They have to get down to the voting booth to elect some liar who'll pass the law that will levy the tax to pay for the gun that will shoot some other poor wretch who forgot to kiss the right ass. Other than that, they are good people and love their dogs. So, what can you do? If you point out the hypocrisy, you'll be called a hate monger. If you say, 'no, I will not check off those names,' you'll be put on the list yourself and someone else with fewer scruples will stand by the door. What are you going to do? You see? What are you going to do! . . . You understand?"

He must have read my face because I don't think I said anything. I was very conscious of the tape recorder going and didn't want to say something stupid.

He said, "Look. I had an aunt. Amy Kelly. Sweet lady. Sewed sweaters for the homeless in Chicago. Donated canned goods every month and a pint of blood every three. Voted Republican. Worked her life away. The sort of person everyone ignores. And that was her favorite phrase. 'What'cha gonna do?' But she meant it! To her it wasn't an expression of capitulation or resignation. It was a question. And I heard it. I heard it!"

So, what was I going to do?

American Cheese
and the difference between an orange

As a matter of fact, Otto's last effort was not a 'horror film.' *The Big Cheese,* which came out briefly in theaters last year, was more a thriller than anything else. You knew who the bad guy was from the first establishing shot as the camera panned over the cheese processing plant in La Crosse, Wisconsin and, in passing, you saw the unfortunate young woman with whom the villain has been dallying pushed into a vat of liquid cheddar. The idea of the Wisconsin cheese manufacturer, Olly Johnson, attempting to gain control of the entire American cheese market by purchasing or killing off competitors seemed absurd enough on the face of it. The character of Mary Stark, the small New Hampshire cheese producer who had previously escaped Johnson's clutches back home in Wisconsin to take refuge in the Stark family's old New England haunts but now refuses to play along with his schemes, was clearly meant to be heroic, despite her individual foibles.

It is Mr. Johnson who informs us early on, like an opera villain confessing his evil doings to the audience, as well as himself, as he dresses in a tuxedo for an evening business event —standing in front of a full-length mirror and begging his own mercy with the mournful plea—that he has never been the same since Mary left him. A chilling moment! The inevitable collision with the ever hungry and love-starved Miss Stark was a hoot and, to my mind, deserved better treatment by the critics as well as the distributor. I would have called it Shakespearean. But the current wave of 'new feminism' is too puritanical to allow for such basic human folly, much less such a fall from grace. Protests at the film premier in Manchester, New Hampshire and La Crosse, Wisconsin, set the tone. A social media shaming made it politically incorrect to enjoy the film.

The only counter might have been an expensive ad campaign extolling Miss Stark's principle as well as her ample physical attributes. Apparently, Otto did not have the funds or the heart for such a fight, even though word of mouth among the targeted young male audience had saved the picture from any actual losses. Still, I would have liked to hear Otto's explanation of what had gone wrong. Was it just a lack of money?

In any case, I'd received a phone call from 'Mary Stark,' while I was driving, and when I got a chance to check, her message was waiting for me immediately following an unpleasant one left by George Peal's secretary.

"Hey there! How's it goin'?" I recognized the cheery voice before she said, "I'm Teresa Nilsson. I've never met you but you may know me better as 'Mary Stark.' I worked with Otto in *The Big Cheese*. I thought you might want to talk with me because I saw quite a bit of both Mysty and Otto over the last year and I know I can tell you a few things."

She left me her number at a hotel in L.A. I called her as soon as I'd walked Arty and consumed my first beer. By that time, I had a few questions in mind.

Miss Nilsson would only be in town for a day or two. I learned from a quick peruse of the Internet that she lives with her boyfriend and several dogs up at Carmel-by-the-Sea, so I thought she wouldn't mind if I took Arty along for the interview. We met in Malibu at Abalone Joe's because it was a shorter drive for her than my own.

Miss Nilsson is quickly identified in a crowd. She is one of the more frequently featured torch bearers for 'big hair' who proudly live among us. Naturally, she's blond, but the color is nearly an orange. But naturally. (She manages to stress that point in all her advertisements.) Even still, the hair is the second natural thing one notices. And nevertheless, Arty was more interested in her legs. We sat on the patio at the end, away from the other tables, where Arty could sprawl on the flagstones at her feet.

After introductions I asked her how she got my number.

Her hands raised, "From Mysty. I went to see her. She looks terrible. You have to do something."

I ordered the cheapest thing on the menu: a sandwich and a beer. She ordered the house special and a white wine.

"What is it you wanted to tell me about Otto and Mysty?"

"She didn't kill him."

"I already believe that. What is it you think I should do?"

"Something. I don't know. She looks terrible!"

I see other eyes turned to us, but I think it's mostly the hair. I doubt if many of the Abalone Joe customers ever saw *The Big Cheese*. Or perhaps it was Miss Nilsson's previous wide-screen cinematic efforts which involved workout routines for the 'Gracious Me' breast enlargement system. This is her own company, based in Oshkosh, Wisconsin, and apparently has made her independently wealthy. I read on-line that her boyfriend is the web designer she hired to market her product.

"Do you have any idea of your own who might have done it?"

There was no hesitation there.

"I think it was Phil Reeves. I told Mysty that. He's a

weasel."

"Other than his taxonomy, why do you think that?"

"It's just what I told Otto a few weeks ago. He's been cheating. You know everyone who works for Otto gets scale plus a percentage. He's always done it that way. It's why everyone wants to work for him. It's a quarterly kiss in the mail as an investor instead of the big lump with all the taxes removed. So I read the posted returns from Lightwave in *Variety*. The picture made twenty-four million. Otto's budget was seven. After the smoke clears, he'll get back about twelve. That leaves about five million when the bills are paid. I can do my own math. I was in for half a million, myself. I should have been getting eight to ten thousand dropped in my account in August. I only got six. So I called Billy Norton, you know, the guy who plays Olly Johnson, and I asked him to check on his deposits as well. Same thing. Except Billy was only in for a quarter. So I call Otto. But his receipts were fine. He didn't know what the matter was. You know, Otto's square—was square. He said he'd call Phil and find out what was happening. But I never heard back. And then he was dead."

I bet Teresa Nilsson could do her math.

"I'll try to find out more."

"Somebody ought to try. That lawyer of hers, Mr. Peal, is a waste of time. And he's rude."

"What did he say?"

"That everything I said was anecdotal. Four thousand dollars and counting, is anecdotal. My guess is that Mr. Peal is used to dealing with too many Hollywood bimbos. I told him, if Phil Reeves is cheating me, you have to know he was cheating Otto as well. That's what I told him. A cheat is a cheat and a liar is a liar."

"Have you called Mr. Reeves?"

"Sure. Right off! He doesn't want to speak with me. I

texted him but he doesn't answer my messages."

She excused herself then, saying she had another appointment with a client, and was gone with a turn of her hips between the other tables. Her wine glass was half empty. Her plate was half full. I didn't know which was worse. The bill stared at me from the leather folder. But I had them put Miss Nilsson's filet chevon in a doggy bag. Maybe Arty would get it and maybe not.

Lt. Ortiz called again. He had just read about my encounter with the thugs outside of Philip Reeves' office.

"You don't want to fool around with any gangs. They'll cut you up."

"I'll do my best."

"You had an appointment with Reeves for a specific time?"

"Yes. I thought I said that."

"You did. I just wanted to be sure. Those guys aren't going to hang around. It sounds like Mr. Reeves has a problem. You want to stay away from him if you can. If you can't, don't make any appointments."

"Are you going to be able to investigate Mysty's case?"

"We'll see. I've got the file on my desk right now. I'll do what I can."

"Thanks."

"I'll call you back."

Jake Abbott
the best defense is a good offense

'The Mysterious Circumstances Defense Fund' was established by Audrey Biedermeier on Tuesday. Mysty has now found a new lawyer, but Miles Anthony would not have been my first choice. I only know him as another of the 'Hollywood lawyer' crowd. Whatever his hourly rates are, he has agreed to take Mysty's case, and his fees would, at least for the moment, be paid by the Defense Fund. Audrey informed me that a dozen individuals, including Teresa Nilsson, had already contributed to the kitty. Obviously, phone calls had been made since Mr. Peal had fired me. Nevertheless, I apologized for my own lack of funds for the cause.

For my own sake, the more interesting development is this: Miles Anthony has a licensed private investigator on retainer. Someone with professional expertise was certainly needed. But then this new prospect was quickly dashed when I met with Jake Abbot on Tuesday evening.

This man dresses like he's color blind, shops at Goodwill, and has poor taste. He's wearing a heavy brown tweed jacket and light tan cotton slacks. Other than that, he's all of five feet tall, has a shaved head, and fronts a full-blown black beard that further widens an already round face. The lifts in his wingtip shoes might get him up to five-two.

On the plus side, Jake prefers to eat at The Kelpy Dog. I brought Arty along with me again for some dinner. I soon discover that Jake likes cats. Arty applied his nose to every exposed surface of the man's body before we had dinner in our hands.

I had to ask him, "How did you get in the private eye business?"

He says, "There aren't enough parts in the movies anymore for dwarfs. I would have been okay, I guess, but I missed out on *Lord of the Rings* because I'm afraid of flying and New Zealand is a bitch by boat. I get seasick too. Besides, DeVito has all the good parts wrapped. I mean, what else was I gonna do?"

This question had metaphysical properties to it that I thought to avoid. Still, there was the hint of a smile in his eyes. He was putting me on.

I say, "There's always the circus."

He doesn't flinch. "Yeah. Smart ass. So tell me what you know."

I told him as best I could in an hour and a half. In the dark, the wind was coming up from the ocean in a steady draft and I think we were both getting chilly. He asked me if he could see my notes. I told him I'd send those along when I got home.

Then he says, "How was the fishing down in San Carlos?"

"I don't fish. I did a little swimming."

"Did you go over to where they filmed the *Oddissey*? Great place, eh! I loved the *Oddissey*. Frickin' fantabulous!"

This reference was not a coincidence. He had informed me of several things at once.

"Yeah. Beautiful. Do you know Charlie Parrot?"

"Papa? Not really. But I know his brother. Don. He tried to kill me recently. I shot him in the leg and told him I'd aim higher if he ever tried that again."

An interesting bit of intentional color.

"What was Don doing?"

"He's selling drugs and sex. Like his old man used to."

"Was shooting him something you did in the line of work?"

"Yeah. Sure. You think I go around shooting people? No. He was badgering one of Mr. Miles' clients. You know her. Sylvia Place. I'm the one got her in up at Ryson Clinic. I have a friend there. But I hear she's getting better."

"I only spoke to her once. She looked pretty worn out."

"That's the heroin and the oxys. You can blame Gorgeous George for that."

"George Rooney?"

"He is the original black hole. Everyone he touches gets sucked up. The guy can act the shit off the stick, but he's still who he is. He's the reason I had to shoot Don Carlos. George convinced him that it was Sylvia that owed him some money. I had to re-convince him it was on George. It was George that placed the order, see? So that was that."

"You don't think he'll come after you again?"

"Sure he will. Don is the one who looks bad right now. But sometimes you can't finish something off without spending a lot of time with a District Attorney, and Miles keeps a good relationship going there. I'll bide my time. Don is a dirt bag and he'll try again, but then I'll have just cause. And that will be that."

This was a curious fellow. I didn't have much more on my side than the notes I would be sending him later, so I decided to ask him outright.

"I'm sure Miles is the sort who pays well. So why are you wearing a jacket with a hole in it?"

"That?" He pushed a finger through just below the breast pocket from the inside. "That's where Don missed me.

208

And actually, I didn't buy it. My girl friend gave it to me. I can't get rid of it now, eh. Or do you mean the whole getty-up? That's for the second look, you might say. You know? If I was just a short guy in nice clothes, no one would remember me. Hollywood is full of 'em. But the beard they remember. Besides, my girl friend likes it. And that's a ticklish situation, I'll tell ya. The pants are a different story. I ripped the ones I was wearing when I climbed a wire fence early this morning. I wasn't able to get home, so I stopped at the Goodwill over on South Figuerosa. They've got some great stuff there, but I was in a rush. Okay? You can't run with your ass hanging out, especially if you've got a big beard. That doesn't play well."

"At least I got the part about Goodwill right."

"What? I look that bad? Geeze."

I found out the next morning that Sylvia Place was one of the contributors to the Mysterious Circumstances Defense Fund. And it was Sylvia who had found a good lawyer.

Thanksgiving
which we are about to receive

Charlie Morris at the *Tab* took another short piece the Wednesday before Thanksgiving. The only development of substance was that Mysty had a new lawyer. Beyond that, attention spans being short, I restated what was known in as brief a capsule as possible on my way to a between-the-lines appeal for donations. I think Charlie knew what I was up to and let me get away with it.

'The case against Mysterious Circumstances is not complicated. First, she was found alone at the scene of the murder of Otto Biedermeier at the time of his death. Second, she was holding the murder weapon in her hand when the police arrived. Third, the house was otherwise locked and secure. Fourth, she had been heard arguing with Otto earlier in the day. The subject of the argument was money and perhaps the ring that was now missing.

'But none of this is relevant to those who have come to her defense. Their belief in her innocence is compelling. It is a matter of the character. And it is only a matter of time before her release. Time is the matter now.'

The bottom line for me was that Mysty was spending Thanksgiving in jail. I called to check on her that morning and when she got back to me she tells me that at one p.m. they served dry turkey slices—white meat only, cold gelatinized gravy, some sort of bitter cranberry flavored jam, and extruded sweet potato paste. When she detailed this, I assumed correctly that it was meant to get me off my butt and out the door. If not today, then tomorrow, bright and early. But at least she sounded a little better than she had previously. There was an edge in her voice. She was in a fighting mood.

Later in the afternoon, just before I sat down with the kids and some neighbors for the full turkey deal Laura likes to spend two days pulling together, Jake Abbott calls me to ask, "What else do you have on the Bosch painting?"

I tell him, "It's in the notes."

"You didn't call anyone at the Getty Museum?"

"No. Not yet. But say, don't you have something better to do today?"

"Like what? Like the dinner thing? Yeah, sure. But I'm Canadian and I already missed that a few weeks ago. I would have done it today, maybe, before Miles called me. Now, he's been talking to Mysty and he runs down the details on what Mysty is eating for dinner and lays a guilt trip on my head like you wouldn't believe."

Having received the same treatment from the source, I tried to make him feel better.

"You can't do anything today. Everybody's home. Where's your girl friend?"

"Rene's gone to her mother's. Her mother doesn't like me. She thinks I'm too short for her daughter."

"Well, people get over things like that."

"Rene is six feet tall in her socks."

"And you're telling me that because?"

"So you can judge for yourself. Maybe her mother's right."

"Well, how about Jerry Stiller and Anne Meara?"

"Jerry is taller than me."

At this point I am realizing the guy is probably feeling a

little lonely. I'm already feeling bad about Mysty, and on impulse I say, "So why don't you drive up to Santa Barbara and have some dinner here?"

There is a split-second pause before he says, "I thought you'd never ask. I'll be there in an hour."

At least I didn't have to watch football.

Jake brings out the mothering instinct in Laura. I saw that right away. And he's far readier with quips and tales than I am. He had us all well entertained. Including the neighbors, who are a fairly dour couple. Even the kids stayed at the table to listen. I think we all expected stories of life as a Hollywood private eye. Instead, he tells us about a trip he once took as a high school student to Russia. This was just before the Soviet Union fell, and basic necessities, like toilet paper, were best had via barter. And that was the same way they had tried to get a turkey in Leningrad because it was October and the weekend of Canadian Thanksgiving. What they got instead, was a swan, freshly murdered on the Neva, and only identified correctly after they had eaten. As it happened, their tour guide had instructed them on the best things to bring on the school trip, and apparently a couple pair of jeans was worth tickets for twelve to the Bolshoi ballet. Unfortunately, the production they had tickets for was *Swan Lake*. The swans had all the girls in the group sobbing and they were forced to leave in the middle of the performance. The day they flew home, Jake was the only one who still had a pair of jeans but that was because his were too short, and nobody wanted them.

He didn't even crack a smile when he delivered the punch line.

Jake was born in Saskatoon, Canada. While I was at New York University during the '90s, Jake was working the oil fields of Saskatchewan along with guys from Texas and

Oklahoma. He does passable accents, and his mimicry can distinguish someone from Ponca City or Lubbock. His dream then was to get to the United States, preferably somewhere that was warm. He had never gone to college but is well read. As he says, there isn't much else to do in Saskatoon, especially in the winter, except to read. Even television sucked, though they did have movies.

He had actually come to Los Angeles in 1996 with the idea of getting parts in the movies. This worked, only in part. After a few years he did an accounting of things and discovered he'd spent more money than he had earned. He was an illegal alien at the time, and to stay there in the warm, he made the mistake of marrying a girl from Seattle with bad habits.

Impulsively I asked, "What kind of bad habits?" A risky question.

He shrugged and gave me a look for having asked.

"She liked shoes. And she liked to have the shoes match her dresses. And the dresses never matched her blouses. That kind of thing, eh."

I relented. Letting him off easy because the kids were there when he said it.

By the time he got divorced, she had spent every dime of the money he had saved from back in the oil fields. That was when he had signed up for classes at the Private Detective Training Institute. Unfortunately, this had been another colossal waste of time and money, but at least it got him certified with the State of California.

"But, actually, everything I know about being a private eye I learned from Mickey Spillane."

I figured this was his comeback at me for asking about the bad habits of his wife.

"Like what? Which one do you like best?"

"Not the books. They're fun. No. The man himself. I

had to go out to Hilton Head in South Carolina to investigate these shenanigans for Miles, see. I had a little time on my hands there, waiting for some information, so I went up the coast to Murrells Inlet, where Spillane lived. He wasn't writing anything much at the time and I was curious what he was up to. A very friendly guy. We drank sweet tea and lemonade and talked our heads off."

"What was the most important thing you learned?"

"Actually, it was the only thing. We talked about Hollywood mostly. The guy had some stories, let me tell you. He should have written an autobiography. He had the material. He'd even worked for Barnum & Bailey when he was young. On the trampoline. But the one thing I learned from him about being a private eye was just about the last thing he said to me when I left. He said, 'Keep your head down.' "

Jake kept a straight face but the smile was in his eyes.

After a hesitation almost everyone laughed except for the neighbors.

"I knew you were headed somewhere with that."

"No, Not the point, eh. The point is you gotta laugh at your own shortcomings. Otherwise, that's what you become."

A philosopher too! That should have shut me up awhile.

Instead, I said something inane, "Well, at least you can't be seen as easily in a crowd."

"Maybe. But that's why I grew the beard? I don't want them to miss me. If I have to, I'll shave it off. Even if Rene doesn't want me to. I really only keep it because it tickles her so much." He let a beat of time pass before continuing. "But being short can be an advantage. The biggest part of that is people underestimate you."

Which makes a point of the most interesting thing about Jake Abbott. He doesn't drink or smoke. He said he'd seen enough of that as a youth and didn't want any part of it. Laura couldn't even get him to drink a little wine. He cleaned us out of apple cider instead.

We were all sorry when he left. The usual afternoon dinner had stretched into the late evening.

But then, the next day, he calls me and apologizes.

"Sorry. I took advantage yesterday. You have to do that, now and again."

"How?"

"Because I lied a little bit. I wanted to see if you were really as square as you seemed to be. I wanted to know if I could trust the stuff in your notes."

"What did you lie about?"

"A couple of things. It doesn't matter. Most of it was true. But thanks again for inviting me out to your home. It was good. Your wife is pretty special. So are your kids."

"You did work the Bakken oil fields, didn't you? That was funny stuff."

"Yeah. I did."

"And the stuff about Russia?"

"Yeah. All good."

"Your girlfriend's mother?"

"Hates my guts. Even more now that I didn't go there for dinner, yesterday. I'm gonna hear about that for a month of Sundays."

"What then?"

"I'm an alcoholic. I don't drink because I'm a drunk. It's why I flunked out at the University of Saskatchewan after two years. Why my marriage went bad. It was never good. But it wasn't her fault. We were both drunks."

"Is that all?"

I actually said, 'Is that all?' I don't know what I was thinking.

"Is that all? What do you want? You wanna hear that I murdered my parents or something?"

"You didn't, did you?"

"No. Not yet. But my father still drives me nuts."

"Okay."

"Okay? Geez! Really? Okay! How did you get to be so square?"

"My parents. That, and watching old Frank Capra movies."

"Yeah. They're good, aren't they. I've seen 'em all."

The Man Who Laughs
in the warehouse of nightmares

Jake's girlfriend, Rene, has left him. She left a note and says she is going to live with her mother while she finds someplace else. I get the details of this when we're driving over to take a look at the warehouse together. Rene has left all her stuff at Jake's apartment, but she has thoughtfully taken his car. He's unhappy, though by his own accounting, it was not unexpected. I listen to this story with as much compassion as I can. I don't know the man well enough yet to offer gratuitous suggestions on such sensitive matters, even in jest.

I say something like, "It's probably for the best." I've heard this line before, and it seems to fit most situations of the kind.

Jake laughs, "Nah. I like tall woman, but I love that car!"

Smartly, I say, "I do too."

He says, "Nah. It'd be too small for you. I've got a Mini Cooper. Golden yellow. Sweetest wheels you ever saw. I just hope she doesn't park it where some jerk will cut the ragtop for fun."

I've always wanted a convertible. Driving 'family cars' and mini-vans all my life has been the bane of my existence, but I don't say it. It might sound like whining.

Traffic from Sherman Oaks, where Jake lives, is rotten. Not unusual, but I see on the GPS that there is an accident. I get off the Ventura Freeway as soon as I can and head down a back street toward the Ventura Boulevard, and pick up the 101 again in Hollywood.

This time I park close in front of the big brown spider on the garage door. And the bum wearing the Boston Red Sox cap is there again, sitting on a milk crate in the shade. When I pulled out another dollar bill, he shook his head and waved it off.

"Keep it." His voice was coarse.

But then he snatched it before I could put it away and says, "I'll buy a candle for Otto down at St. Joseph's."

This made both Jake and I turn at once.

Jake says, "How do you know Otto?"

The bum shrugged, "He was my friend."

This is an older fellow. Fairly tall, thin, with a face deeply tanned and shaved only a day or two before. He has on a flannel shirt ripped at one sleeve and soiled jeans. The dark stain I see on the shirt sleeve might be blood. His sneakers look brand new. No socks.

I had not yet started to open the door, but thought it would be better to talk with him inside, when I noticed that the metal jam on the door was caved in. By the look of it, most likely crowbarred.

Behind me, I hear the gravel of the old fellow's voice.

"They were here last night."

Jake says, "Who?"

"Hoodlums. A gang."

"Could you tell which one?"

"No. It was dark."

Both the bolt lock and the catch of the door lock had been forced out of the frame. The first key wouldn't work but my weight was enough to open it up. The alarm panel lights were all green. It had been deactivated. Mr. Bob was lying on the floor to one side, his body nearly severed at the chest by a single cut of a very sharp blade. The frayed end of the rope of the noose he had dropped on from the ceiling when the door opened now dangled just above our heads. The lights had been left on.

I pulled out my phone to call the police, but Jake held a hand up.

"Let's look around first."

The fellow with the Red Sox hat followed us in. One of the loosened iron straps from the oak panels on the inside of the door scraped at the cement as he closed it behind us. It was an ominous sound Otto would have appreciated

Jake asked, "What's your name?"

"Dan."

"Dan, how long have you known Otto?"

"About ten years, I think. Fifteen maybe. I helped him move some of his pieces in."

To get a better idea of that, I asked, "What was the first thing you moved. Do you remember?"

"The big sponges. Great big purple sponges, man. They was heavier than they looked."

"*Brood Parasite!* That would be 2003. You've known Otto for thirteen years."

"I knew 'em before. I was in that *Otherwhen* movie of his. I was the one with red hair. I still had red hair then, but they dyed it redder. Later on I was his gofer, you might say. He called me his assistant. Nobody noticed but I was the dead man in the prison cell in *The Man Who Laughs*. Otto had me bring him pizza—."

When Dan gestured, I could see a clear plaster over about a dozen stitches on the back of his forearm.

"How did that happen?"

"One of the guys had a knife. I shouldn't 've come so

219

close. My fault."

"Did you call the cops."

"Me? No. I wouldn'ta done that."

It was immediately clear that some of the canvas curtains had been ripped down. Or cut down. Several of the removable limbs from the hanging tree used in *The Cattle and the Cowed* were strewn in our way. A clothes dummy that appeared in several productions had its neck in the noose. The fiberglass body of the shark from *Apples for Oranges* was on its back, with the jaw torn loose at one side. The crowbar used to break in might have been applied as well to the door jam of the brownstone from *Park Slope Adventure*. A splintered edge gaped to the empty space beyond. The hooks where the rubber suits from *Swamp Monsters in Love* had hung were empty. I saw one of those tossed aside in the debris. At the back, the plastic bins of smaller items had all been pulled from their shelves. Prosthetic hands and zombie wigs were dumped together with rubber vomit and an effectively bloodied hacksaw. A stuffed pheasant used in *Dr. Caligari's Dog* was now missing its head again. One bin that had been nearly full of phony handguns was dumped and the contents sorted by someone in an attempt to find something useful. I estimated that half of them were missing. The white pillowcases marked with the model numbers that Mysty had used for each gun were scattered.

Beneath an upside-down bin lettered 's' and amidst all the plastic snakes and spiders my eyes caught on one of the small white dish towels that I knew Mysty had wrapped the knives in. I tugged at it and it unraveled onto the floor. A stiletto skated across the cement.

Jake had wandered away as I went through the debris from the containers and was in the bedroom set from *Orphan Andrew* when I yelled. He hustled toward me, holding a thick folder of papers to his chest.

We both stood still a second staring down at the knife.

Dan came up behind us.

"That's a stiletto, I think. It's the one Gwynplaine uses in *The Man Who Laughs,* I think."

That would be an 's' for spiders, snakes and stilettos. It should have occurred to me.

Jake used the dishtowel to pick the closed knife up and put it in his jacket pocket. But he did not say another word about it. Instead, he near whispered to me, "Come here."

I followed him, stepping through a torn curtain to the bedroom set. The plastic cover there had been ripped away from the bed itself and the bed evidently raised and let down somewhat carelessly, perhaps to look beneath.

"Lay down on that."

I did.

"What do you see?"

Above me the skylight mirrors angled sun away to the far side of the room.

"What?"

"On the wall, dummy."

The pale gray plaster of the free-standing wall to the bedroom was marked in pencil. This was the same scribbling I had noticed before and taken little note of. There were dozens of different figures there, including what appeared to me to be a dialog.

"This is probably one of Otto's visual jokes. The writing on the wall. He was always using visual puns"

"What's it say?"

"Where the blue light fails to white."

This was a line from *The Difference,* a very good zombie movie that Otto had made a few years ago. There were about a dozen other such references, some repeated in slightly different form.

Jake reached over me.

"No! The numbers. There!"

These were numbers in short stacks. At the top of one of the groups was the figure twenty-four million, five hundred and seven thousand. Below that was a figure of seven million three hundred and twenty thousand, and below that, a straight line, and then a seventeen million figure, and below that one that was twelve million and change. Five million, five hundred and thirty thousand was marked at the bottom of the stack. This was underlined twice.

"Do you see it?"

It took a minute. Jake was standing beside the bed, bouncing on the balls of his feet and growing impatient when it finally dawned on me.

"Teresa Nilsson."

"Righto! Otto must have been lying right there where you are now when he figured that out. You see how dark the underlining is? It breaks the surface of the plaster. Someone was cheating him."

"Do you think it was Reeves?

Jake shrugged, "I don't know. But now, you can call the cops."

Dan was standing just behind, staring at the wall without comment, until Jake said this. Abruptly, he turned about face, like a soldier on parade, and headed for the door.

I called a locksmith as well, the same ones with a sticker on the bent door jamb and stressed to them that it was an emergency. The fellow that answered told me everyone had an emergency. But they were there within an hour and, after driving new bolts into the cinder block walls to secure the frame, they were finished before the police were done. For their 'emergency service' he wanted an extra two hundred dollars on a bill of three hundred and fifty. I had started to write the guy a check before Jake opened his wallet and pulled out five one-hundred-dollar bills.

"Can you give us a cash discount for the fifty?"

The guy had agreed before Jake told him he needed a receipt.

The cops seemed more interested in mechanical spiders than attempting a report on what they saw. Jake kept the knife in his jacket pocket. He had stuffed the folder from the office into the back of his pants so that it made him look like he had a back brace beneath his jacket.

Dan had long disappeared by the time the cops arrived, but later I spotted him standing across the street with the small crowd there that was taking a look at what was going on. I waved at him as we left.

I would have taken the time to think a little more about it then, but Jake wanted to drive right over to see Philip Reeves, first thing.

I tried to think it through on my own.

"Did you see that the alarm panel was off?"

"Because they knew the code? Somebody told them? Who do you think? The same crew that slashed your tires?"

"Maybe. What was in that folder you took?"

"A script. Something Otto was working on. I thought I'd read it." But we were on Wilshire Boulevard and almost there when he suddenly changed his mind. "No good. Hold on. We should wait until I hear back from the people at the Getty Museum. We should know about that before we talk to Reeves."

That seemed right to me. "I can drive you home. I have the dog sitter until five."

"Thanks. But hey! We're in the neighborhood. Let's stop by and say hello to Donitz. I haven't actually met the man myself. You can introduce me."

We parked in an empty space on the alley.

Jake stood back and looked at the small house as if it were an object of importance—as if he were an aficionado of architectural styles.

"What he has here is a 'John Byers Adobe'. Solid. Efficient. Spanish revival. Affordable in its time. Not cheap, now. He must be leasing. I can't imagine he owns it."

"You know a little about architecture then?"

"No. I looked it up, before. But you gotta take everything into account. I couldn't get anything out of the City Clerk's office yesterday."

I rang the doorbell. No answer. I knocked. I heard a sound and so I knocked again.

Jake had gone around to the living room window.

He says, "The table by the couch is on its side."

I turned the door nob and it opened.

Again, I heard the sound I had heard before. Jake pushed by me.

"Hello? Anybody home? Hello?" I see he has one hand on the gun in the shoulder holster beneath his jacket.

I saw a bare foot, and the bathroom door on the hallway closed and locked. I could see through down the hall from there to the office. No one was at the desk. But the bedroom door was open, and even with the curtains drawn, I saw that this was a mess. More the disarray of a struggle than a lack of housekeeping skills.

Jake spoke at the bathroom door, "Judy? Are you okay?"

The voice from inside was strained, hoarse, as if from crying.

"Who are you?" The voice was angry.

"My name is Jake Abbott. I'm a private investigator and I work for Miles Anthony. He wanted me to talk to your father."

Jake slid a card beneath the door.

After a moment she said, "I'm not dressed."

Jake turned around to the open bedroom and scanned the confusion there. "What do you need?"

"Leave. Leave me alone."

Jake says, "I can't do that. Something has happened here. I'll call the cops."

"No! Don't!"

She opened the door with a towel pulled around. Just for a moment she seemed stunned to see Jake. Maybe it was his height. She wasn't much taller herself. Perhaps she was still in shock from what had happened to her. Then she looked at me and anger was visible before her face collapsed to some level of resignation. I could see that her lip was split. The gold ring was not in her nose.

"Let me take a shower. I'll be okay."

Jake says, "We'll wait."

Jake took the opportunity then to scan almost everything in sight and took several pictures with his phone, including of Truman Donitz's office, while I straightened things in the living room after he got a couple of pictures of that.

With the towel around her again, she crossed over to the bedroom. The tattoos on the back of her shoulders were bright with reds, greens and blues. I could see a dragon lying there, perhaps asleep, from shoulder to shoulder, with its tail dripping down the back of her right arm."

While she was dressing, Jake says, "I think she reads mystery novels."

The fact that he had immediately related what we both had caught sight of to the Stieg Larsson books was yet another surprise. How can you like both Mickey Spillane and Stieg

Larson?

I say, "Maybe she just saw the movies."

"Maybe. But the books are on a shelf in her room."

I was going to have to be sharper.

When she comes out, she's wearing a terrycloth robe. Her hair is still wet.

Immediately she sat in her chair at the computer and hit the keyboard to turn it on. Then she says, "You didn't look?"

Jake says, "Nah. Not fair to look. But I thought about peeking."

She says, "I meant the computer."

He says, "So did I."

I just watched. She glanced over at me sitting on the couch a couple of times but mostly watched Jake where he leaned with his back against the corner at the entrance to the hall. I had noticed that Jake did not like to sit.

She says, "You can see that dad's not here."

Jake says, "What happened?"

"What do you mean?"

"What happened? Something happened. Someone else was just here."

There was a bruise on her cheek that was still turning darker.

"Nothing! It doesn't matter."

"I think I should call the cops anyway."

"Don't!"

"What happened?"

She looked at me again and then at Jake.

"Wallace Martin was here. He raped me."

Jake had read my notes and he already knew that Martin had raped Mysty as well.

"He shouldn't be on the street. He's dangerous."

"You don't understand."

"I don't understand a lot. Too much. Help me out."

"Martin knows things. He could put dad in jail. Dad wouldn't survive in jail. I know! I've been there."

"What things?"

"I can't tell you."

"If it involves the murder of Otto Biedermeier, you had better say, or you'll be making yourself an accessory . . . but you know that."

"I know."

Jake gave it a breath. I finally caught up myself.

Smartly, I say, "What are you going to do?"

She says, "I don't know. I'm tired. Right now, I want to sleep."

Jake says, "How long have you been out of rehab?"

This changed her face back to the scowl I'd seen after we first arrived.

"Leave me alone!"

"You know, this is one of those moments, don't you? Don't give in. If you need help, I can get you help. I know people."

"What do you know!"

The challenge was in her voice and the set of her jaw.

Jake shrugs, "I'm a drunk. I've been there. At least for some of it. Everyone's different. But sometimes you need a little help. Even somebody with the kind of steel you must have in your bones."

This statement caused the scowl to fade. She took a visible breath.

"I won't. I just need to sleep. Let me sleep."

Jake nodded at me, and we left.

I wasn't so sure about it, but Jake told me while I was driving him back to Sherman Oaks that he liked the tone of her voice. She was a fighter. As much as she had been through, he thought she could handle it. He liked that.

Stupidly, I got smart again. I said, "But she's a little short for you, don't you think?"

It hit the mark. He says, "Don't be a wise guy."

Truth is the daughter of time
and the mother of invention

Arty had his head over the back of the seat between us. I knew it was going to be a long day and I could not be expecting Laura to keep him at the shop. Of course, the kid next door had thoughtfully disappeared. Arty will pretty much ignore you when you speak, unless you look at him directly, so he entertained himself with the possibility of spotting another dog and would periodically turn in the back to one of the side windows, only to return to his forward vigilance, mouth open, tongue out, with salmon treats lingering on his breath.

Jake leaned away from this toward his window and asked me, "Did you ever read Josephine Tey's *The Daughter of Time?*"

"Years ago. Yes."

"Great book, eh?"

Not a lot of people bring up reading books anymore. But I was driving in a neighborhood where kids are likely to attempt spontaneous suicide out from between parked cars and so I didn't look over at his face. The voice was earnest enough.

"Yes. Why do you ask?"

"Did you go through Otto's papers? The ones in the file at the warehouse?"

"No. I didn't see the file."

"In that 'office set' he had there?"

"No. I suppose I just thought it was a prop. I should

have looked."

"You should have. You're a writer. You'd appreciated it. There's a lot of material there that I think he never used. Titles for things I never saw. It was all on the floor where the thugs dumped it. And I found a screenplay he'd written, in the pile there. It's based on *The Daughter of Time*."

I immediately imagined the murder of the two young princes in the Tower of London and thought that could be done up in very creepy fashion.

"Too bad he won't be making it. It would be a terrific movie. Can you pass it along to me before you return it? I'd like to read it too."

"Yeah. Sure. But the problem was the budget. He had several letters in the same folder to people in England talking about just that. He was trying to get the costs down. He wanted it to be set in the time it happened, but he was trying to avoid a costume drama. He was looking for a castle in England where he could film it like a play. Sort of a home life of Richard the Third. You should ask Mysty about it. She probably knows what he was thinking. It's an interesting idea."

The best I could answer with was, "It's a difficult story. So, is that what you had stuffed in your pants at the warehouse yesterday?"

"Right. I had to borrow it. It's one of those books you remember, eh? So, anyway, in this version he's retelling it from the point of view of a housemaid at Middleham Castle, King Richard's childhood home, and a place where he'd sought refuge before. Purists would hate it because it takes liberties, but this version is terrific! The housemaid is actually a physical embodiment of the idea in the title, taken from the Francis Bacon quote. 'Truth is the daughter of time, not authority.' Tey's idea was that Richard was not an ogre and she would prove it, by God! Remember, Richard's wife, Anne Neville, was there with him as well, and Middleham Castle is where they buried their only child, a ten-year-old boy. The child is now a ghost to them both, but neither will admit it to the other. The Queen is still bereaved over the child's death and blaming herself, and she's having no more relations with Richard. See? Now, the housemaid, unknown to Richard, is his half-sister through the philandering of his father. Her mother has told her the tales and she knows this, but the King doesn't, and he's struck by the housemaid's compassion toward him. In a world where everyone is his enemy, she alone shows friendship. Richard makes advances toward her, but she refuses him, knowing he is her half-brother. The King mistakes this for revulsion at his deformity and never understands. There's a long monolog over the grave of his boy—which is overheard by his wife, and they reconcile, just before the battle of Bosworth. Very touching stuff. Very Shakespearean."

"But that's not the original story!"

"No. But it's taken from it. It shows that Richard would not have killed his nephews in the Tower of London. That he was innocent, which is just what Josephine Tey believed and why she wrote the book. It makes her case that it would have been beyond Richard's character to harm them. And the rest of Tey's reconsideration is there too. Otto even has the modern-day detective laid up in the hospital and he tells both stories at once. Both are on stage at once, as it were, as they talk across time. But here the detective is a woman who is recovering from a disastrous pregnancy. She's lost the child she longed for. She'll never have another. And she's the one who has uncovered the long-lost notes of the maid—overlooked by the scholars because she was not a principal player—and because she was a woman. And naturally, the detective and the maid look just alike. Otto staged it so he could have used the same actress for both parts. Very smart. The point was to make something of the story beyond the detective's research. Hard to film that. He even plays a trick with Richard's deformity and makes it read like another version of Cyrano's nose. Richard is so self-conscious about his physical appearance he can't believe anyone sees him for the man that he is. It's what makes him such a fierce warrior. But, when his wife finally convinces him of her love, it's too late."

"Sounds like it would have made a good chick-flick."

"Yeah. I think so too. And good old Otto gets a nice dollop of sex into everything so there's something for everybody. But Tey was a homely looking dame herself. And Otto describes the maid and the detective as homely in the same way. Not very Hollywood. But typically, Otto. Thing is, the maid can't believe the king she loves would see anything in her other than a bed warmer while his wife ignores him. Even so, she gets this close to incest before she puts an end to it. But neither of them can see beyond their own self-consciousness. Isn't that the way. Most people can't be that critical of themselves . . . Look at me, just for instance. From my perspective, being short is simply more efficient! Eh? But does anyone else see it that way? Not likely."

I didn't look at him just then, on purpose. He might have been waiting for me to put my foot in my mouth, but I kept my mouth shut. So he finally picks the thread of it up again.

"So, I don't know a whole lot about the woman. Tey, I mean. But there's a line in the book that Otto repeats in the script that I think you'd like 'The truth of anything at all doesn't lie in someone's account of it. It lies in all the small facts of the time. An advertisement in the paper, the sale of a house, the price of a ring.'

I had to glance over at him then. "Pretty good."

He was looking smug. "Right, eh."

"But you're reducing the motivation for Otto's murder to greed."

"Sure. I bet it is."

"Couldn't it be hate? Or jealousy? Or revenge?"

"Maybe. But you've got to work with what you've got. Look. Most murder is manslaughter. Unintentional homicide. Often done in the commission of a crime. You don't need a lot of motivation for that except carelessness, stupidity, and bad timing."

"You could have both. Or more than just one."

"Sure. But the mix is the thing that makes it difficult. Say, for instance, Phil Reeves was cheating Otto on his receipts. Just say. How is Reeves going to deal with that? Not by going to Otto's house and stabbing him to death. Am I right?"

The return call from the contact at the Getty Museum that morning had not been what either of us expected. A copy of the Bosch painting, 'Removing Rocks from the Head,' had been reproduced especially for Otto himself. The director had contacted them for a copy in September. And most curiously, the woman in charge of this said, for some reason the subject was suddenly very popular. Someone else contacted her a few weeks later, asking for the very same thing. This second request was made only days after Otto's murder, but she wouldn't tell us who it was that ordered it.

"What's your thought?"

"I'm thinking it's a process of elimination, eh? You've done most the work already. Let's go talk to Reeves."

"Why do you need me for that? He doesn't like me."

"As a witness. Besides, I don't want to take my car over there and get the top ruined by some thug."

"You got your car back?"

"Sure. I stole it back last night. It's in the garage for an oil change and a tune."

"What about my tires? I just got new tires!"

"Arty wouldn't be happy in the Mini Cooper, anyway."

This was not a satisfying answer, but I was happier to be in on the investigation than sitting home.

We speculated more on what might have been going on with the painting, but Arty was not impressed. Abruptly, about a block and a half away from Reeves' office building, Jake says, "Stop here. I'm getting out."

Ever quick, I answer, "What?"

"I saw something. Go ahead and park the car but don't get out."

And then he's gone, though I could tell that Arty had an eye on him for a minute as I pulled away.

The street is quiet in the midday sun. The palm trees are making stencil shadows on the parked cars and the street. I don't see a thing, so I took a space on the next block, a few doors away from the office, and waited. Arty was anxious now. Suddenly, he's barking and dancing at the side door.

The first person I actually catch sight of is in the alley at the corner of Reeves' building, trying to be discreet, but not doing a good job of it. Or perhaps he wanted to be seen. In any case, Arty has him pegged. This is the shorter of the fellows who were around my car when the tires were slashed. I tried to calm Arty and stayed in the car with the doors locked.

Just then, it occurs to me to look around and I see one of the larger fellows involved in my previous encounter crossing the street from behind the parked cars there and he's coming toward me pretty fast with something like an aluminum baseball bat in his hand. I figure I'm about to lose a window, so I start my car and pull out. He was practically on me, before he stops short and suddenly looks back. That's when I heard Jake's voice—sort of a bellow—and stepped on the brakes. In the rear view mirror, I can see Jake coming on, but practically sauntering up the street. He's speaking Spanish and I think using slang. I don't know. The one thing I picked up through the closed windows was a name—Don Carlos. Now, the fellow at the corner of the building had already come out into the street to get in front of me when I started to pull away, and he's stopped cold as well. Arty is barking like mad. Both these fellows then turn on their heels and retreat toward the alley that runs beside Reeves' building, and Jake calmly sidles up beside me.

"Go ahead, park it again. No problem."

"There were three of them before."

Jake shrugs, "The other one was probably in a car in the alley. They're gone now, eh."

"You sure?"

"I'm sure. The next time we see them, Don will likely be along for the ride. But stay here, now. Reeves won't be in his office, with all this going on. I just want to leave a note. Notes are always good."

I waited about ten minutes with Arty at constant alert, along with my own fears the thugs had lingered, before Jake got back. The questions had started to pile up.

"That was a long note."

"No. I just said, 'Don't try that again.' It's my favorite phrase for things like that. They use it in the movies all the time. He'll tell Don and that'll make sure Don shows up sooner than later. I want to get this over with. But the psychiatrist across the hall was very chatty. I think she needs business."

"How did they know we were coming?"

"My guess is, from the woman at the Getty Museum. She very likely called Reeves to say I was inquiring. I think he got that copy of the painting made pretty damn quick and that would have cost him extra. I pressed her to tell me who'd bought it, but she wouldn't tell me. I probably bugged her for insisting. Some people are sensitive."

"So, basically, you're telling me I was your getaway driver on this caper."

"No. No. You got it backwards. I was your bodyguard. When the woman at the museum wanted to know my name, I told her I was you."

"So you mean the bad guys are looking for me?"

"No. Not now. I don't think so. Anyway, I made an appointment with Reeves for tomorrow. I told him who I was. And Don will be there, even if Reeves is a no show. But I think he'll be there too. Don might insist on it."

That took some digesting. I had driven him back at the garage in Sherman Oaks by the time I knew more.

"What are you going to do with the knife we found at the warehouse?"

"I gave it to Miles. He can handle that."

"When? You did that this morning? Before you took the car over to the garage?"

"Yeah. Just after I went over to check on Judy."

"You didn't tell me that?"

"You didn't ask."

"So. How's Judy?"

"She'll be okay, I think. Rape isn't something she's going to get over quickly. But it seems this isn't the first time for her. She's been living hard. She was an addict for more than a couple of years. Two or three times, maybe. I'm not sure I heard right. She started crying. Her father bailed her out a couple of times anyway. And she was turning tricks to pay for that. Anyway, I figured I better get over there early before her dad got back from Vegas. That's why I took a cab out to Rene's Mom's house in Ventura last night. I knew I had to get up early. Judy was already awake when I got there. We had a long talk. I took her out to breakfast."

"So, along with everything else, why did you have to get your car tuned today, if it was already running?"

"It's a stick. Rene can't drive stick. I was worried that she'd really screwed things up. I love that car!"

I waited around with Arty to see if Jake's car was ready and then we drove separately to Otto's beach house. At least Arty would get a chance to get wet as recompense for being cooped up in the van for most the day.

Jake has been to the beach house a couple of times before now. I wasn't sure what he was looking for this time. But he wanted me there to talk to.

Immediately inside, I looked again at the Bosch paintings, as if I would be able to tell a difference. Jake started right in moving furniture and getting down on his hands and knees.

I wanted to help, but I didn't know exactly what to do.

"What are we looking for?"

"See, the basic mistake we make is to think the house has been properly searched. The cops only looked for evidence concerning the murder. That's clear now. Miles finally got their report."

"When did you read that?"

"When I was waiting for you to pick me up to go over to see Reeves."

"You're very busy."

"Well, you know, Miles keeps me on retainer. It's not exactly a salary but it's a good draw. I'm supposed to clock against that and then chill for awhile when things are getting resolved. But this isn't working out that way. I mean there are too many moving parts to this thing, and they're all connected somehow."

I was curious about the practical matters of being a private eye. The stuff they never talked about in Mickey

Spillane novels.

"You have health insurance?"

"Yeah. How about you?"

"Yeah."

"That's good . . . So . . . Anyway, what we know now is this: the painting is probably accounted for—"

"How so?"

The copy there is what you saw when you first went through the place, right?"

"Yes."

"And Otto had a copy made two months ago. Actually, he only picked it up about a week before he was murdered. So that's probably when he switched paintings in the house. Then Reeves shows up a couple of the days after the murder and switches his own copy for Otto's. Mysty didn't notice because she's used to it being there and likely she hadn't looked too closely at the damn thing for a long time. It's an odd picture. A little disconcerting. I wouldn't look at it if I didn't have to. Otto was an odd duck. Interesting guy, though. So, anyway, I think he took the original down to sell it. He needed money for his next movie. Miles is getting a court order to take a look Otto's bank account. We should know pretty fast if he made any large deposits."

I was still just standing there watching him squeeze cushions and run his hands into tight spaces.

"So what are we looking for here?"

"The ring."

"The ring? That was in the safe."

"Sure it was. But it probably wasn't there when someone robbed it. The picture would be different now if it was."

"What picture? The Bosch?"

"No, clown. I'm talking about the way everyone is

238

acting."

"You're talking about Donitz and his boy Martin."

"Right."

"Not Reeves?"

"Not Reeves."

"But Donitz went to Vegas a couple days ago. Maybe he's gambled all the money away."

"Yeah. But Miles tells me, that was probably the day after the City of Angeles paid off on some fees for legal work he did as a court appointed lawyer. Probably gets something every month. He's been doing a lot of that kind of thing lately. Otto was probably his last big client."

"Then, why would he kill Otto?"

"He didn't. You already figured that out, eh? He didn't kill Otto. Martin did."

"So we're looking for the ring because Donitz doesn't have it. Otherwise, he wouldn't be living off court-appointed service fees. And we know Martin doesn't have it because he's hanging around too, looking for another payday from Donitz."

"So get busy looking for the ring."

The thing about this that was clear to me was, "If Otto took the ring out of the safe, it was to keep Mysty from selling it until he got the money from selling the painting. But he wouldn't have put it someplace she couldn't find it if she needed it."

He stopped and stood. "You're right . . . So where would she be able to find it?"

The first thing that came to my mind was, "How about in the sea glass she collects. Her 'treasures?'"

Both of us were suddenly dumping the sea glass out on every flat surface. It's beautiful stuff piled out on polish wood, from white and pale blue to amber and near black. Arty helped sniff. But there was no ring.

Jake was down on his knees again, but at the coffee table where he'd dumped a jar. I was at the lunch counter between the dining room and the kitchen.

He stops and says, "So what's the most important thing Mysty owns? The most important to her."

"I have no clue."

"Think. She must have said something. I don't remember anything in your notes."

"No . . . It's not something in the notes. But she did say something once. I was just interested in Otto then. I didn't write it down."

"What?"

"She told me it was the only thing she had that was worth anything. I remember how she called it 'Her magic.' She was evidently a pretty good magician. I never got to see her perform except in the two movies, but she told me once that she kept her magic in a box. That's exactly the way she said it. 'I keep all my old magic in a box.' And that reminds me, I've always heard that magicians never give up their tricks, except to someone who might carry them on. But what she did was unique. Magic on the high wire. Nobody else does that."

"Where do you think that box is?"

We both went to the bedroom and started turning that over. But half an hour later we were pretty sure there was no box of magic tricks there.

I finally get the right idea, "Why don't we just call Mysty!"

Jake looks guilty for letting the thrill of the hunt overcome him.

"I'll have Miles call her."

We both went down to the water then and let Arty swim. The late sun is warm, but it was in our faces, so we turned our backs to it and got to see that Mrs. Dean was giving us dirty looks from her balcony. Likely more for having the dog with us.

I asked Jake. "Did you ever talk with Mrs. Dean?"

"She wouldn't open the door. But I read what you wrote about it. I decided I would leave that alone."

I pulled a couple of chairs out from under Otto's balcony, and we sat in the shade where Mrs. Dean couldn't stare at us, and we talked about cars. This is a subject that has been on my mind lately.

I said, "I don't know, but seeing that Mini Cooper of yours has me thinking. I want to get a car that'll only fit one other person. And maybe a dog."

"What do you want to do with it? Mine's too small, for you and your wife and the dog. Isn't there something else you ever wanted—I mean a bigger car you ever really wanted more than anything else?"

"Sure."

"What?"

"Well, it wasn't a car, exactly."

"What?"

"A truck."

"What kind of truck?"

"Like my dad had for his business when I was a kid. A 1986 Ford f-150. He sold it when I was away at college. I really loved that rust bucket. He called it his 'bucket.' He threw everything in there—anything he didn't have another place for."

"What was so good about it? It looked like a bucket, right?"

"No! It had style! The front tilted in just a little. And it was two-tone, red and white. The gear shift was on the steering column. It was huge inside. When I was a kid I could lay down on that seat, door to door. And it had its own smells. It was another world."

Jake nodded slowly, "Yep. That's what you want then. You're like a little duck. That's what's shaped your brain. But I really hate those bench seats. Makes me have to use my seat belt to keep from sliding around. I hate seat belts."

It was nearly an hour before Miles called Jake back.

Mysty's magic box was in a hollow book. Actually, a box in a book. But I suspected that Otto had something to do with making the hollow. Mysty's tricks were all written down there by hand and described. The props themselves weren't necessary because they were easy to get.

"What book?"

"*The Seen and the Unseen* by Richard Marsh."

"Never heard of it."

"She says it's on the top shelf in the second section. She said it's just out of reach. You'll need a chair." He gave me a dirty look. "You can stand on the chair."

I almost left Arty in the water. He had his eye on me, though, and he was up the stairs right behind me, shaking the water out of his fur along the way and making Jake not so happy to be bringing up the rear.

But more importantly, the ring was there.

The fulcrum beneath the lever that moves the Earth
or Archimedes knows best

What motivates people? Greed is not enough. I argued with Jake about that, just as I once did years ago with Otto. But the root of cynicism that was planted deep in me by years of public-school education kept coming to the surface.

I'd said, "All the crap they make in Hollywood today is just that, crap!"

Otto was having none of it. "You think it was different when Warren William was playing Perry Mason? I assure you, it was worse. They had no idea then that some ambitious graduate student from NYU would one day be studying their habits. The film department didn't even exist until after I was out of there. What makes it look better to you now is the black and white of hindsight. It makes them mythic. But you don't know them. You can't smell the peanuts on their collective breath. Their only interest was selling tickets. They were mere human beings, after all. Not even demigods. And some of them were sad human beings at that. But at least most tried their best under the circumstances, most of the time. They worked in a film factory that produced a product. That's why I decided to go my own way as an independent. That, and because it was the only way I could be in charge of my own fate."

The recording skips there. We were likely eating just then, and the conversation went elsewhere, but later it picks up the theme once again with Otto in mid-thought. "Say you've got a story based on a play that's never been produced. To star, you get a rich kid from Manhattan with mommy-daddy issues who has trouble pronouncing an 's' but wants to be an actor because the work is easier than digging ditches, and given a naturally slack face and twitches, he's already managed to get the 'bad guy' roles down pat. And then you get a young Swedish beauty with an eye for the main chance who doesn't mind sleeping with whoever might get it for her. Then you take a wayward Hungarian who knows how to get film in the can on time and under budget but really wants to be an artist. He can paint with light on film. Add a few good company players who know their roles before they even read the script, and a few script writers who are just trying to make a living re-writing whatever they're told to and put them all on a back lot in Burbank, six thousand miles from where the story is supposed to take place, and you are just as likely to get another forgettable waste of good celluloid as you are a classic like *Casablanca*. What makes the angels suddenly decide to sing? I don't know. But back when I was at our old alma mater in New York, I used to go over to the WNTA studio where they happened to have a copy of that film and I studied every lap dissolve and fade, over and over again. You know, it's always a lot easier to say what went wrong with something than what went right. So, I studied what went right. And to my mind, it was all on the director, Michael Curtiz. That's when I decided what I wanted to do, even though I'd started out just loving the images themselves—because in the end, the cinematographer shoots what the director tells him to."

I've wondered more than once if that conversation changed my life.

While Otto was telling me that Michael Curtiz had set him on his own path, I was thinking that what I loved most about that film, or any film, was the dialog and story. Someone had once called the story in *Casablanca,* 'sophisticated hokum.' But they couldn't make the film without the story, could they? And I'll bet what any one of those actors would have said was, it couldn't have been done so well without them, either. What makes the angels sing, I think, is just the idea that what you're doing is important. If enough people think that at one time, it happens. But without it, they aren't likely to do anything.

All of that was in my head now only because Jacob Abbott is a mystery to me, and I told him so. What makes him tick? What makes him do what he does?

Jake tells me, "It's a lower center of gravity."

It takes me half a second to realize he is playing with the words again and I couldn't help myself, "But don't you have any higher expectations?"

"No. I keep my head down. Like Mr. Spillane told me."

"Look, there's a story here. People don't act randomly. They have motivations. That's the way stories work. If we understood what moves them, we'd know what happened."

He shakes that off, "I wish you were right. The world would make some sense. But whatever motivates them at any one time, most people don't have a clue. No idea. It's just what they want to do, or it feels good doing it."

"You think so? So, tell me, why do you think anyone would kill Otto?"

There is no hesitation in his answer.

"Because they didn't know him."

But I didn't understand yet. "Donitz told me himself that he cared for Otto's family. Why would he involve himself in something so contemptible—something that would so obviously hurt them?"

"That was just an eye for the main chance."

Wasn't that the phrase Otto had used once to describe

245

Ingrid Bergman?

"No! 'Follow the money,' isn't enough. Everyone doesn't do that!"

"But most people do, when they get the opportunity."

"That seems very facile. Very glib. I don't know you very well yet, but I don't believe you actually think like that. Are you really that cynical?"

Jake has the shorter person's habit of tilting his head to the side when he looks up at you. He studied me from that angle for a moment.

"Thanks for asking, but I think it's you that doesn't understand. It's what people do. Most people. A lot of the time. They sell their souls for pottage and find a hundred excuses for it. If I'm cynical, it's because I'm tired of the excuses . . . So, why did the woman cash her mother's Social Security checks to buy oxy's? I really don't give a damn. If she's okay with her mother's pain, then I'm okay if she rots in her own hell. But in general, no. I'm not cynical. I spend a lot of time trying to find the innocence in people. It's what I do. It's what I like doing. And if I find out her mother treated her like shit and pimped her out when she was twelve, I can understand a little better. If I find out she had to teach herself to read, I might even start to like her. 'Not guilty' is a legal verdict. It doesn't mean a thing to me. Miles knows that. That's why he keeps me around. He likes to know if he's doing the right thing."

"Who are you talking about? Sylvia Place?"

"It doesn't matter who. That's not your business. But I'm with you on this. The story makes a difference. Not all the time, but I buy that. That's my job too."

"It can't be a lot of fun."

"No. Fun isn't any part of it."

"A tracer of lost souls, then?"

"Yeah. That sounds about right. Because even though

most people sell themselves too cheap much of the time, there might be some moment of redemption. You never know how the story ends."

"Like *Casablanca*. Otto told me once that they didn't know how the film was going to end until it was done."

He brightened. "I love that film! Eh?"

"Then you believe there's a God?"

"No. I'm not religious. God, if there is a God, shorted me on that conviction. But I do have faith in what I know. And people do have souls. I know that. I've seen it."

"Even Donitz?"

"Especially him. There were a lot of years when he could have dropped working with Otto for short money, and simply catered to the self-indulgences of Hollywood. He stuck with Otto and helped make all of his films possible. But things didn't work out for Donitz. His soul got sick. The gambling is a sickness, eh. But you'd need a shrink to see that. I'm thinking that Donitz changed an awful lot after his wife left him, and maybe that's not all there is to it. Audrey told you he used to bring Judy up to Red Rock. A lot. And Audrey told you that he was like a second father. And Otto was often away making those films."

"Do you mean, there was something else going on there?"

"Yes. But no. That's not likely. Jessie was Otto's girl. I'm just saying that Truman might have loved Jessie too."

Naturally, I'd never thought of that.

"It's funny. Judy told me that she loved Jessie. When she was little, she used to wish she had a mother just like Jessie. She even remembered saying that to her father once. It upset him. And afterward, she wished she hadn't said it. She also said that her dad had tried to be a good father, but things went wrong."

"And I believe her. And I'll bet you what went wrong wasn't just the money."

So that's when I understood that Truman had loved Jessie too.

Philip Reeves did not show up for his appointment the next day. I was there. Jake was there. Don Carlos was not. We sat around for an hour and Jake spoke to the psychiatrist across the hall again. When he was back in the car, first thing he tells me is, he thinks she's a little kinky.

"I thought all psychiatrists were kinky."

"They are. But I think this one has her own kink. She likes short men. She wants to go out for drinks later."

I say, "I can't. Laura tells me we have guests for dinner."

Jake doesn't bother to answer.

"Because they didn't know him."
and horses can fly

Laura wakes up before I do. Always has. She calls this the 'tyranny of the door.' She has to be at the shop by eight-thirty in order to open at nine. But why does she have to get up at six? It's a ten-minute walk to the shop. I've never understood that.

This morning she tells me my phone was ringing in my jacket pocket and she answered it. There was a very nice young woman on the line who wanted to talk to me. I was groggy but I had to ask how she knew the woman was young. It seems they had chatted a bit. It was Alma Biedermeier, calling from Prague. At twenty minutes after six, I'm not ready for such enthusiasm.

I say, "Hello."

Alma says, "Hello!"

I want to say 'Goodbye,' but instead I say, "What's up?"

"Guess what? I'm in Prague! And guess what I'm doing? I'm at the very same place that Otto went to more than fifty years ago! The Clementinum. I'm probably even sitting at the very same table! Only you can't just look at the old bound newspaper volumes anymore. It's all digitized! Just like Vienna! Everything! All on computer! You can search for anything you want! And I'll tell you what, if Otto had been able to do this in 1961, he could have saved himself a lot of trouble."

"Instead of making films, maybe he would have settled

249

for making 'Ottomobile' commercials."

"Why?"

I wasn't ready to explain bad jokes over the phone.

"So what did you find?"

"Well, I'll tell you. I found out that Carroll Desmond and Isabella Byrne were also married in Prague! Same as Josef and Alma Biedermeier! But in April 1937! And Isabella Byrne's father and mother were in attendance." Alma waited after this, as if I would react. When I didn't she went on. "But, that's not even the best part! In June, 1937, they started the *Bohemian Circus Fantastisch!* Together!"

"Interesting. What time is it there?"

"You don't understand—It's just after three o'clock."

"I understand. It's just after three o'clock."

"No! You don't understand yet!"

"No. I don't."

"I have a copy of the very first advertisement announcing their new circus! And guess what? Listen! Not a single name is the same as the other two advertisements we know of—except for Desmond and Isabella."

"So?"

"Did you just wake up?"

"Yes."

"You need some coffee. Listen! At the bottom they announce that they'll be going on tour. On tour! To Vienna and Trieste! It says so!"

"Yeah. So. Did you learn to speak Czech at Harvard as well?"

"No! A very nice young man has helped me. But listen! You don't realize what this means! I think Otto had it all wrong! Circus people in Europe are like family. They live together and they work together. They depend on each other. They have to be that way. They don't just skip around from one circus to another. And many of the circus people at that time were Jews and gypsies. It was a way to earn a living when other trades were banned to them."

"I understand."

"No. You don't! I can tell. Listen! Carl Koch! Remember him? The name on Otto's program? He was a trapeze artist here at the *Circus Royale* in 1938! I actually found him first! I thought I recognized the name. He was very popular, but they let him go. They fired him! But do you know why?" She waited. I waited. "I'll tell you anyway! Because he was a 'disrupter of the public spirit! I guess that translates it. And why? The young man has just explained it to me. He was embarrassed by it. It was because Carl Koch was a Jew!"

"I think there was a lot of that going on at the time."

"Yes! But you still don't understand. Carroll Desmond started the circus in 1937! None of the names on the programs are clearly Jewish. All of them are very common German and Polish names. But go on-line yourself! I found Myra Zubran, the trapeze artist from the 1938 program, living in Florida. She died in 2009. Her obituary is in the *Miami Herald*. It mentions that she was a circus performer in her youth and that she escaped the holocaust. In lieu of flowers, it says to send donations to her favorite charity, a homeless fund at the Temple Israel."

I had no words to say.

She waited until she realized I had finally understood, "You see! And I think the *Bohemian Circus Fantastisch!* was started just to move people out of harm's way. Circus people! The whole idea was a ruse! That's why they had to hire new people all the time. Because, when they got to Trieste, everybody left. Trieste was a major exit point during those years. All except for Carroll and Isabella. His horse act was the key that made it all work. And they ran the circus! Like an underground railroad!

By 1937, the movement of Jews and Gypsies was totally restricted. Don't you see!"

"Yes. I do." I had to admit, "I finally do."

"And do you know what? I think Otto's father was not Joseph Biedermeier! I think it was Carroll Desmond!"

"I think you're right. I need some coffee."

"But he never knew."

"Maybe."

I called Mysty, and when she called back, I asked her about Alma's new discovery. Mysty was quiet. She knew very little about it. There was a famous Jewish circus strongman she remembered people speaking of, named Zishe Breitbart, though she had never met him. But she did not remember Otto ever saying anything about this. At least, not exactly.

"There is a book, I remember. Otto had a book at the house about something like this. He even read part of it to me. It was about Jewish theatre and circuses and that sort of thing. That was several years ago. But I'll tell you something else that you should not forget. For every performer there are many more involved in putting on a circus show. That's how Wallace started. He was a roustabout. He only learned to do a little magic when he hurt his knee. There are canvas men and riggers, hostlers and gandy dancers, prop hands—even a small outfit like that would have needed three or four hands to keep every act moving. Back then, even more. Show horses don't pull wagons. I'm sure acts would pitch in at the gate and do what they could, but they had to be ready to go on. And they probably had other acts not on the bill. Not everyone gets the ink. I didn't myself, for six months or more. But my guess is you have to be talking about sixty or seventy people, at least. More! And they would all know what they were there for. You can't keep a secret under the canvas."

At first the news was exciting. But this quickly passed as the fact of it sank in. So I called Jake and told him about Alma's call and Mysty's speculations about the numbers involved.

Later, Jake called me back with some things he'd found on-line about the *Circus Blumenfeld*, and the *Circus Gebruder Lorch*, both of which had disappeared during the Holocaust.

I couldn't sleep. The fact was, I had overlooked something very obvious.

Arty was awake in the kitchen with me while I looked on my laptop for other links to Jewish circus performers on the Internet. He waited attentively. Finally, I took him with me for a midnight adventure.

In the movies, this is where the character always gets himself into trouble. Normal people don't go lurking around after dark. But actually, I'm not sure why. It is a pretty nifty time to be out and about. It's quiet and things can have the look of film noir about them.

I drove down to Malibu, to Otto's house.

This was a glorious night to be out. A still night. Clear. A quarter-moon nearly as bright as a full one, with the clouds illuminated from above in highlight. Pure Hollywood.

I should have noticed the car parked just up the road, but my mind was on the scenery, and Arty is not that into cars.

I parked on the gravel and moved the stone by the key lime. But the key wasn't there. I actually picked the stone up and used the light on my phone to be sure.

By this time Arty is at the door, waiting. I suppose, because he's not the least bit upset, I assumed everything was okay. But now that I'm there, I didn't want the adventure to be over. I would have to come back for the book that Mysty had mentioned on another day. Anyway, there was always the beach!

I called Arty and took him down the path between the

houses.

It was only at the bottom there, in the near black of the shadow where the two buildings come closest together, that Arty stops cold and growls. I stopped halfway and called him back. But he stayed where he was. I heard whispering. Then the growling stopped. I waited another second. Basically, I'm suddenly scared out of my wits. I should have turned immediately to run.

And then I hear, "Sorry, eh? Bad idea. I was going to spook you. It seemed like a good idea at the time. But I forgot about Arty."

I couldn't see Jake but the sound of his voice let the air out of my lungs. Totally deflated me.

He had already taken the book off the shelf and read a chapter or two by the time I arrived.

"Why didn't you park outside?"

"Habit. Sorry. Rule: never park too close unless you have to."

At which point a very bright flashlight came down the path directly at our faces. The police had arrived. Unfortunately, Rebecca wasn't on duty and these two officers weren't particularly pleased.

After making excuses and showing I.Ds., we walked Arty along the beach and back again in the moonlight and the only thing wrong with it was that I was with Jake and not Laura. But you can't have everything.

The book was *Jewish Identities in German Popular Entertainment, 1890 - 1933* by Marline Otte. Pretty good. There was no mention of Carroll Desmond because he had started his circus several years later. Still, it made the situation for Jews in the period very explicit. Otto had left scraps of paper at various points in the volume, mostly involving the use of horses in circuses at the time.

When I called Mysty back the next day to tell her about my adventure, she had remembered that Otto worked on a screenplay a few years before about a boy in the holocaust who escapes on a white circus horse. Magically, and unknown to the boy, the horse could fly.

David Ortiz hits a home run
but it helps to know how to play ball

David Ortiz speaks in an uninflected manner. On the phone, this is almost a monotone, except for the way he will speak more softly at times. He says, "Look, this isn't my patch. I don't really give a damn about the rich pricks in Malibu. I'm doing this for my sister. She'll make my life a living hell if I don't do something. And it's not like I don't have to take care of the cases I'm already assigned to. So this is totally on my own ticket for now. Understand? You'll excuse me if I'm not pleased to be doing this instead of being home. Timing is everything. This case is already in the 'pending' file. As far as the department is concerned, it's resolved. Or was. There is no active investigation ongoing. That's why they've finally let me take it. And the detective who had it before is already working other cases, so there's no help there. Detective Packer doesn't give a fuck about the ring you found. So, he's let me have it. But if it means my sister will give me some peace, I'll check it all out again. Just remember, they're not paying me for time spent. Understand? But now you've shaken things with that ring, so I have a request in on it. If I get it officially, they'll cover some overtime. Until then, I'm on the short rope. We have a new baby at home. My wife expects me to be there. I can't be sitting on a curb in Oxnard watching moonbeams."

I think I understood. He was going to help. "Thanks."

"Yeah. Sure. I hear you have notes. Jake told me you

have notes."

"I do. You can see them, but there are a couple of things in there you'll have to keep to yourself."

"I'm a police officer. I can't withhold evidence."

"It's not that, exactly. It's a matter of privacy. Not everything people say should end up in the *Tab*."

In lieu of the notes I would email later, I told him what I thought was important. It was clear to me that he had already read a good deal of the police report.

He says, "The thing for me here is not to waste my time. I can't do that. Your friend Jake can do all that. He's getting paid for it. What I have to do is go talk to Donitz. And then I'll look in on Mr. Martin, if I have the chance. The thing with Reeves is another matter. I can't really deal with that. That's Drug Enforcement. That's another department. I'll call somebody."

"Thanks."

"You tell your friend Jake to keep his gun in his pocket."

"I'll mention it."

"He's a pain in the ass."

"He's an interesting guy."

"He's a pain in the ass. He shot somebody over in East L. A., a while back. That made a real mess for me."

"Was that Don Carlos?"

"Don who? No. That was Peter Britchard, the same guy that was in the television show in the '90's. A total asshole. Your friend Jake gave him a new one. That was a hell of a lot of paperwork. The studios have lawyers."

I saw Jake later that day.

I asked him about Britchard.

Jake says, "A real asshole. At least the grass won't grow on his grave. They cremated the son of a bitch."

"What did he do?"

"That was drugs, too. He was a pal of George Rooney's."

"Why did you shoot him?"

"To keep him from shooting me."

"Geez! How many people have you shot?"

"In the last year?"

"Holy crap! You've shot so many people you keep count by the year?"

"No. I just thought you wanted to know about recently. I don't know how many I've shot. I don't keep count. The paperwork is all the same. Sort of runs together. Just as long as it's self-defense and you can prove it, you're clear. But I can at least remember the ones from this year. Don Carlos'll make four."

"You've already shot him."

"No. That was in the leg. I mean, when I finish it."

"Maybe you won't have to."

"That's unlikely. He's just another fish in the sea. You've seen that picture of the little bitty fish and the little fish and the larger fish and the bigger fish and so on. Don Carlos thinks he's hot shit but he's not the biggest fish. If he doesn't stay on top of his situation, someone else will do it for him."

I still couldn't comprehend what he was telling me. "You already shot three people this year?"

"Well, two were at the same time. A couple of gangbangers up at Lake Tahoe. They were about to kill a cop, so I got royal treatment for that. And then there was Britchard. That was in January."

Except for old Arthur Burgess back in Levittown, I had never knowingly spoken to anyone who had killed even one person. Curiosity had me.

"Does it bother you?"

"Only when I miss. Like I did with Don Carlos. I wasn't aiming at his leg. So now we have to finish that up."

"What do you mean, 'we?' "

"Don't worry. If I miss again it'll go pretty fast. Your kids are old enough to take care of themselves and your wife is probably tired of you."

"Thanks."

This conversation took place while sitting in my van in the dark, about half a block from Philip Reeves' office, at three in the morning.

Jake's theory was this. According to the psychiatrist across the hall, Reeves practically lives in his office. "Which means he lives in his office unless he's staying with someone else. I don't think he pays two rents."

The next day, which was already today, Thursday, Reeves had a court hearing concerning a law suit for embezzlement that Miles Anthony was bringing against Reeves on behalf of Mysty Circumstances and the estate of Otto Biedermeier. This date had now been moved up in deference to the investigation of the murder. Miles Anthony was no slouch for pulling strings. Of course, Reeves could be a no show for that appointment as well, but Jake thought he might be there so that he could get a delay in order to take care of other business. That meant Reeves might go to his office to pick up some paperwork. Again, according to the psychiatrist, Reeves had not been around his office since the day we met the thugs who work for Don Carlos out here on the street. Which led to another thought.

"So, is she kinky?"

"That's none of your business."

"You brought it up."

"That was before."

"I see." Jake Abbott was a gentlemen. But obviously the

shrink was into a little kink.

Just about then, Reeves showed up in the rear view mirror at the far end of the block and walks right by us on the opposite side of the street and then across to his door.

Jake waited until Reeves was inside before going across himself. I stayed in the car. I was supposed to call him if I saw anyone else. And I did. Almost immediately. Three of them came out of the alley, where there is a large mirror attached at the corner to avoid hitting pedestrians, and they went into the building almost on Jake's heels.

After texting Jake, I saw the lights in the vestibule go out.

I called David Ortiz. I guess I woke him up, but at least he answered for once.

It was while I'm speaking to Ortiz that I first hear the sound of guns. He hung up on me.

Flashes repeatedly filled the vestibule. The glass shattered in place, catching the brief lights in a filigree. The gun sounds were a hollow booming and reminded me of the firecrackers we used to set off in the sewer pipe at Levittown on the Fourth of July.

If I'd only called 911, we might have had someone show up in fifteen or twenty minutes. Ortiz had called someone else, and an unmarked car showed up in less than five. Both officers had their guns drawn when they stepped out. But as I already figured, it was too late.

By dawn I had given my accounting of events to three sets of officers and was finally allowed to go home.

Jake had been taken away in a squad car almost immediately. I saw Philip Reeves escorted to another car just after that. Other people stood back at the sidewalks and the twisting lights caught on their faces and eyes. The ambulances waited, the strobe of red and yellow blending in with the blue and white from the squad cars in a silent celebration against the underside of the palms and the stucco of the buildings. I suppose the corpses could wait too. By then, I was gone myself.

Jake called and woke me up about ten o'clock.

"So the total is now six. But Don wasn't there. If he was, he got out before the cops came."

"Christ!"

"I could use him, right now. That was very close. When Don Carlos ruined my new jacket, I didn't even know he was around before it happened, so I didn't have time to worry about it. This time was different. I knew they were coming in. That was the hard place they talk about."

"What did you do?"

"I kept my head down."

And that was it. That was all I was going to get out of him.

"So, how did you get home?"

"Cab. But my car's still over in Malibu, where you picked me up."

He wanted me to come and get him again.

I told him I had to shower first but I'd be there by noon.

Arty is always happy to be out of the house. He sat at the door waiting for me to leave, so I wouldn't forget him.

I was over in Sherman Oaks a couple of minutes early. The air is clean, and I have the windows open to a nice breeze off the ocean.

And who do I see?

I see Charlie Parrot, leaning against the wall of the garage, smoking a cigarette. He's wearing a nice black leather jacket and tight gray pants. His fist is in his jacket pocket.

But he doesn't know me, so I drive on by, texting while I do it, which is a trick. The cars are only parked on one side of the street there and Arty sees another fellow on that side behind a big SUV and starts barking like crazy. All I managed to type was 'Don Carlos.' But I pressed the send button before something punched me hard in the back. Then I hit a parked car, and that was when Arty went right out the window.

I got the door open with my left hand, but my right wouldn't move, so I tried to step out, even though the bumper of the van was still sliding against the car I'd hit first and it was headed for another. The next contact practically threw me into the street, onto my back, and that was where I really first felt any pain. I've never been shot before.

Later, Laura was very sympathetic, but she wasn't interested in me. I was already taped up and not much good to anyone, anyway.

So there I was, looking up from the asphalt on a quiet street in Sherman Oaks, when I saw Jake step out from the other side of the house and say, "Hey, Pepe!"

Jake fired his gun almost with the words spoken.

Don Carlos was out on the sidewalk by then with his gun in his hand, already coming out of his pocket. It was still half-way in his pocket when he started to fall, face first.

I actually heard the third shot, even though the other fellow's gun had a silencer on it. Arty had knocked him on his back, and he couldn't get the extended barrel around fast enough, so the bullet went somewhere into the atmosphere.

Jake shot the man where he was. Arty seemed to know immediately that the fight was over.

Arty came over then and sat with me in the middle of the street. But all I'm thinking is, does that make eight? Or is it seven?

The blood-dimmed tide is loose

and everywhere the ceremony of innocence is drowned

Jake says to me, "I only know one poem. I learned it in high school to please Sister Mary Margret. That one poem got me all the way to college. It even got me dates. Everybody thinks you're smart if you can recite a poem, and that one is the bomb. Let me tell you."

"Which one is that?"

" 'The Second Coming.' "

"Yeats."

"Right. See? Everyone knows that poem. It's like the Mona Lisa of poems."

"More like the Starry Night."

"Whatever. Listen," Jake's baritone dropped a notch. "Turning and turning in the widening gyre / The falcon cannot hear the falconer; / Things fall apart; the centre cannot hold; / Mere anarchy is loosed upon the world, / The blood-dimmed tide is loosed, and everywhere / The ceremony of innocence is drowned; / The best lack all conviction, while the worst / Are full of passionate intensity."

Percy was quite impressed at the rendition and gave Jake a nod from the end of the bar.

Jake had tracked down Philip Reeves at his half-sister's home in Rancho Cucamonga. My being told to take it easy for a few days meant that he had driven up to Santa Barbara to see me. I wanted all the details. I was more than a little upset over missing a key part of the story. It was a Saturday, and the kids were all over the house, so we went over to Percy's and had a beer there.

"How did you figure on the half-sister?"

"That was easy. Reeves doesn't have any more family left. And he's such a creep he hid out at her place even though he knew those animals were looking for him—she has a family. Her husband is a teacher at the high school. She works at an insurance company. Three kids. He'd already borrowed money from her a couple of times. The husband was real pissed. He told me the deal."

"Why? Reeves was a successful guy at some point. What happened to him? What's his story?"

"No story. It's the drugs again. The story ended for him when he became an addict. After that he was just another one of the living dead. The zombies Otto put in his films. They're all the same after that. Their souls are gone. They'll do anything they have to for a hit. It's boring. They all talk about it like they're different. Their situation is somehow unique. You hear it a few dozen times and you realize every one of them is the same. But I'll tell you something interesting. It goes all the way back to George Rooney."

"How's that?"

"It's a friggin' circle. Reeves was already dabbling in cocaine when he found out Rooney was looking for a regular source. And Reeves knew that Charlie Parrot had a brother in the business because he heard Otto talking about it when they were making *Storm Warnings* back in 1986. You know that one was all about the drug trade in Hollywood and the confusion between reality and film. Otto was already sick about it way back then. So Reeves became the intermediary. He got the drugs from Don Carlos and passed them on to George Rooney. George Rooney couldn't afford his own habit, so he recruited some of the sweet young things he was playing with. Like Sylvia Place. It was a full circle of death."

"Why didn't Otto notice what was going on?"

"I don't think they saw each other that often. Not anymore. Reeves still put the numbers together. I suppose he managed that. You've spoken to Mysty. She didn't like him, but she didn't want to upset Otto because she'd already made a deal out of disliking Donitz. She was reluctant to push the matter. She's sorry she didn't. And Audrey hadn't actually seen the guy in ten years until the funeral. She told me she was shocked. He looked dried up to her. And he was."

"So why did Reeves talk to you?"

"Because I'm his savior! Yeah! That's what he actually told me. I took out Don Carlos. He was home free! But he's the fool. Whoever Don Carlos gets his stuff from will come after Reeves now. It never ends."

"What did he tell you?"

"About the painting? Just what you figured. He went in a couple days after Otto was murdered to steal the painting. Of course, he only stole a copy. But what does he know about Bosch? It was only worth $1000. About what Otto paid for it. Otto had already sold the real thing for $380,000 to help finance his next picture. Funny that it was the same reason he hid Mysty's ring so she wouldn't sell it. Reeves had promised Don Carlos he would have the money that he owed him, so he was in big trouble. Now, he's gone into the VA rehab. He's a vet. But I'll bet he doesn't make it through the month."

"What about Donitz and Martin?"

"The cops are on that. Your friend Ortiz is on that. He called me and told me to give him some breathing room. I don't think the two things are connected, but our fun and games with Don Carlos has got the department wide-awake again. He's on it."

"Did you tell him about Judy Donitz?"

"No. But he's spoken to her. He asked me what I thought was going on and I said it wasn't nice. He knows about Mysty now. He has it figured that Martin did something to Judy."

"I think the deal is, Truman Donitz came home from Vegas and found out what had happened. He knows it's his fault. You've gotta wonder how he's going to deal with it."

"Whatever he does, it won't be the right thing. He's spent too much of his life now in the wrong."

"You think Judy will survive?"

"Not sure. She won't leave. Not yet. As far as she's concerned, for better or worse, her dad is all she has."

"You talked to her again?"

"Yeah. Sure. If Ortiz wants me to stay away from Donitz and Martin, I have to keep up somehow."

"What about Mysty?"

"What about Mysty? Does she understand yet?"

"About the knife?"

"Yeah. I think she does. I think Miles explained it to her as well as he could. I think she understands it wasn't her fault. But she still said, 'I killed him.' "

"That's what she said to me when I spoke to her."

"Miles had a doctor talk to her about it. With the loss of blood, Otto wasn't going to survive anyway. Her taking the knife out was just the last thing. It was just bad luck made worse because it gave Martin an alibi for being somewhere else when Otto actually died. Miles told me the doctor could not understand how Otto managed to live for as long as he did. Anyone else would have been dead from the first instant Martin stabbed him. But Otto still had a will to live."

I received a letter this evening. This has become a

266

special occurrence. You can spot an actual letter in a pile of junk mail simply by how plain it is. That, and the handwritten address. And the size is always wrong for a billing notice. The only fancy thing about this letter was the stamp. It was Irish. My son had pulled it out of the dross and brought it in to me and now stood and waited, as if for an answer. He wanted the stamp.

Seeing who it was from, I handled the unopened envelop a moment and considered the possible contents before ripping it open.

The note inside was short and folded around a photocopied newspaper article from 1937.

The photocopy was boldly marked '!' in red marker at one margin. At least Alma was consistent.

She wrote, 'I thought you'd like this. It fills in a few blanks, I think. And it's 9 am here, so I very considerately decided not to call you.'

The *Leinster Leader* article from June 20, 1937, was more than a simple marriage announcement. Unsubtly, it was also a political statement.

'Our own Carroll Desmond, unjustly sought in the 1919 murder of Patrick Herrigan of the Royal Irish Constabulary, has for some years been 'on the lam' from the Dublin constable's office. Word is now in hand from Prague, Czechoslovakia, that Mr. Desmond has married his childhood sweetheart, the very patient Isabelle Byrne of Maynooth, long the heartache of many a lad in those equestrian precincts. A full account of the marriage has been received from the bride's father, Thomas Byrne, owner of the Clane stables, who was in attendance, along with his wife Mary Elisabeth.

'Isabelle Byrne is known for having won the Irish National Jumping Championships for 1929 and 1930. She has been most recently a trainer at her father's stables.

'It is noteworthy that, in the intervening years, Mr. Desmond has risen in the very rigorous ranks of riders and trainers on the Continent, to become a 'master of the horse,' after working for a time at several stables, and before finding a place with riding schools in Hanover, Westphalia, Warendorf and finally at the Spanish Riding School in Vienna with the famous Lipizzan horses, where he has been since 1934.

'We wish the bride and groom well and appeal to the authorities to at last allow the Treaty to extend beyond our shores to those lost sons of Ireland who stood against tyranny and were made to leave their homes by the troubles.'

On the verge
a wink of green

Late the next day, restless from sitting around with one arm immobilized, I went out for a drive and took Arty with me. I didn't have a purpose, but I think well when I'm driving and pretty soon I found myself down on the beach in front of Otto's house. A reddening sun was floating on a pale orange sky when I finally had a hunch. Rising over a dark sea, the cliffs of Point Dume were warmed by the color. At this point, all that I had were hunches.

It was after five o'clock when I called Donitz's office, and got no answer. I called Jake. He had the same ideas.

"Things are falling apart, but the center of it is there," he says.

I got to Donitz's office before Jake did and knocked, but again there was no answer. Jake came up behind me and started pounding and wouldn't stop until Judy finally opened the door. All the while, Jake is talking to her through the door as if she's right at the other side.

"Look, honey, this is not going to get better. You know that. It has to stop. Someone else is going to get hurt. Killing Otto was Wallace's mistake. We understand that. But Otto's not the thing now. It's way beyond that. It's your father now. He's going to get hurt. Wallace Martin is dangerous. You know that."

She might have been asleep before, but at least she was wearing a bra. Her body tattoos disappeared like a tight shirt into a pair of loose trunks. I wasn't sure exactly what all the tattoos were meant to depict, but she favored blues and blacks.

She looked at both of us with all the resentment she had left to muster. "What?"

With her head slunk down, the sleeping dragon claws reaching from her back onto her shoulders bracketed her anger.

Jake spoke first, "We need to find your father."

"He's not here."

"We need to find him. There's something wrong. I'm afraid something bad is going to happen. He could get himself killed. Can you call him?"

Her phone was already in her hand, likely to call the police about my pounding. She looked directly into Jake's face and called her father. There was no answer.

She says, "He probably thinks I just want money. We had an argument before. I needed a couple of bucks."

"Can you text him?"

"He doesn't do that. He gets frustrated with his fingers. I do all his texting for him."

"Can you text him anyway?"

"And say what?"

"Say that Wallace Martin is going to kill him."

That took the slump out of her shoulders.

She says, "That's where he's going! He's going to meet Martin now!"

"Where?"

"At a parking lot. I heard him say he'd meet him at the parking lot."

"Where?"

"How should I know? Martin asked him for some money. Dad said yes. Martin said, meet him at the parking lot. That's all. When he hung up I figured it was a good time to hit him for some salary. But he went ballistic!"

L.A. is covered with parking lots but only one, about half-way between Santa Monica and Oxnard, ever came up in conversation with Truman Donitz. We had to take the chance. I said this out loud, but Jake was already moving as if he'd made the connection himself. He was gone before I turned my key in the ignition. I called Lt. Ortiz. No answer. I called his sister. She answered. I told her the deal. She hung up on me.

What was I going to do?

I took off for Point Dume. Arty had his head up over the back of the seat. He seemed to know something was up and he watched traffic, car by car, as if one of them was going to be important.

What else was going on, I only found out later.

Lt. Ortiz had a tail on Wallace Martin when he left his apartment in Oxnard. Ortiz himself picked that up as Martin came down Route 1 and followed him right to the parking lot below Point Dume. Below, was the point.

The parking area I've gone to many times before with the kids is the one below. The other one, closer to the top and much smaller, is usually full. But I drove right to the upper area, perhaps because it was faster, but without a second thought. And this seemed to be confirmed at first because I see Jake's Mini Cooper there, already parked illegally. I parked behind him and was out with Arty on his leash when Rebecca Ortiz pulls up behind me, with her lights strobing. She shook her head at me and headed into the park.

A cold wind pushed steadily from the ocean. The red-eyed sun now stared at me from just above the seam between burnt-orange sky and blackened water.

Arty took off after Rebecca, and I was lucky to keep a hold on part of his leash and pulled him closer. Jake had disappeared. Despite the stiff breeze off the water, there were other people out for the view, and the paths of the park above

271

were fairly busy, mostly with couples trying to be romantic in the chill. I saw more than one of the guys with his jacket off because he'd put it on his girlfriend's shoulders. Other than the flash of lights from Rebecca's cruiser across the brush, the scene was pretty calm.

What had happened is this. Martin had driven to the parking lot below and left his own car to get in with Truman Donitz who was waiting for him there. Donitz had a gun and was probably busy trying to work up his gumption to shoot Martin. He shouldn't have bothered to wait. Martin shot Donitz first, as soon as the door was closed behind him.

It was right then that Martin gets out again and sees that Lt. Ortiz is driving down the lot toward him, lights flashing, and another police car is blocking the entrance.

Martin scoots down between the other parked cars and heads for the path up from the beach to the public area at the top of Point Doom. My guess is he probably thought he had a chance to highjack some transportation up above and get away. But somewhere near the top, he sees Rebecca Ortiz coming down a fenced path toward him. She doesn't recognize him yet because the light is behind him and he's just another dark figure among others.

That's when I come running into the scene—like a one-armed jerk.

Rebecca has taken a path the long way, by the cliffs, figuring if Martin were there, he'd stay off to the side. But I suppose he was feeling some urgency. I come right down the main way from the entrance at the road. I ran right into the sonofabitch. He hits the ground under my weight, but I lost more breath than he did. Arty immediately goes for his legs. His gun came right out of his pocket onto the sand of the path there and he reaches for that. I try to stop him but I only had the one arm free and he has me for muscle anyway. We both can hear Rebecca yelling then, saying it's the police, and for him to stop. But he gets a hand on his gun and stands up despite me on one leg in a desperate tackle, and Arty on the other. He doesn't shoot down at me, though. He shoots at Rebecca, who immediately drops out of sight. Then he kicks me off, and kicks Arty away, and heads over the steel rope that marks the path ahead. There are several screams from people around the park. Arty's leash had pulled out of my hand, and he must have been right behind Martin, because I lost sight of him in the low bushes toward the edge. I was yelling at the top of my lungs for Arty to stop.

The blood sun had grown large against the pastel orange of the sky and begun to melt like wax at the bottom, leaving a long drip of color on the water—and with this, briefly, a fire tongue that licked toward us. For a few seconds, the only real movement or sound, more than wind and my own voice, was behind me as people ran from the park. Trying to see against the waning light watered my eyes, but I went over the steel rope myself then looking for Arty and continued to call him.

Down the near slope, maybe a hundred feet to my left, I could see a dark figure scrambling across the edge in the scraggle of bushes, his body reddened at the back by the sun as he made his way across. I was sure this was Jake. But directly in front of me, about fifty feet down the slope, I see something else. I heard Arty then in his closed mouth growl but couldn't see him for the bushes between. A silhouetted figure there abruptly stood, arm extended, and fired a gun—the flash of it was startling—before something hit him from below. And then the figure was gone. There's not a sound then but the wind in my ears. I called for Arty again. My heart sank.

And it was at that moment the last coal of the sun flattened in a puddle of light at the very rim of the ocean and winked out in a flash of pure green.

I stood there at the end of that step of rock, staring out across the dark of the brush and cliffs below me, trying to see something—anything.

Suddenly then, Rebecca was standing on the rock edge beside me.

Very calmly, like nothing else had happened, she says, "You know, I've never seen that before."

I was sure she meant the color, and not something else, but I was finally speechless. The space beyond the darkening of the cliff edge, all the way to the distant wine-flecked surface of blackened ocean, had now lost all dimension. There was no sign of Arty. No bark. Just the silence of the wind. And then, as if from nowhere, the distinctive figure of Jake rising from the ledges below and coming directly up the slope toward me.

Only then did Rebecca just matter of factly hand me Arty's leash. Arty is at the other end, behind me, looking very happy to have found yet another female to protect.

Her brother, David, appeared at the path from the beach, moving slowly, his flashlight playing between the scrub and ledges.

Finally, against a brief hush of the wind, a radio call on the device at Rebecca's belt came from an officer somewhere below. Someone had fallen from Point Dume.

Later, Laura has her mouth agape as I tell her about all of this. It seems to me she is more impressed by it than she was when I told her I'd been shot.

The removal of rocks in the head
is what monkey wrenches are for

I gave a sheriff's deputy my statement, but I couldn't go home. Not yet. Not with all of this in my head. I looked for Jake but he was not around, so I called Laura and told her I was safe, just in case one of the television news crews had picked up my name, and then went back to Santa Monica to speak with Judy Donitz. I can pretend it was to try and offer her some comfort along with the news, but this would not be true. It was to comfort myself.

Jake's Mini Cooper was outside the door of the Donitz house. She answered immediately when I knocked. She was dressed this time, and it was clear she'd been crying. Behind her on the couch I could see Jake, who gave me a partial wave and a nod, and she left the door open to me and walked back and sat at her desk. I sat down in the chair by the magazines, where I had once waited to speak with her father.

She was staring at the dark screen of her computer and tapped keys randomly before turning to me. Her voice was clear.

"He wasn't a bad man."

Reflexively I said, "No," but couldn't think of anything else to add.

She was looking at me, and not at Jake.

"It was Martin who killed Otto. Dad didn't want that."

"I know."

But Jake shook his head. "Your dad was responsible. It happened because of him."

Whatever Jake had told her before I came, he did not want it made easy. At least she nodded.

She didn't look at Jake.

"I asked him once why he gambled. He said he did it for me. So that he could leave me something. . . . I told him that was bullshit. And after a while he said I was right; that was bullshit. But he didn't know why. He didn't understand it. I told him that was bullshit too."

I didn't know what she wanted me to say. But it was Jake who answered her.

"I think you were half right. He wanted something else than what he had. But he didn't want to work that out. He just wanted it to happen."

She nodded again.

Jake said, "It's like wanting to be hit by lightning. You want everything to change. Even if it's a random chance what you'll get, and you're willing to bet on it because you don't like what you've got, but you still don't understand what you want."

She finally looked at him, "Why are you so smart?" The challenge in her voice straightened her back

"Maybe I'm a genius. At least I know what it's like when things don't work out. Your dad made his choices before, too many times, and they all went bad. He wanted to be a good lawyer and ended up protecting thugs by playing the rules in court. He loved your mother, and that didn't work out."

"I wasn't what he wanted, either."

"No. I don't know why, but I think that's right, or he would have done more to protect you. But I think he loved you anyway. He just didn't believe that was something he could rely on. "

She clenched her jaw.

"Him rely on me? Me? You don't understand anything. You don't even know what happened!"

"Not all of it."

She slumped. "What's to know? Wallace was a nut. My father knew it. He hired him anyway. I told him. What did he think was going to happen? My father is to blame for all of it. Everything!"

I had to say, "I still don't think he meant for Otto to be killed."

"No. He didn't mean it. He never meant anything! Everything was just chance. Everything was bad luck. Never his fault. My mother was right. My mother was a bitch, but she was right about him. He was a successful lawyer because he was always good with excuses."

I said, "I think he was trying to help Otto. Trying to control Martin until they could do something."

She shrugged, the bones in her shoulders moving forward instead of up. "Maybe. But then Martin brought that bag of stuff from the safe and dumped it there on the desk. They woke me up with the arguing. I saw it all there. And then Dad gave Martin the money that was supposed to be for me— the money he promised me—and told him to get the hell out. To get as far away as he could. When Martin was gone, Dad started ripping open all the folders. He was yelling like a mad man and I came out of my room and asked him what was going on. He said that the ring wasn't there—that Martin had taken it."

Jake shook his head, "It doesn't help to know it, but he would have taken your money to Las Vegas anyway."

"Yeah, . . . sure. But you know, . . . you want to believe some things. Sometimes."

I spoke then without realizing, "And Martin never had the ring."

"No. Probably not. When he came here—the day he raped me—he didn't have a dime. He took money from my wallet for gas. He said I was paying for it. That I was paying for what he had done to me. . . . And I was."

She did not smile at that but I understood it was meant as a sad joke. The oddness of simply talking to her after all that had happened was plain to Jake as well. I looked at him, feeling a little lost in it. But I think she just wanted to be talking to someone.

I said, "Otto didn't go to the party that night at the last minute. He was upset. That's why he was still there when Martin broke in."

She reacted to that the way Jake might. "He didn't have to break anything! Dad had a key. He even had the combination to the safe. Otto trusted my father with the combination. Can you believe it? How can that be?"

"Otto knew a different man, I think. Your father had changed."

"Yeah. Maybe. I guess I used to love him too."

I said, "I'm sorry." I was.

She straightened, "No! You don't know! I was thinking about that. I was thinking about all that tonight after Dad left. One way or the other, I was trying to figure if I should stay and try to help, or just get out. And then I thought, when Martin told him that he killed Otto, Dad was still more concerned about the ring. The money mattered more. . . . Really? He knew Otto before I was born. Otto was his friend. He used to take me up to Red Rock and Jessie would take care of me, and that meant nothing to him anymore. I meant nothing to him. . . . You know, after Martin raped me, I told Dad. . . . Do you know what he said? He said, 'What did you expect, running around here half-naked?' I ought to be more careful! . . . Yeah! But he was right about that. What did I expect, running around here at all?" She suddenly looked at Jake. "I said, why are you even here?"

She was asking the question of herself, but Jake responded as if the question was directed at him. "I thought you should know about your dad. I'm just trying to understand what happened."

She grimaced. The tattooed claws at her shoulders closed. "Do you? Now? Do you understand?"

"No. I don't. But I think I can see what happened. How it happened. Understanding it is something else."

A police cruiser had pulled up outside and the blue of the strobing light broke the blinds in a cold pulse.

Mysterious Circumstances resolved
December 7th, 2016. A Hollywood Tab exclusive by Thomas Lenz

Otto Biedermeier did not believe in leaving his stories unresolved. In a Biedermeier picture, there is no doubt about who is saved and who is damned.

You have likely read by now of the most recent developments in the Biedermeier murder case. Mysterious Circumstances, the filmmaker's wife of twenty years, previously charged with her husband's murder, has now been released from custody pending further investigation. Ms. Circumstances is presently staying with family in the Los Angeles Area.

At this time, Wallace Martin, Ms. Circumstances' former husband, is the primary suspect in the stabbing of the filmmaker early in the morning of October 16, and Truman Donitz, the longtime attorney for Mr. Biedermeier, is believed to have been his accomplice, or, at the very least, a key participant in the crime.

It is now further alleged that Martin then murdered his associate, Donitz, on Sunday evening, December 4th, immediately after which Martin himself died in a fall from the cliffs at Point Dume while evading arrest. The previous murder of film director Otto Biedermeier now appears to have been the result of a failed attempt to steal a valuable ring owned by Ms. Circumstances, a crime planned by the two confederates.

The missing ring has since been recovered. A missing

painting, mentioned in prior reports, has been traced, and was previously sold by Mr. Biedermeier to raise funds for his next motion picture. The missing test films from the director's many productions have now been located in the archives of the USC Cinema Studies department, where they were donated by the filmmaker himself.

But these events are only the culmination of a larger and far more complex story.

Famously, in one of the director's most popular films, *Bare!* released in 1984, what begins as the simple tale of a New Hampshire nudist colony being terrorized by a family of black bears, ends up being a moral saga of human predation, enlightenment, and salvation in the Garden of Eden.

To those who objected to the nudity but not the violence, Biedermeier answered, 'In your fear of embarrassment you subvert the whole endeavor of human civilization, leaving codes of fashion to govern our very existence."

To understand the greater loss of Otto Biedermeier, the man himself, we must first realize what we have found.

The man who became Otto Biedermeier was one of many orphans of the storm of war that destroyed his parents and the world that knew them. He was adopted and raised with the name Lincoln Kelly in the heart of America, on a farm in Illinois. But it was out of a love of visual imagery discovered through photography, that the truth of things beckoned. After studying film as a means of communication, well before that discipline was an accepted degree, he graduated from my own alma mater, New York University, in 1961, with a BA in English literature. Writing was to be a main strength throughout his career, often done on location to meet the demands of what sets and props were readably available, thus saving production costs.

As Biedermeier has said, it was the story that mattered, "in the Wild West, or on the planet Mars—it was still the story —mere human beings trying to get along as best they can as human beings, while facing the odds. The conventions of the horror genre let me get down to basics. The universe is mostly cold. Heartless. It's only the friction of life that gives it warmth."

However, his very first project, a documentary, was begun with a singular objective, to discover his own identity. It was to become the pursuit of his life. And though he succeeded as an independent filmmaker beyond all expectations, defining the very limits of our humanity in the face of the absurd, a context he always saw as closer to the truth than society would admit, he ultimately failed.

However, I believe Otto Biedermeier would see even this defeat as a fitting end. To him, from the very first, it was the quest that mattered, not the victory. Defining the purpose was everything. Achieving an end is never wholly in our hands. As he once told this reporter, "We are not gods. We are men. As a director, it is too easy to believe you are god. A slap in the face is always welcomed. Having reveled in making the perfection of a baby, it's always good to change a stinky diaper."

Truly, what we know now is perhaps a little more than what Otto Biedermeier learned on the very first leg of his journey in 1961, peddling a bicycle, from Trieste, through Vienna, to Prague, accompanied by Jessie Fleming, his future wife and long-time collaborator. Because he presented that first film as a documentary tracing the course of a long forgotten one-ring circus in the year 1939, we assumed that he had rightly chosen his own name from those on the fragile program that was recovered from the clothes he wore when he was found as an orphan in 1945.

It is my belief now, for which I have yet no physical proof, that Otto knew who his actual parents were, and that his taking of the Biedermeier name was a conscious choice—a decision made about who he wanted to be—and that his father was more likely to have been Carroll Desmond and that his mother was Isabella Byrne. But he had chosen to be Otto Biedermeier instead, son of Josef and Alma. Why?

Because he mistakenly assumed that his actual father, the 'Zirkusdirector und Stallmeister,' Carroll Desmond, had forsaken those who had followed him. He was ashamed of that heritage and took the part instead of the 'Unglaublich Josef Biedermeier, Zaubererr,' and the 'Fabelhaft,' Alma Klage 'Zauberer Assistent,' to uphold the memory of the betrayed in the only way he could.

I suppose, unless some scrap of a lost letter were to be discovered, we can never know what the boy who became Otto Biedermeier actually knew or remembered. He did not say anything about the matter in his *Ottobiography*. But he did allude to this when writing about the deaths of his first wife and son —at least what was revealed in the therapy sessions for his depression, though he later disparaged the experience in *Deadly Projections*: 'On that psychiatrist's couch—actually a hard wooden chair—I admitted to remembering one particular dream of my childhood, prior to that first meal I ate in the mess tent with the American soldiers. That dream makes me certain that I am older than they thought when I was rescued. At least by a couple of years. I was likely malnourished and much smaller than I should have been. What I recalled was a dream of cold night and wind and leaves that I guessed to be autumn. It was on a night when I was near the horses, which I think I often was. My adoptive father, Jim Kelly told me later that this must have been to calm the animals, because I had described the nightmare to him when I was awakened by it, which is the only reason I think I remembered it again in the psychiatrist's office. My father told me then that horses are often calmed by the presence of a child, or a dog.

But here is the thing: in my dream, I am not standing on the ground. This makes some difference to interpreting the dream, and I argued about this with the shrink. He believed I was reading too much into it, that dreams are seldom literal. And perhaps so.

But in this dream, there was a great commotion, and uniformed men had come in the night, men in dark uniforms and with white faces, and they were taking people away. There was crying and yelling. And I could see a large man with a mustache, standing to one side of this and silently watching. Some of the people spoke to him angrily as they passed. Others looked to me! Accusingly! The horses behind me stomped their huge feet and snorted like wild beasts.

And one of these people being forced to leave was another small boy but in his own mother's arms, his bare legs dangling as he stared back at me. He was crying, but he spoke a name to me. He even reached a hand toward me. He said, 'Otto.' I'm quite sure of it. But I was crying then as well, and I have no idea why he spoke that name. However, the man who stood to the side and watched still said nothing. And when the people were gone and the horses had calmed and it was silent once again, that large man continued to stare back at me, but still he did not speak.

I had awakened with this nightmare more than once, and always awoke crying. My adoptive mother, Eileen Kelly, came to the kitchen where I had just related this to my father, and she made warm milk for me. And the nightmare faded. But I think it is out of such simple bad dreams that all of the phantasms of my films are made.'

This was not a careless recollection that Otto had

chosen for his book. It had a purpose. And much of that is very obvious. Many of his films take place on dark and stormy nights—standard fare for Halloween tales. But his villains do not often speak. They seldom say 'boo!' It is by their very silence that they frighten.

And there is another theme you will find in nearly every one of over thirty films. Betrayal. There are always friends who should not be trusted. Yet too, there is always the one who comes through, despite the worst. I think it is this that gives deeper resonance to his work after the fright has faded, because there is always the curiosity in any viewer to know who finally will do what needs to be done, and the encouragement of knowing that someone will, as someone always must. But more than that, I think of the nightmare that the young Lincoln Kelly had and I find myself easily in the thick of speculation.

It would not be fair for me to assume, without admitting my own ignorance in the matter. Certainly, Otto said what he wanted to say about it. It was his business, after all. But mine now is to understand his story and to say what I believe it to be.

After all, he did not remake himself as the son of Carroll Desmond, the great horse master, even though he did always love horses and riding, and might have guessed the origins of this love for himself.

Otto chose to be the son of Josef Biedermeier and Alma Klage. His choice was true even if it was mistaken. Otto believed that Carroll Desmond had betrayed Josef Biedermeier in his moment of need, perhaps to save himself—or even to save his own son? A man of such righteousness could not have lived with that. Not one who believed that standing by one's friends—being true—is the sole means of salvation.

But the measure of the man was cut from better cloth. He was his father's son, after all.

M16 —

About the author

It is hard to be serious about so unserious a subject as oneself. Though I now live in New Hampshire, I was born in New York City and raised there, with intermissions in South Carolina. Through the years, I have had a fair number of mundane jobs from mowing lawns to shoveling snow and house painting—all of it good material for stories. My favorite of those occupations was being a night clerk at several hotels, which is the background to a failed novel that I will continue to work until I get it right. For higher education I attended an experimental college in the hills of Vermont (it was all the rage at the time). For an all too brief period of about ten years, I was publisher, editor, and chief window-washer for several publications produced under the aegis of Avenue Victor Hugo, the new and used bookshop I have conducted on Newbury Street in Boston for most of my life. *Hound* was my first published novel, issued by Small Beer Press, along with its sequel, *Slepyng Hound to Wake*. I have completed seven other novels (some begun well before *Hound* was conceived), two novellas, and two books worth of short stories since, none of which has found a home with the mainstream publishers. As part of my revolt against establishment publishing, its sales psychosis, and the whole 'query' system of our day that reduces literature to the refined product of writing workshops and a politically correct zeitgeist, I published the novel *The Dark Heart of Night* for myself and found the process pleasing enough to continue. In order that I might keep the bills paid, I will continue to sell other people's books through our on-line bookshop site and our small barn in Lee, New Hampshire, and to publish and write so long as I have the mind to. My dear family has been, for the most part, quite tolerant of all this.

www.ingramcontent.com/pod-product-compliance
Lightning Source LLC
Chambersburg PA
CBHW030650260626
47157CB00007B/2576